I've travelled the world twice over,
Met the famous: saints and sinners,
Poets and artists, kings and queens,
Old stars and hopeful beginners,
I've been where no-one's been before,
Learned secrets from writers and cooks
All with one library ticket
To the wonderful world of books.

MY FRIEND MADAME ZORA

"She must have been six feet tall, and she was gauntly thin and narrow and so hung about with necklaces and floating, gauzy scarves that she had the appearance of an uncompromisingly angular, cast-iron lamp standard that had been elaborately clad in black crepe for some important funeral." This was Janet Sandison's first impression of the mysterious clairvoyant Madame Zora, who was to involve Janet and her husband Twice Alexander, home on leave from the Caribbean island of St. Jago, in a series of events, uncanny, semi-tragic, or just plain hilarious.

JANE DUNCAN

MY FRIEND MADAME ZORA

Complete and Unabridged

ULVERSCROFT
Leicester

First published in Great Britain 1963 by
Macmillan London Ltd.,

First Large Print Edition
published April 1985
by arrangement with
Macmillan London Ltd.,
and
St. Martin's Press Inc.,
New York

British Library CIP Data

Duncan, Jane
    My friend Madame Zora.—Large print ed.—
Ulverscroft large print series: romance
I. Title
823'.914[F]   PR6054.U46

ISBN 0-7089-1280-X

Published by
F. A. Thorpe (Publishing) Ltd.
Anstey, Leicestershire
Set by Rowland Phototypesetting Ltd.
Bury St. Edmunds, Suffolk
Printed and bound in Great Britain by
T. J. Press (Padstow) Ltd., Padstow, Cornwall

This book is for Thomas Smith.

Dear T.S.,

I have used the elements of your post-1945 story as you said I might. The condition that you laid down was that I must make a nice, happy book out of it because everything had ended happily for you, and I hope that what follows is nice and happy enough to please you.

May I present the book to you with my affection?

JANE

1

WHEN I look back upon the few months of 1951 during which the events in this story took place, I invariably find myself thinking of a jigsaw puzzle, but a jigsaw puzzle on a very big scale. It is as if I were sitting alone in the auditorium of a theatre, looking at a vast empty stage, and then my friend Monica comes in from one side, stands with her back to me and begins to gesticulate. She waves an arm this way, crooks a finger that way, and at each movement a piece of scenery moves in from the wings or drops down from above and at some movements people come upon the stage and become part of the picture she is constructing. It is with astonishment that I realise that one of these people is myself, moving like a puppet, creating part of this picture of hers without my own awareness, as if I were being manipulated by some powerful but unknowable force. It is a queer thing to look back to this time. It is like looking into a new dimension. It is a little uncanny and becomes more uncanny still when Monica admits that when she looks back to that time she sees herself as a puppet too. This admission is very queer indeed, for there is, one would say, very little of the puppet about my friend Monica. She did not look or sound like a puppet on the evening in early August 1951 when she walked into the kitchen of my home and said: "Well, well, well! Welcome home to Reachfar! How are you? A little thinner in the face but it suits you—makes you look more unpredictable and a little less forthright and reliable . . . Well, all you Sandisons, what do you think of her?"

Without giving my family time to reply, she threw herself into my husband's arms, and after they had embraced each other in a way that many wives would resent, she gave tongue again: "And you've got even bulkier, Twice! I didn't think it possible."

My husband is called Twice because both his Christian name and his surname are Alexander, and Monica brings out the worst in him. Holding her at arms' length, he said: "You're looking a bit bulky yourself—when's it due?"

"Not till late January." She backed away from him and wrinkled her beautiful nose. "You're not supposed to notice it yet. This is only August. And in front of all these people, too!"

This made my family in the persons of my father, my Aunt Kate, my Uncle George and our friend Tom join in a shout of laughter, for one of Monica's many foibles is her whole-hearted delight in her ability to produce babies, and the moment that this, her second pregnancy in the two years since her marriage, had been confirmed, she had walked the mile and a half from her home at Poyntdale up the hill to my home at Reachfar, telling everyone that she met on the way that she was going to have another baby.

Down the years since I first met her in 1939, I have come to associate Monica in my mind with what, loosely, we call "trouble". By this I mean that I cannot associate her with placidity or an existence that is even in its tenor, for there is something in her that breaks the smooth flow of life as surely as a thrown stone breaks the glassy surface of a slow-running river. She cannot be otherwise and each time I see

3

her, after a separation, I cannot be other than wary of her, as if she were the exposed end of a live electric wire.

On this occasion, I was seeing her again after an interval of sixteen months, for Twice and I had just come home on leave from the West Indies and this was our very first evening at my family home in Rossshire, to which we had driven from Southampton. My mind does not seem to retain detailed images of people. All it retains are impressions and, in the case of Monica, I had retained an awareness of her great beauty, but now I was overcome by that beauty of hers, in its living form, as I had been overcome by it the first time that I ever saw her. And it was a riper, fuller beauty now. Her marriage to Sir Torquil Daviot, our neighbour and the principal landowner of our district, was obviously a success and his pride in her and contentment with her were about him like an aura as she stood laughing in the middle of the floor, her dark red hair picking up the firelight in fitful streaks as the peaty water of a Highland pool picks up the glow of an autumn sunset.

4

"You look as elegant as ever, baby or no baby," I told her. "How are the others?"

Torquil was a widower with two children, Lydia and young Torquil, when Monica married him, and the first child of their marriage, Janet, called after myself, was something of a favourite of mine.

"How is Jay-ell?"

"We are not calling her that any more," Monica said. "She is plain Janet now."

"And nothing plain about her," said my aunt. "She's as bonnie a bairn as I've seen this many a long day."

"Aye, she is that," said Tom.

"And red hair on her," said George.

"And going to be a clever one," said my father.

"She is a spoiled brat," said Monica. "Lydia and young Torquil make a perfect fool of her, but wait till they go back to school! . . . Let's not talk about children —they bore me, really, and I don't know why I keep on acquiring them. . . . I didn't come up here tonight to talk nursery. . . . How was St. Jago?"

"I didn't come home on leave from St. Jago to talk St. Jago," I said. "What's doing around these parts?"

5

It was pleasant to sit by the home fire in the house where I had been born and hear again about me the familiar names of people and places in the district that had been overlaid in memory by all the new and strange experiences of a tropical island and its exotically different way of life. It was like a voyage of rediscovery, like walking round a garden that one had known long ago, to find this small tree grown almost beyond recognition, that plant multiplied unbelievably and, with a nostalgic sadness, the flower that had grown in that corner dead and gone.

"And old Cripple Maggie is still alive?" I asked at one point.

"Aye, an' living-like!" said Tom. "It is myself that is of the belief that it is the whisky in her that's at the bottom of it. She is what ye might be calling preserved in it, like—like yon cherries in brandy that the ould cook at Poyntdale used to be making."

"Och and Hamish is chust about as good as ever he was," George, my uncle, said. "Last week, when I was down at Achcraggan, I met the two o' them on the County Road on their way home with the wee cartie and the horsie and them singing like a couple of linties."

Hamish the Tinker and Cripple Maggie, his wife, were two of the classic survival characters of the district who had maintained their individuality in spite of the best efforts of the Government and various welfare and charitable bodies to "better their lot". They had been given a smallholding of ten acres with a small modern bungalow upon it, and their two sons and one daughter worked the land like a garden and kept the house like a new pin behind its starched lace curtains, but on more than one winter night Maggie and Hamish had still been found sleeping in the comfortable little stable with the "horsie" and a drop of whisky to keep them warm as had been their habit down all their carefree years as travelling tinkers.

"We had a spot of trouble with them at the Old People's Outing," Monica said now. "We took the old people up the glen this year to see the new power station and dam," she explained, "and I must say I blame myself for not remembering how many pubs there are between here and Loch Ruidh. As the buses flew past pub after pub, Hamish and Maggie got more and more restive and disappointed, so I'm told—I was following in the car with old Hugh the Tailor and Mrs. Macrae and Mr. Siddon—you wouldn't know him, Janet—he's Ina Siddon's—she was a Gillespie—he's her father-in-law and only came here to live last year. Those three have arthritis and can't walk. So—"

"But there's no arthritis in their tongues!" my aunt put in. "Hugh the Tailor has never stopped speaking yet of what a night of it they had."

"Anyway, I missed the carry-on in the bus on the way up," Monica said, "but after supper—we had supper laid on at the Village Hall at Ruidh—we couldn't find Hamish and Maggie. In the end I had to hire the local car and send Mrs. Macrae and Hugh and Mr. Siddon home in it and I went off with the policeman to look for Hamish and Maggie. We wouldn't have found them yet if they hadn't got to the singing stage, but we heard them. They were sitting on a rock above the river, as tight as a couple of lords, with a bottle of whisky and a great enormous salmon they had caught lying between them. Where

8

they got all the whisky no-one will ever know."

"What did you do?" I asked.

"Oh, the policeman was frightfully nice," said Monica. I have yet to see the policeman—or any other man for that matter—who is not frightfully nice to Monica. "He just said, 'Get them out of here for goodness' sake and put that damned fish in your car before the ghillie gets the smell of it!'" Monica giggled. "So I got Hamish and Maggie home all right, but I kept the fish."

"And very good it was too, yon bittie of it that you sent up to us," said Tom. "That Outing that you and the W.R.I. leddies gives is a grand thing, Monica, all apart an' separate from Hamish an' Maggie's salmon. It is myself that enchoyed every minute of yon drive to yon wonderful electric scheme and seeing a-all the people o' the district that I havena seen since long."

"And that reminds me, Janet," Monica said, "I've promised a lot of my old people that I'll bring you to see them and I've told the W.R.I. you will open the session with a talk on house-keeping in St. Jago before you go back."

"The hell you have!" I said. "Now, look here, Monica, Twice and I have a lot to do this leave and—"

"You don't have leave to do things you have to do," she argued. "The idea of leave is recreation and I think it's stupid—"

"You shut up! And if you think it's recreation to talk about keeping house in St. Jago, you're demented! You had no business to go saying—"

"Torquil!" said Twice in a loud voice. "Here we go! We're off already. Let's all have a dram and, for Pete's sake, you two, try to remember this is a glad re-union, not the same old fight we were involved in sixteen months ago."

"Och, never heed them, Twice, lad," said my aunt. "They've fought all the days they've known one another. . . . The glasses are in the right-hand cupboard of the dresser there as usual." And then, because Monica and I were still snarling at one another: "Hold your tongue, Janet! You're older than Monica and should have a little sense although she's got none. Anyway, it isn't much she's asking you to do and her work among the old people is a real blessing to the district."

And so, of course, in the end, I went on several rounds of visits with Monica and again, of course, I enjoyed them, for I like most old people and these of our district had known me since I was born and I had a whole fair countryside and way of life in common with them.

And I came out of my rounds of visits with an even increased admiration for my friend Monica, whom I had always admired in almost every possible way. In marrying Sir Torquil Daviot she had, I thought, taken on what, in the slang of our day, we would call a "tough assignment". It can never be easy, I feel, to marry a widower and become a stepmother, for, having been a stepchild myself for a part of my life, I know how difficult stepchildren can be even when they have no malignant intentions. But this side of her marriage apart, Monica, an Englishwoman and a "foreigner"', had stepped into the place of a local woman of well-known and respected family, whose death at the birth of her second child had made a deep and lasting impression on the long, hard memories of our district. Then, preceding Aileen, that first wife of Sir Torquil's, in the memories of the countryside went Lady Lydia, Sir Torquil's mother, who was still alive although too crippled with the too-common arthritis to leave her house. From the time of Monica's marriage, I could foresee the difficult terms on which the people were going to accept her, if ever they came to accept her at all. "Leddy Torquil"—as the district had called Aileen—"is gone, poor bonnie lassie," they said, "and the Laird has married this Leddy Monica from England—her father is a marquis, so they say—and she brings a lot of money with her, from what we'll be hearing. Och, well, Leddy Lydia was from England and the daughter of a duke, but a finer, kinder leddy was never seen in the countryside and if this new one will do half as good she will be all right."

Even in 1951, when the welfare state and social security were phrases in common usage, the older people of our district still looked to the "Big Hoose" of Poyntdale as to a fount of comfort in trouble and advice in dilemma, for our district is far from the surging movement of the big whirlpools of the cities. It is a backwater and into it new ideas slip slowly, borne on weak, wayward, uncertain side-currents. The pension, drawn at the post office every week, was a wonderful dispensation from that remote, nebulous thing called the "Government", but you could not be sure that you would get it if there was nobody at the Big Hoose at Poyntdale who would help you to fill up the necessary form.

"Monica," I said as we drove along the back lane behind Achcraggan on our way to the last call for the day, "I don't believe in waiting till people are dead to throw bouquets at them. I have to congratulate you on this whole situation here—your marriage, Poyntdale and your handling of the people round about—especially the old ones. They are a difficult, cross-grained load of chips of Highland rock and I think you're marvellous with them, so there!"

"Thanks a million, ducks," she said. "You could not have said anything that could please me more."

"I wish I knew how it's done," I added. "After all, these people here are about as foreign to you as my West Indians are to me and all that happens with me is that I get more and more muddle-headed and disoriented among them."

13

"No. Your West Indian situation is far more complicated, Janet. The things I do here are obvious and easy—the hospital stuff and the W.R.I. and so on. The visiting around among the old people is the only thing that is really my own idea and I do that because I like it and I think it takes on value because I believe in it, really believe in it in a deep-down, implicit way." She drew the car into the roadside and, stopping, took a packet of cigarettes from her bag. "Have a smoke. . . . The welfare state is all very fine, it looks after the mechanics of life, but life isn't all mechanics. The welfare state can do nothing for loneliness—plain, ordinary, human loneliness— I think it's the most terrible thing in the world. Wasn't it James Joyce who spoke of the 'soul's incurable loneliness'? . . . For the genius on his mountain peak it may be incurable, but for the rest of us it isn't. There are windows in it where the light of common day can get in if it will try. That's all I'm doing with these old people, breaking through their loneliness, and I do it because I know, in my own experience, what a hell it can be. . . . The welfare state tries to cope, with the old people's homes and all that, but the people here don't want to go into homes. They are not gregarious enough by nature and the homes have the stigma of the old poor-house in their minds still, so they stay around in their own little cottages and their pensions ensure that they have food and warmth. But as they get less and less able to go out and about, loneliness sets in and they simply don't know what's the matter with them, but they become unhappy. And it's not much fun to eat alone so they cook less and less. And— well, I just can't bear it for them and that's why I do this. Quite often, old Mrs. Lumsden, for instance, is as cross as an old witch when I arrive and tells me nastily that she is busy washing blankets but to come in all the same now I'm here, but if I miss a week of visiting her, she tells me the next time I go that the worst of people nowadays is that you can never depend on them from one week to the next."

"How many of them do you visit?" I asked.

"Between forty and fifty."

"For Pete's sake! I didn't know there were that many people in the district."

"Don't be a clown! The depopulation of

the Highlands applies mostly to youth. What with longevity and sheer cussedness and one thing and another, there's a person of over seventy in this district to every two of any other age. Dammit, they come tottering home here from the ends of the earth to spend their last days, like that old bird in the ten-gallon hat we spoke to in the High Street. He hasn't been home for fifty years, but he flies in from Alberta, aged seventy-one, six weeks ago and has already fought with everybody in the place." She started the engine of the car. "Well, we'd better get going again. Gosh, Janet, it's marvellous to have you back and just be with you like this!"

"And it's marvellous to be back, Monica."

"Look, this business of living out in St. Jago—do you simply loathe it?"

"Oh, no! In fact I like it, but in a queer way. I can hardly explain it. . . . When you were a youngster, did you ever have a crush on a much older man or a foreigner?"

"My dear, all the time! From the age of about fifteen I was never out of love—but why?"

"That's the sort of feeling I have for St.

Jago—of being fascinated in a hopeless sort of way with something I simply don't understand. When I am there, I am so muddled in my mind half the time that I become exasperated with the climate, the insects, the negroes, the lush vegetation and all the rest of it, but if anyone were to tell me that I could not, ever, go back there, I should be terribly sad. Silly, isn't it?"

"And when are you and Twice due to go back, actually?"

"It's not certain—October or November or so. But we've a tremendous amount to do. Now that Twice is going to be permanently stationed in the West Indies, we really ought to sell Crookmill." Crookmill was Twice's and my home in south-west Scotland. "It's madness keeping it on and having all this bother with tenants and things. Then Twice has a lot of business to see to down in the Midlands and London."

Monica stopped the car at the roadside again. "Listen, while Twice is messing around in the Midlands, what about us having a week or so at Beechwood? Mama would love to see you again and I want to get away for a bit before this baby gets too big and Beechwood on my own with the family gives me the creeps. Jan, do let's arrange it!"

"Well, we'll see," I said. "Look here, if we're going calling on whoever it is, let's go. . . . Where are we going anyway?"

"To old Mrs. Gilmour."

"Granny Gilmour? Is she still alive?"

"Don't be silly! She's one of the younger, spryer ones. She's only seventy-five."

I took thought for a moment. "I suppose you are right. One tends to think of all the grandmothers as being the same age as one's own grandmother, but of course Bella Gilmour married very young and Guido was younger than I was. . . . Start the car, Monica. We'll be late and Torquil and Twice will be worried."

"Oh, let them be!" said Monica. "I don't know why Torquil has to treat me like an idiot as soon as you come on the scene. He never does otherwise."

"Neither does Twice me without you," I said.

"Like Torquil me when you. Why is it they them? But never mind that now. Have another cigarette and give tongue about this Guido you mentioned."

"Why?"

18

"Because I'm interested in him, that's why. At times I think I am only half-witted. I sometimes forget that you were brought up up here and I had completely forgotten that you were a contemporary of Guido Gilmour's."

"Not Gilmour," I said. "His name is Guido Sidonio—Bella Gilmour married an Italian sailor during the 1914–18 war and Guido is their son. Wait a minute now— he'd be five years younger than I am—yes, four or five years, that's right. He'll be about thirty-six or -seven now. Is he around here still?"

"No," Monica said. "He's dead. He was lost in the Mediterranean. He was a para-trooper."

"Oh. Why were you asking about him then?"

"Everybody knows he is dead except Granny Gilmour as you call her. She just doesn't believe that Guido is dead. . . . Don't get me wrong. She's not dotty like Miss Annie Boyd or old Davie the Mole-catcher who sees Torquil's grandfather on the road every morning and sometimes holds the horses outside the Plough for him. Granny Gilmour is as sane as you are

19

—probably saner—but you won't convince her that her Guido was killed in the war. . . . What sort of a man was he?"

"Look," I said, "let's abandon this visit for today and go down to the Plough and have a snort. We'll come down to see Granny Gilmour tomorrow—it'll give me time to catch up with what I remember of Guido."

"Done!" said Monica and pointed her car towards the Plough Inn.

Being early in the evening, just after the opening hour, there was nobody in the Plough's bar parlour except ourselves, and when our drinks had been brought, Monica said: "I've asked all sorts of people about Guido Gilmour as they call him but nobody seems to know very much about him. All one gets is: 'Och, aye, he was Bella Gilmour's laddie.' I thought he was an illegitimate."

"No. No—Bella was in domestic service in London and she met Sidonio down there. They were married—" I wrinkled my brows, peering down the long lane of my memory. "I remember Guido coming to school as a little boy of five and giving his name as Guido Sidonio. He was a thin, dark, olive-skinned boy—very Italian-looking, but one of the thin, lanky sort, not the short, fat kind. And he was extraordinarily handsome when he grew up."

I looked down into my drink and was silent for a moment.

"Janet!" said Monica. "You're blushing! So help me, you're forty-one and blushing in the most lovely way! I do wish Twice were here to see."

"Oh, shut up!" I said. "Actually, it's sheer embarrassment. Heavens, how awful one was when young!"

"Will another drink help?" she asked and, getting up, she pushed the bell-knob on the wall by the door. Then she stood looking down at me, her long eyes dancing with wicked amusement. "I can hardly wait. After some of the situations I've seen you in back in the war, this Guido thing must have been a snorter. . . . Thank you!" she said to the barman and then, when he had gone out and shut the door: "Tes beaux yeux, my sweet! Do tell about Guido!"

"Oh, the whole thing is stupid and it was nothing to do with Guido anyway. . . . What year did Rudolf Valentino die?"

21

"Who was he? Oh, he was a film star, wasn't he?"

"How perishable is fame! He was the greatest lover the screen has ever known—literally millions of women wept over his coffin, as sincerely as for any real lover, while he lay in state under a blanket of red roses."

"And did you weep too?"

"No, but they revived all his films a year or two after his death—I was at the University at the time—and I saw one or two of them. I don't think I got quite under the spell, but—"

"Yes?"

"It's difficult to explain. I used to come home here for the holidays and somehow —it was a long time after the Valentino revival was all over—I got a sort of thing about a bloke who was up here, a friend of Guido Sidonio's. He had that sort of smouldering look, you know, that Valentino had had and, well—"

Monica bent a cold derisive eye upon me. "Why not say it?" she asked. "You put the eye on him, gave him that soft, wide-eyed, wondering stare of yours?" I did not reply and she went on: "I don't know what Twice

Alexander has done to you since he married you. You go on as if your past had been blotted out, as if it had never existed, as if I had no memory. Great Heavens, have you really forgotten how you used to carry on when we were in the Air Force?"

"Oh, shut up, Monica!"

"Well, go on then! You lured Guido round the nearest dark corner—"

"It wasn't Guido, I told you!" I said crossly. "Oh, I don't know why I'm telling you about all this. It's nothing to do with Guido anyway. It was all this friend of his. He wasn't really like Valentino and yet he was, in a way. Anyway, he made me think of Valentino and Valentino made me think of romantic passion—"

"Later on, it didn't need Valentino to make you think of that. I've seen it come over you at sight of a target map of Berlin!"

"Oh, be quiet! Anyway, this friend was up staying with Guido for the holidays— he was a student friend—Guido was at Edinburgh University at the time. They were both about seventeen or eighteen—"

"And you?"

"I'd be twenty-two or twenty-three— maybe I was even twenty-four. . . . Look

23

here, this is nothing to the point about Guido Sidonio."

"Never mind that. Tell it anyway. I absolutely dote on your past. It wasn't Guido you put the eye on, it was the friend?"

I nodded and felt myself blushing again.

"For Pete's sake!" said Monica. "What happened? What hideous mischief did you work on this misguided youth of seventeen?"

"That's the silly part!" I burst out. "It was he who worked the mischief on me. We walked up the hill from Achcraggan to Reachfar—it was early on an evening in summer. He scared the living daylights out of me and I left him in the middle of the moor and ran like a stag for home and I was terrified to set foot in Achcraggan again for the rest of that holiday in case I'd meet him. I've never been so overcome in my life."

"I take off my hat to the only man who ever scared you," said Monica. "But what happened?"

"Oh, nothing really. That's the silly part. But there was something about him once we were alone up on the moor that scared me to death. I was literally overcome, so overcome that I don't even remember the thing clearly except for the feeling of panic. I was sitting on a boulder under a tree and he was standing up and he suddenly put his hand under my chin and tilted my face up and said: 'You have beauty—the beauty of the tilled earth—'"

"And a very lover-like speech too! What did you say? 'Aw, go on now, do, with your nonsense'?"

"No. I did worse. I simply panicked and jumped to my feet and—and—that was when I ran for it. And so would you have done. Remember what I said about St. Jago? About being fascinated and frightened at the same time? That's how I was with this youth—floundering away out of my depth. He was too—too different. Other young men I knew didn't say things like that and they didn't say things like that like that! He didn't say it as if he were admiring me—he said it as if I were something that he had just discovered, as if I weren't even animate, as if I were a view or something. Oh, I can't describe it. But I still blush inside and outside too when I think of the thing. I started it, but I was afraid to finish it. Very shaming."

"Oh, forget that, my sweet. . . . What was his name?"

"You would ask that," I said bitterly. "Romantic passion and Valentino my foot! That's the worst thing of all. His name was Stubb—Bertie Stubb. I can never think of Valentino, the great lover of all time, without thinking in the same second of Bertie Stubb. He left a permanent mark on my character and biased for ever my attitude to the romantic passion. It is by chance encounters like mine with Bertie Stubb that the axis of a character is forged. He put me off these intense, smouldering-eyed types for good. But all this has nothing to do with Guido Sidonio and don't you go gabbing to Granny Gilmour about it either."

"Of course I won't!"

"All Guido did was to bring the bloke to these parts and generally set the stage. I don't think I ever saw Guido to speak to after that time, Monica. This bloke used to come up with him every holidays and I avoided them. Then, later on, Guido went into teaching, didn't he?"

"Yes, in London. An L.C.C. school. Then he joined the Army at the beginning of the war."

We both looked out of the window of the Plough for a moment at the broad still waters of the Firth which still lapped at the little stone pier across the way as they had lapped when I was a child.

"It's all so long ago," I said after a moment. "When I was at school here, Guido was in the Baby Class when I was a big girl in the Top Class—five years is a generation of difference at that age."

We went on staring out of the window for another minute.

"I wonder if Granny Gilmour is right? I wonder if Guido is still alive?" Monica said quietly, watching the everlasting water.

"Monica, it's terribly unlikely. The War Office didn't make many mistakes in the '39–'45 issue. If they reported him killed, Guido was killed all right."

"It was 'Missing—believed killed', the report. I got Gerald to have it checked," she said.

"Oh?" I stared at her. Her interest in Granny Gilmour and Guido was deeper than I had thought if she had gone to the trouble of having her brother in London check the records. "Monica, why? Have you any—any reason other than Granny Gilmour's idea for thinking he may be alive still?"

"No. But the old lady is so terribly positive. She is extraordinarily convincing, but you'll see that for yourself tomorrow. . . . But queer things happen. Look at Andrew Boyd turning up after all these years—"

"That was different!" I argued. "Andrew Boyd ran away for a petty criminal reason and turned up again when the furore had died down."

"There have been other cases in this last war," Monica said obstinately. "There's a friend of my sister Steff who was married to a Frenchman. He was reported killed in 1944, but when she went to France for a holiday last year she found him, married to a large peasant woman who has lots of vineyards in the Pommard area and doing very nicely for himself, thank you."

"What happened?"

"Oh, they're divorced now—they never got on anyway—but it just shows you."

"But Guido wasn't running away from a wife he didn't like," I said.

"How do you know what Guido was running away from, to, for, by or with?" she asked.

"Oh, all right. Have your mystery. Are you suggesting that Granny Gilmour is in cahoots with Guido in any way?"

"No!" Her voice was sharply protesting. "No. Granny Gilmour has no more solid basis for her belief than you or I might have. She simply maintains that if Guido were dead she would know it. And she does not know it."

"How do you mean know it? You can't know a thing if you just won't know it," I said.

"It's not only with their brains and intellects that people know things sometimes," Monica said quietly. "People like Granny Gilmour especially. Minds like yours and mine, a bit poisoned and blinded by this pseudo-education they inject us with, can't grasp the deep, delicate kind of knowing that might be possible for Granny Gilmour. . . . But never mind that now. Let's have one for the road and then go home."

When we left the Plough, we drove back along the High Street to the shop of

Dickson, Ironmonger and Seed Merchant, where Monica picked up a roll of barbed wire, and we then drove around the little hill where the church stands to return to the shore road, but as we passed the church gates, Monica said: "Oh, there's Malcolm! I want to see him about these young trees," and she turned the car through the gates and up to the door of the church.

"Trees next!" I said. "We won't get home tonight!"

"Who suggested the Plough?" she asked, and jumping out of the car she slammed the door and disappeared into the church after Malcolm.

I got out of the car and wandered down the path at the side of the church that led to the graves of my family. There is nothing impressive about the Sandison plot. It is a row of four stones in all, three old ones, very weathered, that bear the names of Sandisons I have never known and a fourth one which is a square pillar of grey granite and which, at that time, carried the name of my mother, Elizabeth Sandison, who died when I was ten and, below hers, and close together, the names of my grandfather and grandmother—John Sandison and

Catherine Sandison—for those two old people died within the same twenty-four hours.

There was no sadness, now, for me in this little green place in the lee of the little hill beside the sea, only a pleasant, loving nostalgia born of memories of these people that were all happy and gold-flecked with the sparkle of a childhood spent among them and that they had made warm and secure and happy for me. With the August sun slanting on the grass and on the lettering of their names, I did not think of death, but of them as they had been, not static and cold, but warm and full of the movement of the little foibles and quirks of character that, in my memory, had made them immortal. They had not died, for me, but had been overtaken in my mind by a change, so that I knew them as it were in a new way and in a new dimension, with a new knowledge that came to the mind from some other sphere. What was it Monica had said? "It is not only with their brains and intellects that people know things." She was right. I was no longer knowing these people with my brain or with my intellect, but I was knowing them in a way deeper

31

than I had ever known them before. Was this the change, the transmutation in knowing that had failed to come to Granny Gilmour about Guido? Granny Gilmour had an old woman's experience of death. She had lost her two sons in the war of 1914–18, she had lost her daughter Bella, the mother of Guido, in the influenza epidemic of 1919 and she had lost her husband, old Peter the Slater, only a few years ago. Granny Gilmour knew death—but she did not know it for Guido. Was it possible—? I shook my head, as if to shake sleep from my eyes, and saw Monica standing at the corner of the church looking down into the shallow hollow where the graves lay so I began to walk back towards her. When I reached her side she continued to stare out over the graveyard for a moment and then she shook her head, just as I had shaken mine a moment ago.

"That was queer," she said. "I've read about people getting that feeling of having been in a certain place before when they haven't, but I've never had it happen to me until now!"

"What in the world do you mean?"

"When I came out of the church and

looked round for you and saw you standing down there, I had a feeling of 'I have seen this before—a long time ago but I've seen it before—the sun on the grass, the shadows of the gravestones, that beech in full leaf—just as it is now. And somebody standing, just where you were standing!'"

Involuntarily I shivered. "Don't talk rot!" I said. "Of course you've been in this churchyard before and there's always somebody standing in it. This serves me right for encouraging a pregnant woman to drink whisky but, darn it, you only had three small ones. What's the matter with you?"

"Nothing at all. I feel as right as rain. But it was odd, odd how forcibly it came over me that I had seen it before and yet hadn't."

"Monica, try to talk sense! What do you mean?"

"Well, dammit, I know I haven't seen that exact thing before—not in this life—"

"Get into that car and drive us home or you won't see me any more in this life either. Holy smoke, I came home here from the West Indies on leave to rest my nerves and all I get is my favourite friend disappearing into the Celtic Twilight like a whigmaleerie!"

Starting the car, Monica giggled. "What's a whigmaleerie?"

"What you English call a will-o'-the-wisp, I think. I'm not very up in fairy lore, largely because of Tom and George. They don't hold with fairies, as you know, and they reduced them all to hard sense before I was six. But a lot of the words are very nice. Tom and George used to have a wonderful tale about two local characters, Dugald and Angus, who were coming home from the Plough one dark night with a little too much whisky on board. Tom and George were on the east moor—it was lambing time—and they heard Dugald and Angus coming, taking a short cut over to Dinchory, and Tom struck a match to light his pipe. Dugald said: 'God bless me, Angus, yon iss a whigmaleerie so it iss, and it iss myself that iss going right back to Achcraggan!' But Angus said: 'Not at a-all, Dugald, man. It iss the Reachfar moor we are on and there iss no whigmaleeries in it. What you wass seeing would chust be an ordinary kelpie!'"

And so we drove home, while I educated

Monica in a few fairy words such as bodach, uruisk, trow and dwerg, and I thought no more of the Celtic Twilight until the next day, when we went to call on old Granny Gilmour.

There was nothing of the twilight about the bright little cottage in the Church Lane of Achcraggan, with its red geraniums and pink pea-blossoms between the white lace curtains at the windows, and there was nothing of the wispy character of the whig-maleerie about Granny Gilmour when she opened her neat front door to us. She was a firm, round, pink-cheeked little lady with silver hair that still waved from its centre parting into the tight little knot at the back and, it being afternoon, she was wearing a small, gay, frilly apron over her flower-printed dress.

"So it is yourself, Leddy Monica!" she smiled, and then her bright eyes turned to me. "My, if it isn't Janet Reachfar! Dear me, Mrs. Alexander, I should say!"

"Janet Reachfar will do very well, Granny," I said. "It's the first name I ever had and I'm quite proud of it."

"Well, it is myself that is pleased to see you! My, but you're like your mother—

35

but there's a look of ould Mrs. Reachfar too. But come away in. And how are they all at Reachfar?"

The talk was very much as the talk had been on all the other visits I had made with Monica. I found myself, stimulated by the memories of Granny Gilmour, remembering all sorts of things that had long been submerged in my mind, overlaid by the more recent happenings of later life.

When Granny Gilmour discovered that we were making no other calls that day and thus had plenty of time, she insisted on making tea for us, and as she popped about from her little living-room to her little kitchen at the back, she seemed to become more spry and lively every minute.

"And this is my new present I bought for myself," she said, appearing with a sparkling electric kettle and plugging it in as if she had been accustomed to electric power all the days of her life. "To think of Tricity coming all that way!" she said then, and for a moment I thought she was talking of some newcomer to Achcraggan and so she was, although not the sort of newcomer I had imagined. "Was Leddy Monica telling you she took us for a jaunt up to where they make Tricity in Glen Ruidh? What a long way—three whole hours we was in the bus going—but very bonnie country. My, we did enjoy ourselves. . . . Has your auntie got a Tricity kettle at Reachfar?"

"Yes, she got one as a present," I said.

"They're very handy," she said as she poured boiling water into the teapot. "But I wouldna care for a washing-machine. Murdo Dickson was at me for to buy a washing-machine but I told him no. It would be different if Guido was at home, but when it's just me myself I'm not needing it. And anyway, I think maybe they're gey coorse on the clothes."

Throughout the conversation in the hour and a half that we spent with her, Guido's name came out in that way as if he, like so many of the sons and grandsons, daughters and grand-daughters of our district, were away in the south or in England, Canada or Australia earning his living. She had bought a small electric fire for Guido's room which was "right handy for keeping his things aired" and when I admired her plants on the window-sill she said: "I look after them the best I can, but it's Guido that's the best hand with the flowers." Had she been trying to convince me that she was right and the powers of the War Office wrong; that Guido was alive and not dead, she could have adopted no more convincing argument than this attitude of there being no argument involved because she was speaking out of a certainty of knowledge.

"And how is Daisy?" she asked me at one point, reminding me that Daisy Ramsay who helped to look after Crookmill for Twice and me was her cousin.

"I haven't been to Crookmill yet since we landed, Granny," I told her. "You see, we had the Smith children from America with us and we brought them straight up from Southampton. My husband and I are going down to Crookmill next week, though. We are going to have to sell it, for it seems that we'll be in the West Indies for the next few years and we can't afford to keep it."

"Daisy will be right disappointed," she said. "She's fair settled down down there —she never even bothers to come home for a holiday now."

2

WITH her remark about Daisy's disappointment, Granny Gilmour had hit a painful nail very fairly and squarely on the quick and, a few days later, when Twice and I had driven through Inverness and were on the road south for Perth, Stirling and eventually Crookmill, I said: "Twice, what are we going to do about Loose-an'-Daze?"

"Loose-an'-Daze" was our combined name for Daisy Ramsay and her friend Lucy Wilton, the joint caretakers of Crookmill. They were both widows of about sixty, both pretty in different ways, both silly and woolly-headed about many things, but both extremely capable in a domestic way and of a kindliness and loyalty that is very rare.

Eighteen months ago, when we had gone abroad for the first time, we had left them in charge of the house, they being delighted to have its roof under which to live on their limited means, and they had let the main part of it for short periods to various people who were seeking a home in the district. These rentals had not been without their tribulations, many of which Twice and I knew—although we did not say so to each other in so many words—were due to the idiosyncrasies of Loose-an'-Daze who, I could imagine, would expect every tenant to behave exactly as Twice and I had behaved, which is, after all, asking the impossible of everyone. For myself, I could imagine no worse fate than to have to live under the eye of Loose-an'-Daze if I liked my breakfast earlier than their former master or preferred strong tea when their former mistress had preferred it weak. Although the very apotheosis of the muddle-headed, their silly pretty faces could take on all the scornful disdain that any two particularly embittered camels might express. From our point of view, they were excellent caretakers had we been able to afford a house that we would occupy for, perhaps, three months in every two or three years. As two people who could run the house as an investment that would even cover expenses, they were a total failure.

Nor, at Crookmill, was the Loose-an'-

Daze combination all that the unwary tenant had to contend with. In 1947, when Twice and I had rehabilitated the place, which was a near-ruin, we had fallen into the toils of an old stonemason called Matthew, which he himself pronounced "Mattha", and of these toils we had never broken free. In the first place, he had been introduced to us in an advisory capacity about the alterations to the old stone walls of the house, for he was nearly eighty and, in theory, retired and being looked after by his spinster daughter in a lavish way on funds supplied by a son in America. Mattha, however, was very spry, very ill-tempered and highly ill-suited to idle retirement and he fell upon Crookmill, Twice, me, Loose-an'-Daze, our dog, our garden and everything connected with us in a dragoonish, bullying fashion which none of us had the strength of character to resist. He conscripted his grandsons who lived in Ballydendran, the local town, to dig the garden and chop the firewood; he oversaw the man who came to read the electric meter and accused him of being "nae better nor a Government-trained swindler"; he accused the coalman of overturning our gatepost with his lorry; he quarrelled incessantly with Loose-an'-Daze and, in general, made life as difficult as a cross, unreasonable old man can make it, but somehow, in the teeth of all sense and reason, both Twice and I were devoted to him. He had, somehow, something of the old, gnarled, cross-grained but rock-like quality that made the old Crookmill building the delightful place it was and this quality made Mattha part of it. Without Mattha, Crookmill, to us, would not be the same. "God knows what we can do about Loose-an'-Daze," Twice said now. "It's awful how disillusion catches up with a bloke. I always thought one of your greater charms was your trick of collecting faithful hangers-on and look where it's landed us!"

"Me?" I squealed. "I didn't collect them! It was you that got Kate to send Daze to us and it was Monica that brought Loose."

"But it was you that attached them in this limpet-like way. And what about Mattha? You can't blame him on anybody else—he's entirely your own work."

"Never mind that now," I said, being very cool and businesslike. "There's no point in holding a post-mortem about a lot of ancient history. There they are and what are we going to do about them?"

"Mattha will be all right," Twice said. "He'll miss the fun of creating the devil round the place but he'll just have to miss it. At least he's provided for. But what about these two silly women? We've got to get them absorbed somehow. . . . What about Monica's friends and relations? She's got as many of them as Brer Rabbit and they're all wealthy—wouldn't some of them be needing housekeepers?"

"None of them will be too keen about Loose. Most of the Loame family have suffered from her before as you well know. She was always getting into trouble of one kind and another and spraining her ankles and missing buses and being unreliable and they're all sick of her. Twice, it's funny that she's never been quite so unreliable at Crookmill. D'you suppose it's the influence of Daze?"

Twice snorted. "She may not have sprained her ankles at Crookmill, but she and Daze and their influence nearly broke all our hearts and sprained all our sanities at one time, if you remember. . . . I wonder if they're still chasing every middle-aged man that they see?"

"Oh, lord, I hope not! Actually, they did settle down a bit that time after Blair the banker two-timed them so badly."

"I know, but they've been more or less idle the last sixteen months," Twice said distrustfully, "and Satan finds some mischief still—"

"I wouldn't call them idle," I said sourly. "Look at the number of tenants they've sickened off."

"Don't. I wish I could hate them for it and go there and throw them out on to the road bag and baggage with lots of righteous conviction. But I can't. Life isn't that easy."

Off and on, throughout the journey which took most of the day, we talked of Loose-an'-Daze, but it was all quite pointless and when, in the late afternoon, we pulled up at the little bridge that led over the stream to the path across the garden to the house and they, flanked by Mattha and our dog, Dram, came running out to meet us, the idea that we should change all this, so that this scene would never be repeated, seemed more ridiculous and remote than ever.

"I said they would be here in plenty of time for supper—" said Loose.

"—and not just have cold meat and salad!" said Daze.

"But a proper meal—"

"—instead of a lot of makeshift nonsense about not knowing the time—"

"Ach, haud yer tongues for the love o' giddness ere ye deave us a'!" said Mattha.

Here, I thought, is life at Crookmill, completely unchanged, for, always, there was something of the Greek drama about those three—the strophe and antistrophe of Loose-an'-Daze interrupted now and then by the voice of doom from Mattha in his broad Border dialect.

And now a new voice broke into the drama. Dram, the mastiff dog that Twice had given me three years ago and who had not seen me for over a year, was standing beside Mattha, his golden coat shining, his head cocked and his high-borne tail waving slowly from side to side in a questioning way, but as soon as I spoke the words: "Hello, everybody!" his head suddenly changed position, seemed to change shape, even, as bright recognition came into his eyes and ears and he sprang, all eighty pounds of him, at the open door of the car, put his large feet in my lap, bowled me over on to Twice and began to lick my face in a suffocating fashion.

"Holy cow! Dram, get off, you brute!" Twice shouted and, with Twice pushing and Mattha pulling from behind, Dram, shivering with pleasure, was hauled out on to the grass and I too got out of the car.

"What a great big clever dog!" I said and Dram, beside himself now, hurled himself on the grass, rolled over and over several times and then with a loud salvo of barks galloped away up the hill by the stream as if to proclaim his joy from the hilltops.

"Ah wish a' the folk Ah ken wis as wyce as that dug," said Mattha with a sour look at Loose-an'-Daze. "Weel, Ah'm real pleased tae see yee. We wis startin' tae think that yeez wis niver comin' back frae that heathenish place oot there. Hoo ur yeez?"

"Dry," said Twice. "Have you a drink in the house?"

"Aye, Ah huv that, although if ye left it

46

tae some folk yer whistle wid be gey dry aboot here."

"It's in the sideboard," said Daze.

"Left-hand cupboard," said Loose.

"And we'll bring the luggage."

"And Mattha, you'll help—"

"Yes, and not go in there and start drinking—"

"As if there was nothing to be done—"

"Fur the love o' Jimmy Johnson get oot o' ma bliddy road ere Ah get they cases ooty that caur! Ah help ma Bob, if Ah hudnae the patience o' a bliddy saint Ah'd hae killt ye baith lang syne!"

Twice and I both, I think, feeling how remarkable was the fact that this familiar babel could blot out sixteen months spent in a foreign land and induce the feeling that time had telescoped itself, left them quarrelling about the car and the baggage, went over the bridge, up the path and into the house.

It shone at us with an air of true welcome, a welcome that was long planned and into which much thought and effort had gone. It gleamed from the favourite flowers in the favourite vases, from the polish on the furniture, from the basket of birch logs beside the bright fire and from the tin of tobacco on the mantel and the box of cigarettes beside my chair. I felt tears rise to my eyes and Twice, at the sideboard, was being unusually dilatory and clumsy about opening the whisky bottle and pouring the drinks, but, within moments, the three of them were upon us again, loaded with coats and suitcases and quarrelling as if they had never quarrelled before, but had newly come to it with the first flush of rapturous strength.

"Oh, shut up, the lot of you!" said Twice, as if he had last spoken these words that morning and not over a year ago. "And sit down and have a drink."

"There's the supper—" said Loose.

"You stay—I'll see to the supper," said Daze.

"No, you stay. I'll go."

"No, I'll go!"

"You'll both go!" I said. "Twice, give them some sherry and let them go. Otherwise they'll only canter to and fro to the kitchen and drive us all nuts."

"That's the best idea—"

"You see, there's the gravy—"

"And the cream to whip—"

"Tak' yer tongues tae the cream!" said Mattha. "They'll whup it richt enough if they dinnae soor it first!"

With a joint glance of uppity disdain at Mattha they took themselves happily off to the kitchen with their small glasses of sherry.

"My," said Mattha, accepting his whisky, "it's they twae that's had a time o' it gettin' ready fur yeez comin'."

Now that they were out of hearing, his voice was full of an indulgent affection and an almost loving smile wrinkled still more his gnarled old face.

"They had the place fair upside-doon wi' their cleanin' an' it no' needin' it, ye ken, fur they've kept it fair spotless the hale time yeez wis awa'. God sake, but they're an awfy pair. An' ye ken their latest cairry-on?"

"No. What?"

"They're at the horse-racin' an' the fitba' coupons!"

"Gambling, you mean?"

"Whit else? It wad fair gi'e ye the grue tae hear them. They dinnae ken which en' o' a horse rins first or a goalpost frae a referee's weskit, but they won ten bob apiece on the Derby a year back an' there's nae haudin' them iver since. Ye'd laugh yer en' at them wi' the fitba' coupon. They dae it accordin' tae their hoaryscope."

"Horoscope?" Twice frowned in puzzlement.

Mattha gave one of his hoarse, malevolent chuckles. "Aye. They get the hoaryscope in this wumman's maggyzine that they get ilka Thursday—yin o' them is Jiminy an' the ither yin is Saggy-somethin' but Ah niver can mind which o' them is whae."

"And what then?" Twice asked, quite fascinated.

"Bless ye, dinnae ask me! They coont the nummer o' letters in the furst word o' the hoaryscope an' if it's fower letters they put the fowerth team on the coupon tae win. Then they gang tae the end o' the hoaryscope an' coont backwards an' if it's five letters in that word, the fifth team frae the bo'om o' the coupon is pit in tae win. Then they—"

"Think of a number and take away the age of their aunt less the figures of the year she was born in?"

"That's jist aboot it," Mattha agreed.

"And how much do they spend on all this?" I asked.

"Ach, only hauf-a-croon a week—wan an' thruppense the piece—an' it's jist the yae coupon atween the twae o' them. An speired at them whit wey they didnae dae yin apiece an' they tell't me union wis strength. Ah'm an auld man gettin', but Ah niver seen a dafter pair o' weemen then them twae an' yet ye cannae help but like them. . . . Och, weel, Ah maun awa' doon the road hame. It's richt fine tae see yeez back frae that ootlandish place oot there. Ah'll be up the morn gin ye're needin' onything."

He creaked away out of the room, leaving us alone by the bright fire.

Compared with our house in St. Jago, whose style of architecture might be described as colonial Georgian, for Guinea Corner had been built in Georgian times, the rooms at Crookmill were small, low and cosy, for the St. Jagoan rooms were all open on at least one side to a verandah. This cosiness, indeed, was the most striking difference between St. Jago and Britain— the cosiness, the small tidiness, the feeling of wild nature having been brought under cultivation and control. Compared with St. Jago's bush-covered mountains, the rocky lulls of Ross, even, seemed to be thoroughly domesticated. But even while I enjoyed the cosy domestication, the tidy smallness of the garden that lay beyond the windows within its neat stone wall, I wondered if I could live in this house as I used to do without feeling confined.

"Twice," I said, "everything in this country is very small and neat and well-regulated, isn't it?"

He leaned towards the fire and knocked out his pipe. "Including the small one and threepences gambled neatly away every week, regulated by one's horoscope," he said and laughed. "What will these two women get up to next?"

"I must say I don't have much patience with horoscope football coupons," I agreed with him. "It seems so terribly damn silly even for Loose-an'-Daze. And it's fearfully depressing to think there are probably millions of people doing these coupons every week and probably by very similar queer and mystic rules, because it's their only way of occupying their leisure."

"A thing that seems to have been overlooked in this social trend of this century towards more leisure for everybody," Twice said, "is that it takes considerable intelligence to obtain real satisfaction from leisure. Leisure is a state you have to be trained for just as an athlete has to be trained to run a mile in record time, and it takes longer to train people for leisure than it does to train athletes. I'm not sure that the leisure thing doesn't take centuries. Anyway, I've met very few people who have the gift of employing leisure constructively and getting real satisfaction out of it, and the ones I have met have all been the children, grand-children and great-grand-children of a leisured class."

"Like Monica?"

"Yes, Monica's the real thing. As the mistress of Poyntdale, she needn't lift a finger if she doesn't want to, but do you find her reduced to doing football coupons by her horoscope? Not on your life. She casts round and finds something constructive to do that she gets fun out of doing. And I'll tell you another thing—George and Tom have the gift of being leisurely, but your father hasn't got it any more than I have. At Reachfar, he and I had to be doing something we thought was useful, like that thing of fencing the garden, and before we knew where we were we were going at it as if we were being paid for it at piece-work rates. But not Tom and George. They didn't care whether a post was driven today or tomorrow. I could have kicked them, but I envied them. And I can't see why they are like that. They've worked hard all their lives and should have the cursed habit of work just as much as your father and I have."

I laughed. "Tom and George have no real habits. They are the freest men I know and always have been. They have always had an air of never being dominated by their work—they always kept it in its place, treated it as a thing that they would do if they felt like it but not otherwise. I think my grandmother's philosophy about working hard and getting on in the world and all that took much more on Dad than on Tom and George. Those two have the real Highland temperament of the day being more important than the evil that's sufficient to it, if you see what I mean. They seem to say to themselves: 'Well, here's another day of my time in this world!' and they don't bother about what to achieve in it or what its evil is—the day itself is enough and a happy thought and you just go along enjoying it. If you see a fence that needs mending in the course of it and you feel like mending a fence, you mend it, but you don't insult the day first thing in the morning by thinking: 'I'll mend that fence today,' as if the day were good for nothing but mending a fence."

"And you have a good touch of that temperament yourself," Twice told me. "Since I've known you, which is about six years now, I've spent more time sitting talking than I ever spent in my life before. It's great fun, but it doesn't get us any further with this business of selling this place, for instance. We ought to tell these two old football-by-the-stars experts as soon as possible, you know."

"Oh, fiddlesticks!" I said. "We'll tell them tomorrow. Let's have another drink and have our supper in peace for one night."

While Twice poured the drinks I added: "I told Monica we were going to sell, by the way. Knowing half the earth as she does, she might just rustle up the right buyer."

"That's true. And I'll tell them at the Works when I go along there tomorrow. But maybe we ought to give it to a house-agent as well, Flash. I don't want to go back to St. Jago with this hanging round our necks again."

"No, darling, I know. But it'll be all right. . . . The other thing we should do is plan this leave a bit. Otherwise the few months will slip through our fingers and we'll have nothing to talk about to each other when we go back. . . . When are you going to the Midlands?"

"Oh, I'll be up and down and to and fro, but if we go to London, I can drive up from there as well as I can drive down from here. That needn't tie us at all."

"Monica wants me to go to Beechwood and it would be handy for you for Birmingham and so on. I'd like to go. And apart from that, I think Monica should get away from the north and the clutches of her county work and her old people for a bit."

Twice's glance sharpened. "She's all

right, isn't she? I mean, she and Torquil are hitting it all right?"

"Oh, lord, yes! She's happier than I ever thought she could be but—"

"But what?"

"Oh, well, she's pregnant, but she was full of capers that didn't seem terribly characteristic of her. Old Granny Gilmour's grandson that she brought up was killed in the war but Granny refuses to believe it and thinks he is still alive and Monica is getting kind of rattly about it. Then, when we went to the church at Achcraggan, she claimed to have had one of these 'I-have-been-here-before' time-slips. It's all stupid, but I think a change would be good for her. After all, it's a pretty narrow life up there for someone like Monica who used to rattle round the world like a pea on a drum."

"If she starts that I-have-been-here-before stuff with Torquil, there'll be trouble," Twice said. "Crikey, you and I have all the luck. We've just left the black magic and obeah of St. Jago to come here and find half our friends juggling with the time-scale and the other half with football by the stars. At the end of this leave you and I are going to be seen running for St. Jago as to a beloved sanctuary."

"I shouldn't be surprised," I said.

At that moment there was a loud thud against the front door which was at the end of a little passage off the room where we sat, a thud I had not heard for sixteen months but which I recognised at once.

"That's Dram," said Twice and opened the door. "Come on, then, chum!"

Very proudly, like the ambassador of an emperor bearing a precious gift, his head erect, his tail at the high port, Dram came across the room and laid at my feet a very large, very black, very skinny, very dead cat.

"Oh, Heavens!" I said, staring up at Twice who took even longer than I did to regain his speech.

Dram, looking from one of us to the other, was slowly realising that this, the largest prey which he had been able to find —for he knew he must not attack sheep or cattle—was not pleasing us and his tail waved from side to side for a moment, then began to move more slowly, then drooped limply towards the floor and then his proud ears sagged and, last of all, he retired heavily to a corner and sat down with his back to us.

"Oh, Dram, you wick—"

"Don't!" said Twice. "The fellow was doing a fellow's very best. Dram, come here!"

His head on one side, his eyes questioning, Dram came over to Twice who put his hand under the dog's jaw and said: "But you shouldn't have done it, though. No!"

Dram looked at the dead cat and gave a sad sigh, then looked at me. "Oh, all right," I said. "But don't do it again." I went to the door to the back quarters. "Loose! Daze! . . . D'you know whose cat this is—was?"

"It's dead!"

"The poor pussy!"

"Oh, it's bad luck!"

"Right on the hearthrug!"

"Oh dear!"

"Oh goodness!"

With one accord they both burst into tears and fled from the room.

"Holy blistering cow!" said Twice, and spreading out a newspaper he scooped the dead cat into it, and carried it away outside.

At long last, we had supper, with Loose-an'-Daze sniffling through each course, blowing their noses in the kitchen between courses and speaking throughout of nothing but the evil omen of the dead black cat on the hearthrug on our first night home. "Oh, rats!" Twice snapped sharply at last, utterly exasperated, forgetting that this was a word fraught with danger. But Dram had not forgotten. At the very sound, he bounded from my side at the table and was out through the window and as he passed we heard the glass of three panes tinkle to the floor as his heavy shoulder hit the window-frame. Twice looked grimly at Loose-an'-Daze who were now on the verge of nervous giggles.

"Please go away quietly to bed, you two," he said, tight-lipped. "I cannot stand any more. This place is a mad-house."

With a minimum of noise and movement, they cleared the table and went away, leaving us alone among the broken glass.

"I'm very sorry, Twice," I said humbly. "Life as it seems to—to accrue round me is not what you are used to and it's very trying for you. All I can say is that it never accrued in such an extraordinary way before I met you."

He stared at me for a second and then suddenly burst into laughter. "All right. Let's say that this is what accrues round the combination of what Tom would call the both of the two of us." He scraped the toe of his shoe about among the broken glass. "Let's go to bed. I wonder where that damn' dog is now? Dram!"

Like a genie out of a bottle, the forward part of Dram appeared, the head rearing above the large fore-paws on the window-sill, and in the mouth there was a very large, very ugly but still live rat. I loathe rats.

"Don't bring that in here," I screamed at him.

"Go and sit down," Twice told me and I obeyed by leaving the room altogether and sitting down in my bedroom where I began to get undressed. After about ten minutes, Twice came in and shut the door.

"That dog!" I said. "Has he killed it?"

"Yes, and he's in his bed and very pleased with himself. He's going to be a riot when we get him out to St. Jago. The negroes are terrified of any dog and I've never seen a mastiff in the island. I wonder what they'll think of him?"

61

"It's more important to me what he'll think of them! Killing black cats is one thing but killing black men is quite another. . . . And I wonder who that cat belonged to anyway? I don't like cats very much but I don't approve of Dram killing them either."

Twice rolled into bed and picked up his book. "Oh, well, if it was somebody's darling let's hope they never find out about its sad end. But I don't think it was. It was some starving, mangy stray and it's probably happier dead. . . . Gosh, this is a comfortable little house! I'd forgotten how nice it was."

"You stop that!" I told him. "This house is for sale."

The next morning I arose in a very businesslike frame of mind and as soon as breakfast was over and Twice had left for the Ballydendran Engineering Works, which was the Scottish headquarters of his firm, I equipped myself with paper and pencil and began to make a list of the furniture that was to be sold with the house. I had made up my mind to part with and had written down "six upright chairs, 1948 Utility Period" when Loose-an'-Daze insinuated themselves into my bedroom and closed the door behind them in a fashion so conspiratorial that I felt that the waves of secrecy emanating from them must be palpable in the High Street of Ballydendran two miles away.

"There's a policeman outside!" hissed Loose.

"Talking to Mattha!" Daze said in sepulchral antistrophe.

"And Mattha's swearing—"

"—and insulting him—"

I waited for no more but strode out into the garden.

The policeman was standing in the middle of the back-yard, looking like a large, astonished, peace-loving bloodhound, while Mattha faced him, spitting, snarling and growling like a very small, ill-tempered terrier and Dram was sitting on the grass regarding them both, with a flicker of malignancy now and then at the policeman.

"—an' awa' ye go an' stop the wee laddies frae stealin' plooms!" Mattha was concluding his vicious tirade. "There's nae cat got killt here last nicht or ony ither nicht an' if it hud've got killt here it hud nae richt tae be here!"

"Good morning," I said to the constable. "What's the matter?"

"It's Madame Zora, Madam. She has laid a complaint that last night she saw this man deliberately help this dog of his here to catch one of her cats and kill it."

I looked at Mattha. He at once looked away from me, hunched one shoulder and spat into the cabbage patch, and when I looked at the dog he rose, went close to Mattha and lay down with his large head on the toe of Mattha's heavy boot.

"Mattha?" I said.

"We did nut, Ah'm tellin' ye!" he said and spat again. "An' even if we did, yeez cannae prove it! Madam Zory! Madam Zory ma backside! She's plain Lizzie Fintry an' aye wis an' aye wull be noo, fur whit man wid mairry yon? Madam Zory an' her cats! Ah've a gidd mind tae—"

"Mattha—" I began.

"Noo, jist you listen tae me, Mistress!" he said. "Dinnae you tak' ony notice o' him!" He looked in the direction of the constable and spat. "A cat's no' a dacent leeshenced beast like a dug an' Lizzie

64

Fintry can go an' scratch hersel' aboot her bliddy cat as faur's the law's concerned. An' besides, she cannae prove whae killt it!"

"Madame Zora saw your dog doing it," said the policeman. "From her bedroom window."

"An' whae's gonny believe her in a coort o' law if Ah say the dug never did kill it? Are you stan'in' there in yer big bitts an' yer impidence tellin' me that the sheriff'll tak' the word o' a fortune-teller like Lizzie Fintry that made her livin' tellin' lees afore ma word an' me a dacent stonemason tae ma tredd? Awa' ye go hame to yer polis station afore Ah get sweerin' at ye, Wullie Beattie, ye big thowless lump, ye!"

"Madame Zora says that you set your dog—"

"Constable Beattie," I said, "the dog is mine."

"Noo, you listen tae me, Mistress—"

"Mattha, be quiet!" I said and turned to the policeman again. "Dram, the dog, did bring home a dead cat last night and if it was Madame Zora's cat I am very sorry. What do we do now?"

The constable drew breath to speak and

65

then looked at Mattha in silence. Mattha scowled at both of us, spat again and drew himself up to his full crumpled height till he looked like a defiant, wind-twisted old tree.

"Ye neednae bother aboot the dug an' me," he said with dignity. "We ken when we're no' wantit. Come on, Dram!" The two of them moved away down the path. "But the only time we iver killt a cat, it wis sair needin' killin'!" he threw back at us over his shoulder, and the dog, as if in agreement, looked back too before jumping across the stream while Mattha stumped over the little bridge.

I turned back to the policeman and said: "I am very, very sorry about the whole thing, Constable, but I realise that that's no use. What happens next?"

"To tell the truth, Madam," he told me in a confidential voice, "the very fact that the dog is yours and not his"—he jerked his head in the direction that Mattha had gone—"will make a lot of difference. Madame Zora has a spite at Mattha—it comes down from long ago—her father and Mattha's father had a big row once—"

"Are you a Ballydendran man, then, Constable Beattie?" I asked.

"Aye. I was born and bred here."

"You weren't stationed here two years ago, were you?"

"No, I was still in the Army then. I stayed in for a bit after the war but then I got married and came out and joined the Force."

I like finding out about people and hearing their life histories and, by the time the constable and I had had a cup of coffee, I had heard all about the row fifty years ago between Mattha's stonemason father and Mr. William Fintry, Building Contractor, which had consisted in Mattha Senior clouting Mr. Fintry over the head with a mallet, whereupon Mr. Fintry had Mattha Senior charged with assault, whereupon Mattha Senior exposed to the County Council that for the flooring of a certain school Mr. Fintry had used deal and had charged for pine, all of which had led to a major Ballydendran scandal just about the turn of the century.

"And why is Miss Fintry called Madame Zora?" I enquired.

"It's sort of a professional name, like,

Mrs. Alexander. She's a fortune-teller and crystal-gazer and that—or she was—down in London, and she kept a boarding-house place too, I believe. But she doesn't do much at either the fortune-telling or the room-letting now, although she's got a brass plate that says Astrology on the front gate of Dunroamin."

"Dunroamin? Is that the name of her house?"

"Aye. It's up the back lane behind the Free Kirk. It's not a bad name for a house except that Willie Fintry never roamed very much—he spent all his days in Ballydendran. He was born down the Causeway behind the slaughter-house and all the roaming he ever did was up to the lane behind the Kirk. Lizzie—Madame Zora, that is—came back here after he died last year."

"And is she living here permanently now?"

"Aye. Folk said she would likely sell Dunroamin and go away back to London, but not her. She moved in a year bye last July and there she's been ever since, quite the thing."

"Oh, lord, the cat!" I said, called back

as if by a knell to the present and the business in hand.

"Ach, I wouldn't worry about it if I was you, Mrs. Alexander," he told me comfortably. "I'm sure if you were to go and see her and sort of apologise and that, it would be all right."

"Do you think so? And I could offer to get another cat for her."

"She's got about a dozen already, but being a Fintry she wouldn't likely could resist it if she was getting offered another one for nothing."

"An' that's the truest word ye ever spoke, Wullie Beattie!" said the voice of Mattha through the open window.

"You keep out of this, Mattha," I said, "for you and that damned dog have made enough trouble already."

"No' as muckle as that cat made. That cat kill't a hale cleckin' o' auld Jeanie's chickens, that's whit it did."

"Why didn't Jeanie report that?" the constable asked.

"Because she's got mair sense an' less bliddy impidence than Lizzie Fintry!" said Mattha. "Jeanie's no' daft enough to wear oot the polis bitts that ye get oot o' oor taxes walkin' aboot efter things that there's nae proof fur!"

"Mattha," I said sternly, "what did you do with the corpse of that cat?"

"Whit corpse o' whit cat?"

"It was in the coal cellar. Twice put it there last night. It's not there now."

"Ah niver saw nae corpse o' nae cat an' if there wis a corpse o' a cat, ma coal cellar's no' the place fur it. Naeboddy's got nae business in ma coal cellar, as they twae Loose-an'-Daze as ye ca' them can tell ye tae their cost, an' if Ah wis tae see cats' corpses in it Ah'm tellin' ye there widnae hauf be a Battle o' the Boyne aboot here!"

Mercifully, at this moment his attention was attracted by Dram and he bawled: "Dang ye! Dinnae gae diggin' that up the noo, man! Hae ye nae mair sense nor a cat yersel'?" and he jerked away with his rheumaticky walk across the garden and out of sight. When I looked back at the policeman, he was smiling and I smiled back at him and said: "I'll go and see Madame Zora as soon as I possibly can, Constable Beattie—this afternoon if I can manage it."

"I'm sure that'll fix it, Mrs. Alexander.

She knows she hasn't really got a case. But she made the complaint and you know how it is. We have to do something."

"I know," I said, comforting him and full of sympathy for him as he rode away on his bicycle, and only after he was out of sight did it occur to me that probably I myself had greater need of sympathy than he had.

Twice came home for lunch full of sparkle after a happy morning at the Works. He is an engineer and we were on this few months of leave after about sixteen months of intensive engineering on his part in St. Jago, but he still, apparently, found a morning at an engineering works more relaxing and interesting than any other form of activity.

"Well," he said to me over a glass of beer before lunch, "told Loose-an'-Daze?"

"Told them what?"

"About the house!"

"No," I said and looked with intensity out of the window.

"But they'd have seen you listing the furniture," he said comfortably. "I suppose they'll catch on."

"I didn't list the furniture," I said, still looking out of the window.

"Then what the blazes have you been doing all the morning?"

"Smoothing down the law about Madame Zora's cat."

"Whose cat?"

"Madame Zora's."

"Who's she?"

"A crystal-gazer."

He put his glass of beer carefully to one side and studied me closely. "Are you feeling all right?" he asked. "I mean you haven't fallen down or hit your head or anything?"

I merely stared at him in an uppish way.

"Who is Madame Zora?"

"I told you. She's a crystal-gazer that lives in the back lane behind the Free Kirk at a house called Dunroamin."

"Dunroamin?"

"It means finished wandering."

"Finished wandering?"

"That's what the policeman said."

"The policeman?"

"His name is Willie Beattie. And her name is Lizzie Fintry."

"Whose?"

"Madame Zora's. And I have to go to see her this afternoon."

"What for?"

"To apologise about that dog of yours killing her cat."

"He's your dog."

"I didn't teach him to kill things."

"And that's why he brings home live rats."

Dram, who had been looking from one of us to the other, taking an intelligent interest in the conversation, sprang up and pushed his head under the sofa at the word "rats". He could not get it out again. It is too big. He is always getting his head under things and not being able to get it out again. We have never discovered how he gets it in, in the first place. We rose and each took an end of the sofa and tilted it to set him free.

"Siddown and don't move!" Twice then said to him, and he sat down between us again and Twice said to me: "Did this woman actually see Dram killing her cat then?"

"She saw worse than that. She saw Mattha actually egging Dram on and helping him to kill it."

"Good lord! Have you spoken to Mattha?"

"You know perfectly well that there is not the least use in speaking to Mattha as you call it. Madame Zora's father had Mattha's father in court fifty years ago for clouting him over the head with a mallet and if Mattha gets the chance he and Dram will kill all Madame Zora's cats and no power on earth will stop him."

"How many more cats has she got then?"

"The constable said about a dozen, but I don't know how accurate that is."

"And you're going to see her and apologise?"

"That's what Constable Beattie thought would be best."

"You sound terribly depressed, Flash. I shouldn't worry if I were you. After all, I don't think anybody can do anything about a cat getting killed."

"I'm having to do plenty!" I said. "If you think it's easy to apologise to crystal-gazers about their dead cats, why don't you take a crack at it yourself? Besides . . ."

"Besides what?"

"This leave of ours is getting away on the wrong foot. There's far too much magic

74

getting into it, what with Monica having time-slips and Loose-an'-Daze and their horoscopes and now crystal-gazers' cats. I came home here feeling like being welcomed and cosseted and having people interested in me and my travels beyond the seas and instead of that they think of nothing but football coupons and old people's outings and dead cats. I wish I was back in St. Jago!"

"Are you really feeling disappointed in the leave, Flash?"

I do not know precisely the extraordinary nature of the bond that can unite two people to a degree when certain words, looks and gestures have a peculiar private significance, but when Twice speaks the word "really" with a certain anxiety in his blue glance from under heavy eyelids in his down-bent face, I feel that a nerve-like connection is vibrating between him and myself and that, when I answer him, my meaning must be delicately and precisely clear.

I smiled at him now and said: "Oh, not really and not disappointed at all, darling. After all, we're still in the first fortnight of this leave. But I do feel a little foreign and

75

as if the world at home here had gone marching on without missing me from the ranks and that by coming back I have upset its neat formation a little. Don't you have any feeling of that?"

"I think it's the old thing of its being better to travel hopefully than to arrive."

"My friend Mr. Rollin was the first to say that to me," I said, remembering.

Twice smiled. "We've looked forward to this leave for so long and built it up into some sort of blaze of glory and now that it's here it is just some more living—no better and no worse than any other bit of living. Cheer up, my pet. It may get better as we go along—as you say, maybe the first fortnight's always the worst."

I grinned at him. "Unjust, I call it. For the best end of a year and a half I've felt like a stranger and a sojourner in St. Jago waiting for the day when I'd come back here and now I feel like an S. and S. here waiting for the time to go back to St. Jago. Life seems to have turned into a permanent transit camp."

"There's a whole religion based on that idea—forget what they call it—that this life is only a sort of transit camp between one state of being and another and that we wander through it in a state that is really amnesia or semi-consciousness compared with the experience of the real lives on either side of it."

"No, look, Twice, don't you go starting getting funny and fey and other-worldly. Just you stop thinking about things like that. What you and I want to do is take life firmly by the forelock as it comes along and do the thing that seems to need doing each day. . . . What are you going to do this afternoon?"

"Start drawing the lay-out for the mill-house of Paradise Sugar Factory, St. Jago."

"Aw, Twice, can't you ever forget engineering?"

"Easily, given the right stimulus. Any suggestions?"

"Well, I thought you might come with me to this woman about this cat."

"Not me!" He shied like a horse and then added: "Besides, if I did you know what would happen."

"What?"

"We'd get the giggles or something. Anyway, in my bones I know it's better for you to go on your own."

"In your bones you lie in your teeth, you darned coward!" I said.

"And," he continued, "when we embarked on this marriage thing the agreement was that I would earn the pennies and you would attend to all matters social and domestic."

"Dram killing a crystal-gazer's cat on the other side of the hill is neither social nor domestic."

"And it's nothing to do with the penny-earning."

"Then it's outside the whole terms of the agreement," I said, glaring at him. "That's just what I'm complaining about really! It seems to me that half my life and half the things I have to do in it are outside the terms of anything that ever was. I have a feeling that everything is getting away fair daft, as Mattha says. I feel everything is getting out of control."

"Oh, you and your feelings!"

"Dunroamin!" I exploded. "Willie Fintry was lucky. I wish I had finished wandering and knew where I was going for a change!"

3

DUNROAMIN looked to me like exactly the right sort of house for keeping a lot of cats in, for it was a heavy-looking villa of grey stone, with heavily-curtained windows and a garden full of nothing but gravel paths and sick-looking laurels growing out of sour-looking, slimy soil. It had a dark brown front door leading into a brown-tiled hall with brown-papered walls and a stained-glass window on the brown staircase. I mean, if the cats forgot themselves and were unpleasant about the house, one would not have noticed anything—it was all too dim and dark—except for the smell. I must say I noticed the smell right away, even before the door was opened. I think it rose from the coir doormat but it may have been coming from under the laurels. But when Madame Zora opened her front door, I became unconscious of everything except herself—even the smell of the cats ceased to assail me, all my senses being engaged with this extraordinary apparition. I am a tall woman, anywhere between five feet eight and ten inches according to the heels I am wearing, and I am spare rather than fat, so that, in the main, I find other women shorter and stouter than myself and seldom have I met any woman at whom I have to look up. Madame Zora was the exception to all my former experience. She must have been six feet tall and she was gauntly thin and narrow and so hung about with necklaces and floating, gauzy scarves and loose flowing panels on her ankle-length dress that she had the appearance of an uncompromisingly angular, cast-iron lamp standard that had been elaborately clad in black crape for some important funeral. In the dim light of the dark brown hall she presented to my eyes a frightening mixture of the solid and the ethereal. The gaunt, pole-like, black-clad body from ankles to neck seemed to be more solid than normal human flesh, and the floating gauze draperies seemed to be more ethereal than any textile stuff made by human hands and, at the neck, the material of which she was made seemed to change, for the solid black of the dress gave way to a face so heavily powdered with dead white that it was almost luminously green around the deep cavities of the sunken dark eyes. And she seemed to have no forehead, for her hair, of the hard black that only dye can give to human hair, was drawn in a tight, lustreless swathe from temple to temple immediately above her eyebrows.

"Gug-good-afternoon," I stammered, my faculties already impaired as the faculties can so quickly be by the lightning messages which the eyes carry to the brain. "Madame Zora?"

I held out my hand as is my ingrained Highland habit when meeting a stranger but she ignored it and, dramatically, she swept aside a brown velvet curtain that hung just inside the door, so that with a rattle of wooden rings and a hissing "swish!" it struck the wall on my right. Then, spreading wide both her drapery-festooned arms and throwing her head back so that her face became a white plane with two black crescents on it atilt on her scrawny neck, she intoned: "I knew it! I kne-ew it! The dark-haired stranger is here! Welcome, stranger! Enter!"

With a second sweeping gesture, she hit

81

the edge of the heavy brown door, causing it to swing shut with a loud crash and I sprang inside to avoid being crushed like a walnut in a nutcracker. Madame Zora, chanting in a sepulchral voice words about "the dark-haired stranger from far away", had now turned away from me down the dim hall and I felt that there was nothing to do but follow her, but when I tried to step forward, I discovered that the back of my pleated tweed skirt was caught in the door. It was a horrid moment. It was a dull day outside, the stained-glass window looked to the north, it was very dim in the hall of that house, Madame Zora chanting to herself was disappearing down a dark passage beneath a staircase, and out of the darkness there shone what seemed to me to be thousands of little green lamps, all in pairs, all at different levels, and the air was full of stealthy, sinuous movement. For a moment, I had an urge to scream like a banshee and then I had a fleeting vision of Dram with a black cat in his mouth.

"And he was darn right," I said, aloud, I think, and then I shouted into the dimness: "Madame Zora!"

"Follow me! Follow me-ee, dear stranger!" she called back, her voice sounding as if it came from inside a hollow hill. I tried to twist round to get at the catch of the door, whereupon I discovered that it was some patent device fixed at a height of about eight feet from the ground, which I could not have reached even on tiptoe had I been facing the right way and would not have known how to work even if I could have reached it. And the green eyes of the cats seemed to be closing in. I do not like cats.

"Madame Zora!" I shouted.

"Follow me! Follow me-ee!" the voice floated back.

"Don't be a fool!" I shouted, deciding that only desperate measures would be of any avail. "Come back here at once!"

"You spoke, dear stranger?"

"You bet I did!" I shouted down the hall. "I can't move. My skirt's caught in this confounded door!"

Madame Zora materialised beside me, opened the door, I snatched my skirt free, the door clicked shut and, as if this technical hitch had never occurred, she went back into her routine and with a "Follow me! Follow me-ee, dear stranger!" she floated off down the hall again while I, in my heavy brogues, clumped stolidly in her wake.

I think that the room in which we eventually arrived through another door and another brown velvet curtain on wooden rings had originally been a pantry. It was not very large; it was semi-basement, for the back of the house was built into the side of a hill and its only window was a small high one, with bars, that looked out on to a wall of grey stone about a foot away. It was crowded with heavy furniture, ornaments, draperies and knick-knacks, it was dankly and miserably cold and it smelled inexorably and sickeningly of cats.

"My sanctum," said Madame Zora. "The citadel of my soul where I awaited you," with which she sat down, closed her eyes, raised both her arms to shoulder level and in a ceremonious, ritual way placed her finger-tips upon her eyelids.

I am pathetically slow-witted in some ways, but it was now suddenly borne in on me that Madame Zora thought that I was a customer or client or patient for crystal-gazing and that this was the reason for the mystic welcome. And I was embarrassed, because the fakery was so obvious, with the embarrassment that one feels on seeing something that would be tawdry at best shabbily presented, so that all its sleaziness was exaggerated. It was like a second-rate act at a second-rate music hall that had long ago been defeated by the newer, more showy second-rateness of the cinema next door. The two prerequisites, I think, for charlatanism to succeed are that it should be slick and up-to-date. Madame Zora's crystal on its black-velvet-covered table, her fly-blown charts of the Zodiac signs, her yellowed diagrams of the lines on the human hand, were dim with the dust of yester-year and her act as the mystic seer creaked as loudly and unslickly as did the joints of her shoulders and elbows when she lowered her hands from her forehead. She opened her sunken eyes and looked at me and I came out of embarrassment and into pathos.

"My name," I said gently, "is Janet Alexander. I came—I came—because—"

"Because it was your fate to come!" she chanted at me. "We are all bound inexorably to the wheel of fate and it was written that you were to come here today."

Well, she might be right at that, I thought. If Dram and Mattha hadn't gone and killed that cat, I wouldn't be here. Fate is as good a name as any for the trouble I get into.

"I came here because my dog killed your cat," I said, and as I spoke the word I became conscious of two very skinny cats —one tortoiseshell and one grey—rubbing themselves against my legs. "One of your cats!" I amended hastily. "And I'm very sorry indeed. If there is any compensation I can make—"

"Ten shillings!" she said suddenly, in a voice so different from her intoning, fortune-telling one that I almost jumped.

"Ten shillings?" I repeated stupidly.

"I do not bargain. Ten shillings."

"Why, certainly, Madame Zora," I said, recovering my wits. "There is no question of bargaining!"

I was about to add that it was cheap at the price, but thought in time that even for me such a remark would be a little too stupid. I opened my handbag which had in it all the usual things that are found in ladies' handbags and also one or two things that are less usual, such as a small adjustable spanner that Twice had put in there for safe keeping and a half-pound block of chocolate which was our sweet ration for the month at that time, if I remember rightly, but the important thing was that there was no money in my bag at all. For some peculiar reason, this induced in me a panic-stricken feeling that here I was in this house with the bars on the windows, with this queer woman and all these cats—at that moment three more cats sidled into the room and eyed me balefully—and she wanted ten shillings and I could not give it to her and now what? I shivered, took a desperate pull at myself and looked up at her, but before I could speak she said: "What a lot of chocolate!" Startled again, and startled out of my panic, I stared at her and saw that her eyes were fixed avidly on the blue paper that wrapped the chocolate lying in the open bag. A dozen thoughts flicked through my mind. Sweets are still rationed in Britain! She's terribly thin! Look at her eyes! She's hungry! Ten shillings for the cat! She's starving! She has this house but no money! Nobody wants their fortunes told! She's starving! I took out the block of chocolate. "Do have it!" I said. "This dreadful rationing still—we get lots of sweets abroad where we are!"

She was about to snatch the chocolate from me, but just in time she remembered her fortune-telling manner, became suddenly grand and accepted the package with a languid affectation of grace and laid it beside the crystal on the table, intoning: "The dark stranger bearing a gift! A gift wearing the mystic blue—the colour of happiness. Great happiness will be yours, my friend."

I am a very earthy sort of character, I think, and in the face of superstitions about colour and the like I tend to feel something that is compounded of irritation and embarrassment. On the other hand, I can never be scornful of other people's beliefs, no matter how stupid they may seem to me, for I have some very odd beliefs of my own that would undoubtedly seem incredibly stupid to other people, but it would hurt me to have them scorned.

"The colour blue is associated with happiness, is it?" I said. "I suppose that is the reason for the little wedding rhyme:

Something old, something new,
Something borrowed and something
    blue."

"Undoubtedly," she agreed. "Many of the great truths of the spheres degenerate in the small minds of humanity into mere superstition but their essential truth remains in spite of that."

This disconcerted me. The association of a colour with a future state of mind—to believe that blue can lead to happiness—struck me as having its basis in primitive superstition, but I did not argue the matter.

"Blue is an important colour in your life, my friend," she intoned. "I can see its aura all about you!"

"It's a colour I have never worn in many years. I had too much of it in the Air Force during the war," I told her firmly and returned to business. "I am very sorry that I came out without my purse, Madame

Zora, but I shall send the ten shillings as soon as I get home."

She bowed her head in regal assent, but the effect was spoiled by the avid look that she bent at the same time at the slab of chocolate on the table. The voice of Monica speaking of her old people came into my mind. "They can't even bother to feed themselves sometimes and they get hungry and can't think what's the matter with them. There isn't much fun in preparing meals for one and eating them all by yourself."

I suddenly picked up the blue-papered slab and broke it in half and then into smaller pieces. "Yes, it's quite nice and fresh," I said. "Have a piece!"

This time, she did not remember to assume her mystic manner before snatching at the unbroken half and beginning to cram pieces into her mouth and I turned away from the sight, which was extraordinarily repulsive, and began to move towards the door.

"What a pretty vase that is!" I said, pausing beside a very bogus-looking Chinese urn that stood on the floor with a skinny black cat spitting at me from behind it.

"A gift! A gift from one of my many friends!" came the voice of the seer from behind me in the full diapason of its chanting note now, although a little glutinous with chocolate. "Gifts in return for the comfort I have been able to give by virtue of the knowledge that has been vouchsafed to me!" and with this she popped another lump of chocolate into her mouth and chewed vigorously while the cats marched in a procession round her long skirts, looking greedily up at her champing jaws.

"But I see," she said after a gulping swallow, "that you are an unbeliever. Ah, well!"

She heaved a mournful sigh as if she were being forced to watch me jump over the precipice and into the abyss that yawned for unbelievers, and then helped herself to another hunk of chocolate.

"Unbelieving in what, Madame Zora?" I asked.

"In the great art which I practise."

"What is your—er—special branch of art, Madame Zora?"

"I am an astrologer," she said with pride. "I am a member of the Innermost Circle of Twentieth-Century Astrologers or Icta, as we are called."

"How very interesting!" I said.

This was not hypocrisy in any form. I am very simple-minded and very easy to interest, especially in the complications that people think up to make the already complicated business of living more complicated still. "And do you practise in Ballydendran?"

I was a little hesitant about the verb "practise", for astrology was a subject that I had never before discussed with a devotee, and every art and craft has its own fascinating set of words and I feel that it is only polite to try to get them correct.

"Not directly," she said. "I have my professional plate on my gate, as no doubt you noticed, but these small-town communities have no interest in the arts or the philosophies."

I wanted very much to ask how astrology was practised indirectly, but before I could find the words she suddenly reached forward and raised my right hand on the palm of her own bony, dry-skinned hand and said: "You are an artist, of course?"

"No," I said. "Not at all, Madame Zora. I am utterly ungifted."

She shook her head in silent contradiction of my words and went on: "You will not believe me, I know, but you are on the verge of an interesting discovery. Your coming here today is the merest link in a chain, several links of which have already been forged, and when you leave here another link will be complete." She looked at me with her dull black eyes which seemed to be unnaturally dilated, and two of the cats, a tortoiseshell one and a mangy-looking grey one, were prowling about between us, rubbing themselves against her draperies and my stockings. I suddenly found it all hateful, almost snatched my hand out of hers, and jerkily pulled on my gloves.

"Poor pussy!" I said in a sickening, cowardly way to the tortoiseshell cat which stared up at me slit-eyed and baleful, and tried to sidle past it, while Madame Zora, well into her stride, intoned behind me: "And today you came with the blue-wrapped gift! Ah, the gifts, the gifts! Ah, my dear, dear friends!" The voice slipped into a dreamlike timbre. "I have been given in my time so many gifts." She waved her draped arms in a gesture that embraced the room. "All these things that you see around me are my beloved gifts, gifts from those that loved me. That"—she pointed to some sort of African spear on the wall—"was given to me by a great explorer, now gone beyond. And that parchment was a gift from a great Egyptologist."

I was certain in my own mind that the room and its contents were the result of many visits to many junk-shops by a very acquisitive woman of too fertile imagination, but there was something pathetic to me in this escape into an imaginary past filled with fictitious intimacies. The woman was lonely, cursed with that loneliness that Monica had spoken of, that ogre that waits for the faltering feet and mind of advancing age, so I began to admire her possessions, ask small questions about them and generally show an interest in them. In the end, she led me into a room on one side of the front door which was my main objective. This room was furnished in a normal way as a drawing-room, if one can apply the word "normal" to a room so full of furniture and bric-à-brac that it was almost impossible to find a foothold in it, but at least it had no crystals sitting on black velvet or charts of the Heavens on the walls.

"And this," she said, showing me a small carving in pink jade that sat under a glass dome on a table, "was given to me by a Grand Duke of Russia. But for the Revolution—" She stared dreaming out into the laurels that reached almost to the top of the window. "But for the Revolution, my life might have followed a different course, but that was not in the stars. The stars always know—they always know!"

On the whole, I preferred our conversation without the stars in it, so, in order to recall her to the earthly sphere, I made a move towards the door of the room and looked for one last thing to remark upon on the way and I found it. I found it with a rush of joy and I could admire it with my whole heart and soul, for at that moment, with Madame Zora staring in some half-trance through the dirty glass at the sickly laurels, with the cats gathering round our feet on the dusty carpet, it seemed to glow at me and wrap me about with a fresh breeze from my own beloved countryside. On the wall by the door there hung a painting of Poyntdale Bay, a small crescent of the Firth that lay below Reachfar.

"That is a very beautiful picture, Madame Zora!" I said.

She came out of her trance, turned and floated across the room towards me, weaving her way with uncanny skill amid her trailing draperies through the clutter of small tables and chairs.

"Ah, yes, another gift from another friend! Another of my dear, dear friends! Ah, yes."

"Who is the painter?" I asked. "I know nothing about painting but it seems to have a strange—distinction."

"I have never examined it," she said in a faraway voice that seemed to come across a plain of disapproval. "I have no interest in the value of my gifts—they are made dear to me by the givers."

I had now got out into the dim, cat-haunted hall and was wondering how the catch of the door worked and how I would get away, when she suddenly snatched my upper arm in her claw-like fingers, and as I looked into the black caverns of her eyes in her white face which seemed faintly green in the dim light, I wondered if she were going to be sick after all that chocolate on an empty stomach.

"You are going," she said, "but you and I are bound together now! The link is between us! We are bound—bound!"

"Oh, no, we aren't!" I thought.

"It is written in the stars that we shall meet again!" she chanted. "It is written!"

"About the ten shillings—" I said, to bring the conversation back to my own mundane plane.

"Ah, yes. Your gift to me of ten shillings."

Now this is something that I am at a loss to explain, but to discover that the ten shillings, her exorbitant price for a half-starved cat, had already, in her twisted old mind, been transformed into one of her many "gifts", laid upon me the soft finger of pathos. Into my mind again came the voice of Monica: "People say that their minds break down with old age and that they get deaf because their ear-drums get faulty. It isn't entirely like that. It's the loneliness that drives their minds into fantasy very often and they become deaf because there's nobody to speak to them and their ears get out of practice!"

I looked at the old woman standing there in her shabby black draperies in the dingy cat-smelling hall. I thought of her hunger for the chocolate, of the coldness of this house, and I wondered what was the exact amount of the old-age pension. And did people like this woman, owning a house like this, qualify for it? I thought of my father, Tom and George, all over seventy, and of their cheerful way of life in the warm house of Reachfar. And I thought of Monica, driving almost daily round her district in an attempt to counteract just the sort of situation that seemed to be facing me here. I felt that if I walked out of this house and left this old woman, I would be haunted for the rest of my life by the queer white face with its sunken eyes beneath the black-enamel band of hair and, wondering even as I did it how far I had fallen under her charlatan-reeking, obsolete spell, I did one of those things that I do so often and begin to curse myself for doing the very moment I have done them. I smiled at her and said: "I think it would be very nice,

Madame Zora, if you came to tea one day and I gave you the ten shillings then."

"To tea? Yes! Yes!" And then she remembered her professional manner. "And when can this joy come to me?" she intoned.

"Shall we say Friday week?"

She looked down upon me graciously, like a duchess indulging the whim of some member of the lower orders who did not quite know her place but who meant well.

"I shall be pleased to come and accept your gift," she said, magnificently unaware of my desire to kick myself and her too. However, she now opened the door and the fresh air of the grey early evening flowed in.

"But, remember," she said in her chanting voice, "we are but links in the chain, the chain that binds us all to one another."

I went down the two steps out of the house and felt the hard gravel under my shoes with gratitude.

"You will come back!" she said, closing the heavy door. "You will come back, my friend!"

The door closed. I heard the rattle of the

wooden rings from inside as she pulled the inner curtain into place and I stood staring at the brown door, certain that she was floating down the passage to the room with all the cats and the charts of the Heavens, intoning these words: "You will come back! You will come back, my friend!"

I shivered, for the evening was freshly cool after the stale chill of the house and the cat-smelling dankness of the drawing-room. I turned away, ran down the gravel path and walked smartly back the mile and a half over the fields to Crookmill.

Twice was in the living-room with tea on a table beside him when I went into the house.

"Hello," he said. "I thought you must be tea-ing with Madame Zora so I got them to bring mine in."

Mattha came into the room bearing a cup, saucer and plate. "Ah brocht this when Ah saw ye comin'," he said, "because them twae is busy at their fitba' coupon, but if ye're needin' mair sangwiches Ah'll gie them a shout."

"That's all right, Mattha," I said. "There's enough here, thanks."

He looked with sulky malice at Twice.

"Aw richt," he said. "Ah'll get ye that kitlin ye're wantin' for Lizzie Fintry seein' ye're fair set on it."

"That's fine, Mattha," Twice said quietly, and I grasped that they had had a slight argument about a replacement kitten, but before I could say that it would not be required, Mattha turned to me in a war-like way.

"Wis she kinna hauf-ceevil tae ye?"

"She was very nice indeed, Mattha, and to tell you the truth I am ashamed of both you and Dram."

Dram, who had been lying at Twice's feet, got up as I spoke and went to sit behind Mattha's twisted old legs.

"Ye've little need tae be ashamed o' the dug or me aither!" said Mattha. "It wis high bliddy time yon cat wis deid although it wid be jist like Lizzie Fintry tae mak' a falorum aboot it."

"Madame Zora made no falorum at all."

"Madam Zory ma back—"

"Oh, shut up, Mattha! And if you can't control that dog better I'll put him in the charge of Loose-an'-Daze."

"Them twae? If ye wis tae rely on them tae keep the dug auld Lizzie hersel' wad

101

likely be deid lang syne!" He swung back to Twice. "Whit'n a like kitlin are ye wantin' fur the auld bitch? Auld Jeanie's cat's got a wheen grey strippit yins an' Andy Byers the J'iner's cat is a hauf-Persian an' maistly white. An dinnae ken if it's got ony kitlins the noo but it huz them aboot every twae month reg'lar."

"I don't care a hang what colour or sex it is, as long as it's a kitten. One of old Jeanie's striped ones will do and let's get the thing over and done with."

"Guid kens whit wey ye're botherin' yersel' aboot Lizzie Fintry. There's no' been a Fintry born yet that wis iver due thanks or said thanks!"

I felt gloomy and cross and tired of the whole subject. "Oh, dry up, Mattha. And just don't you and that darned dog go cat-killing any more."

"Whae says we iver went cat-killin'? Ah niver admittit it, Ah'll warrant ye! An' if we hud've killt that cat it wis sair needin' killin'. It—"

I stared at him malignantly and after a moment he laid his hand on the dog's head and said: "Come on, Dram. You an' me's in bother an' we micht as weel tak' a bit walk."

"Owff!" said Dram in a voice that shook the house and the two of them withdrew.

"Have some tea," Twice said to me. "I've seen you in better temper. How was Madame Zora?"

"It was all awful!" I burst out. "I'm so depressed I could burst into tears and—"

Twice looked at me for a moment and began to pour me a cup of tea. "Sit down, my pet, and tell all. What's upset you? Was the old dame very nasty?"

"No, just phoney. She's been phoney all her life and now she's getting old and it's starting to crack on her and get shoddy like—like imitation leather when the skin wears off and the canvas starts to show through. It was all phoney and awful." I swallowed a draught of tea and went on more calmly: "She's half-mad, actually, Twice—half-mad in a literal way. One half of her mind is off balance and the other half is still on balance in a mean, grasping sort of way."

"In what way is she off?" Twice asked.

"Well, she calls herself an astrologer and she goes about intoning a lot of stuff about links in chains and writings in the stars and 'You will come back! You will come ba-ack!'"

"Here, stop that! If that's an imitation of what she did it's far too good. I'd rather have tea with a banshee."

"You'll have every opportunity to have tea with a banshee, for that's just what I've gone and done."

"What are you talking about?"

"I've asked her to tea."

"For pity's sake, Flash! What for?"

"Just for pity's sake, although I could kick myself now. Something just came over me and I did it. She seemed so terribly lonely and Monica was saying about how loneliness was such a terrible thing and—well, I don't know what happened. I just invited her, that's all. Oh, drat Monica!"

"Oh, well, it's nothing desperate. It comes under social and domestic. . . . What sort of age is she?"

"Oh, sixty anyhow—maybe more. Her hair is dyed—"

"Lizzie Fintry? She'll niver see seeventy again," said Mattha, coming in with a basket of logs which he set down by the fireplace. "She wis born the year o' the Tay

104

Bridge Disaster, the same as oor Bella, but Bella although an ill-tongued besom is no' sic a disaster as Lizzie Fintry."

"When was the Tay Bridge Disaster again?" Twice asked, for he can always be side-tracked into matters historical.

"Eighteen seventy-eight," I said.

"Are ye sure it wisnae seeventy-nine?" Mattha enquired. "But even if it wis eichty, this is nineteen-fifty-yin an' that still mak's Lizzie seeventy-yin."

"Then she's very spry for her age," I said nastily, looking at Mattha's creaky knees. "Not a sign of rheumatism about her!"

"She's hud things gey saft byes some folk!" he told me and went out, shutting the door behind him in a pointed way.

I went on to tell Twice of the queer, cat-smelling Dunroamin with its chill dankness and suffocating curtains on their wooden rings.

"And the maddening thing about it," I said, "is that although all your common-sense knows it's all as false as bedamned, it gets you. I can quite imagine that during the 1914–18 war, for instance, when so many women were at their wits' end with anxiety, she probably got away handsomely with all that spurious stuff and made a lot of money. And after that too. Probably the only thing that put her out of business was partly old age and partly those magazines that Loose-an'-Daze buy giving the people their horoscopes for free. When you are with her, she doesn't strike you as phoney so much as just plain old-fashioned. I suppose that rackets, to pay, have to be bang up-to-date. . . . The house inside is like a museum. An awful lot of the stuff is absolute junk—ancient Egyptian scrolls as phoney as she is and all that—but there's some nice old furniture and china and a nice bit of jade and oh!—I nearly forgot to tell you—she has a picture of—guess what?"

"The cow jumping through Saturn's nebula," said Twice, very witty.

"Don't be a fool. No. Poyntdale Bay."

"Poyntdale Bay? What sort of picture?"

"A painting in oils—a very nice one. At least, I liked it. Maybe it was just relief at seeing something so normal and home-like in that awful house, but I don't think so. It really was a picture that gave you a real feeling of Poyntdale Bay."

106

"You are sure it was Poyntdale Bay? Did you ask her where she got it?"

"Now, look, Twice, for the first ten years of my life the view over Poyntdale Bay was about all I did see and I know a picture of it when I see it now. It was Poyntdale Bay, seen from the top of Poyntdale Long Ley —you know the field I mean? That big one just west of the big house?"

"All right, it was Poyntdale Bay. Did you ask where she got it?"

"Yes, and she said: 'Oh, a gift, a gift— one of my many gifts!'"

"Don't bleat and keen like that! It makes my back hair rise."

"Well, that's what she said, so I don't know where she got it. But I wish it was mine. I'd love to take it back to St. Jago for the drawing-room at Guinea Corner. It'd be a splendid antidote to all that tropical heat and clutter and madness."

Twice snorted. "It seems to me that you can find plenty of clutter and madness without going to the tropics for it, and if you're going to have this old woman to tea you'd better do it fairly soon and get it over with. We may have to go down south next week."

"Oh? . . . Did you ring up the agents about the house?"

"What house?"

"This house! So you didn't?"

"Did you do anything about the furniture lists?" he asked.

"You know I haven't had time! Why, I'm only just back from—"

"And have you said anything to Loose-an'-Daze?"

"Now, Twice Alexander—"

At that moment, Loose-an'-Daze rushed into the room and picked up the tea-things.

"Sir Andrew's outside—"

"—and a gentleman with him!"

"He's Mr. Egbert—" Loose supplied.

"From London, Lucy says!"

"All right!" said Twice. "Even if his name's Hubert and he's from Timbuctoo, go and open the door and let him come in!"

Sir Andrew Craig, from whom we had bought the ruined cottages that were now our house, was Monica's uncle by marriage, and as soon as he introduced the "gentleman from London" as "Mr. Fitzhugh", I recognised him to be Monica's cousin Egbert, of whom I had often heard but whom I had never met before.

He was a small, dapper gentleman of about sixty-five, probably being made to look even shorter, slimmer and better-tailored than he really was by his proximity to Sir Andrew, who was a big, florid man who always wore very baggy tweed suits whose trousers always looked bald at the knees and very hairy in every other part.

Sir Andrew was an engineer by profession with a number of small but profitable inventions to his credit, and although, as a hostess, I do not think I make a practice of looking my gift visitors in the mouth, I became aware that Mr. Fitzhugh had been brought along to see us because Sir Andrew did not know what to do with him for the hour or two before dinner. Sir Andrew was a widower who lived alone with a few old servants in a hideous Victorian house called "The Crook" and he did not like visitors unless they were engineers whom he could entertain in his workshop, which contained equipment of more value than all the furniture and other contents of all the rest of his large house.

"Fitzhugh's just spending a night with

me," he said in a tone that clearly implied the words "Thank Heaven!"

He put his head on one side and frowned at his guest as if Cousin Egbert were a bolt that did not fit the hole that had been drilled for it.

"So I brought him along to see you," he added to me and then turned to Twice: "Now that you're back here for a bit, you must come up to Millington and Shire's with me on Friday—you'll be very interested in this new planetary gearing they're trying. I had no faith in it at first but—"

He put down the glass of whisky that Twice had just handed to him, took a pencil from his pocket, put on his glasses and began to draw planetary gears (I suppose that that is what they were) all over the blotter on my writing-table. I was left with Cousin Egbert.

"Are you spending some time in Scotland, Mr. Fitzhugh?"

Sir Andrew looked up under his heavy brows, his pencil poised over his drawing.

"Only a day or two," he said. "He's going to look at some pictures in some place in Edinburgh."

"I see," I said.

Sir Andrew went on with his drawing and I looked at Cousin Egbert, wondering if he were deaf and dumb and Monica had forgotten to tell me.

"Not Edinburgh," he said in a high squeaky voice. "Glasgow."

"—and this operates inside this radius here—not Edinburgh?" said Sir Andrew. "But you said Edinburgh."

"Didn't," said Cousin Egbert.

Sir Andrew frowned. "You did! When you arrived you said you'd come to look at pictures in Edinburgh!" he said with emphasis.

"Said," said Cousin Egbert in an emphatic squeak, "I'd come from looking at pictures in Edinburgh!"

"Same thing!" said Sir Andrew. "And all pictures anyway! . . . Now, the interesting thing about this pivot, Alexander, is that—"

"You know Monica?" Cousin Egbert squeaked at me.

"Oh, yes. The Daviot place, Poyntdale, marches on the north side with my home. I saw her last week."

"Known her long?"

"Since 1939, Mr. Fitzhugh."

"Been to Beechwood?"

"Yes, once or twice, but not since 1944. How are they all?"

"All right, I suppose. . . . Sure you haven't been there since 1944?"

"Certain, Mr. Fitzhugh. Why?"

"Couldn't have seen you there then. I didn't come back from Italy till '47. Was in the States during the war. When did we meet?"

"We've never met before, Mr. Fitzhugh."

"Have," he said categorically.

"I'm quite certain we haven't!" I said, trying to say it lightly and politely, but I was irritated by the little man, with his thin, bland, pale face, with its parchment-like skin and the sharp little eyes that were of so light a blue as to be almost like clear water. I became more irritated when he drew an eyeglass from his pocket, fixed it in his left eye and walked round me, staring into my face as if going over it for "points" as the buyers do with animals at the Perth Cattle Sales. My face is not beautiful enough, I feel, to stand up to such a scrutiny, and to hide my irritation and embarrassment I turned away from him under the pretext of going to the box for a cigarette.

Twice and Sir Andrew, well meshed in their planetary gears now, had departed, drinks in hand, to Twice's drawing-office and I was left to carry on a stilted conversation with Cousin Egbert. I enjoy meeting new people; I am willing to talk, or listen to people talk, about any subject under the sun, and I knew from Monica that Cousin Egbert, although eccentric in some ways—he took only one bath a year that the natural oils might not be lost from his skin and he always altered the position of the furniture in any room where he slept so that his feet pointed to the south-east—was still one of the greatest art authorities of the age. He had gone to Italy at the end of the 1939–45 war as one of the Commission sent out to trace the treasures of the Florentine museums which had been scattered, some by the Italians for safe-keeping, some by the Germans in the course of their retreat. There were many things I should have liked to ask him about and get him talking about if I could, but he kept worrying back to this subject of our having met before as a

113

very persistent dog worries at a very hard bone.

"Could have been in the street, of course, or maybe in a train," he said at last. "Probably a train. Seen you for longer than just passing in the street."

"That is possible," I agreed with him wearily, although I thought it very unlikely that Cousin Egbert and I had ever shared a railway compartment. I had not been in a train since 1945, Cousin Egbert went to the United States in 1939, and before that he undoubtedly travelled first-class while I had invariably travelled third.

"Of course," I suggested, "I might have a double."

"Doubt it. Don't believe in 'em."

"And where in Glasgow are these pictures you are going to see?"

"Grierson's Galleries. You interested in painting?"

"I should be very interested if I knew anything about it," I told him. "This will be difficult for you to understand, but I've gone to one or two exhibitions and there's a sort of frustration in looking at pictures and knowing even while you enjoy looking at them that you are missing a lot through not knowing enough about them and how they are made."

"See your point perfectly," he told me. "Like me with music. Important thing, though, is to know you are ignorant and not the pictures or the music. The real Philistine condemns the pictures, not himself. Only way to learn about pictures is to keep looking at them, provided you like looking, that is. Do you?"

"Yes, I do."

"You're in better case than me with music. I hate the noise a flute makes!" he informed me in a venomous squeak. "And the man looks so silly making it and flautist is a silly word—sounds like a woman kicking up her heels in a flounced petti-coat!"

I laughed outright at his pale-faced indignation and he stared at me with questioning astonishment.

"Monica often sees words as pictures," I explained. "It must be a family faculty. I shall never hear the word 'flautist' again without visualising the woman in the flounced petticoat."

A faint glimmer of light seemed to pass across his face which, I realised, was the expression of pleasure that most of us display by what we call a smile. Cousin Egbert did not smile. His mouth stayed closed. Even when he spoke, it opened only enough to emit a few jerky syllables from between his thin lips.

"Like to come with me to Grierson's tomorrow?" he asked suddenly. "See the pictures and have lunch afterwards? Delighted, you know."

I was taken aback a little. The invitation was spontaneous—the sort of invitation that I myself or Twice or Monica might issue—but spontaneity sat oddly upon Cousin Egbert, so, being taken by surprise, I did the thing that came most easily to me at the moment, as I invariably do.

"That's very kind of you, Mr. Fitzhugh," I said. "Thank you. I'd like very much to come."

The next day, Twice drove me to the station, where I met Cousin Egbert and he and I set out on the half-hour journey to Glasgow. As he sat opposite to me in the compartment, I was aware again of his narrow-eyed scrutiny and felt again that irritation, like the irritation that one feels with people like Loose-an'-Daze who, telling of some trivial event, say: "Was it Tuesday? No, it must have been Wednesday. No, wait a minute, it must have been the Thursday because I had just finished putting away the laundry at the time—" What did it matter, I thought, if we had once before sat in the same railway compartment? And I gave my hat a twitch and glared out of the window thinking bitterly that at forty-one no woman could expect a spontaneous invitation to lunch except for some queer reason such as this.

"Think I was mistaken," he said at last. "Don't think we've met before."

I sighed. "I don't think so either, Mr. Fitzhugh. I'm sure I should have remembered."

From then on, we had a very pleasant day. Mr. Fisher, the director of the gallery, and Cousin Egbert showed me a great many pictures and told me a great deal too much about them for my slow wits to keep pace with and, having got me thoroughly bemused, they then retired to Mr. Fisher's office to have a business chat, leaving me alone on a sofa in the gallery, for which I was more than thankful. The chat continued through lunch at which they drank the best part of two bottles of claret and it was arranged that Mr. Fisher would travel to London in the autumn, stay with Cousin Egbert and see an exhibition of Italian paintings that was to be shown at Cousin Egbert's gallery in Bond Street.

When the coffee came, I was suddenly overcome by my feeling of "What am I doing here?" A number of times in the course of my life, I have suddenly been struck, on finding myself in an unusual place in unlikely company, by this question and I have often played the fascinating game of trying to trace the factors that have led to this moment of here and now, but this time the chase after factors was short, for the sole factor in the case was Monica. Her uncle had brought her cousin to see me; the cousin had asked me to lunch and here I was, having had a very good lunch, sitting in the sleepy "ante-room", as it was called, of Mr. Fisher's club having a very good cup of coffee. Still, although it was not a very interesting game of "What am I doing here?" the moment of question had brought the exhilaration that it always brought to me, the feeling of all life having led up to this one instant of completeness in the "here" of space and "now" of time.

"Have you ever had your portrait painted, Mrs. Alexander?" Mr. Fisher asked me suddenly.

I laughed. "No, I'm afraid not, Mr. Fisher."

"A Highlander, aren't you?"

"Yes. From Ross. Do you know the north?"

"Not that far north. I have a little place near Oban." He turned to Cousin Egbert. "Scotland needs another good portrait painter—another Raeburn—before these long Highland heads are bred out of the race. The faces of our people are changing, with all these wars and influxes of foreign blood. Mrs. Alexander has a head that's going out of fashion—you resemble my old grandmother. She was from Inverness-shire."

"A Macdonald, by any chance?" I asked.

"Yes. How did you know?"

"My grandmother was a Macdonald from the Lochaber country. I am said to be like her. Maybe your grandmother and I are remote cousins, Mr. Fisher."

"That the thing you have in your dining-room, Fisher?" Cousin Egbert asked.

"By 'thing', Mrs. Alexander," Mr. Fisher explained to me, "Fitzhugh means a portrait of my grandmother." He turned to Cousin Egbert. "Yes, that's Granny. It may not be a very good painting but it's the only likeness of Granny that we have and there it stays, Fitzhugh!"

"'Snot that bad. Good enough to make me think I had met this young lady before, anyway!" said Cousin Egbert. "Thing worried me. Annoyed me. Don't like being haunted by a thing like that."

Had he any idea, I wondered, how he could worry, annoy and haunt with his persistence the person he thought he had met? However, my good lunch had made me tolerant, I suppose, for, telling myself that without his persistence he would not be the connoisseur he was, I managed to say fairly pleasantly: "You've no idea how glad I am that my face is at last off your mind!" at which both he and Mr. Fisher were obliging enough to laugh.

I left Cousin Egbert with his friend with whom he was to dine before catching the night train to London, and travelled back alone to Ballydendran where Twice met me at the station again.

"Well, nice day?" he asked.

"Very nice, but I haven't come home an authority on painting by a long shot. I always thought that George and Tom were pretty bad at explaining how they knew there was a rabbit in a certain bush or how they knew where we'd be likely to find a covey of partridges on a certain day. I've always thought you were a perfect fool at explaining anything mechanical, to be frank. But art experts are worse than any of you. They pre-suppose that one knows more than even you or George or Tom do."

"Knowing about a thing and teaching what one knows to somebody else are two different things," Twice said. "But anyway, you saw some good pictures?"

"Yes. Some beautiful pictures, but I'd just as soon have old Madame Zora's Poyntdale Bay as any of them—only I didn't tell Cousin Egbert and Mr. Fisher that. . . . And I had a very good lunch. What sort of day did you have?"

"A lot of telephone arguments about shipping dates for plant for St. Jago, mostly. This country isn't what it was. In

121

1946 or '47, remember how you and I used to put our behinds out of joint to try to catch a ship with a consignment of engines? Nowadays, nobody seems to give a damn whether they sell engineering plant or not. Nobody seems to give a damn about anything much."

"You're getting old," I said. "It's a funny thing that as soon as people turn the corner of forty and get to be forty-one, they start saying 'nowadays' in that disgruntled way. . . . People don't have the drive now that we were brought up to have and it's old-fashioned to expect them to have it. Life is easier now. They don't need the drive that we needed. Drive is being bred out of people like the horns being bred out of cattle."

"Highland cattle with no horns'll be pretty funny," Twice said, "but no funnier than a Scots engineer with no pride in his job. Call it evolution if you like and me old-fashioned if you like, but I think it stinks." He drove the car into the garage and we got out to cross the stream towards the house. "In a way, I'm very pleased that I'm not called upon to work in this country any more. St. Jago may be pretty mad and fairly good hell in lots of ways, but one's spared this smug complacent thing—this it-will-be-all-the-same-in-a-hundred-years and come-night-come-ninepence thing that they go in for here."

"Come night, come ninepence! Dad used to say that! You are out-dated, my pet. Nowadays, it's come Friday, come nineteen quid!"

"For you," Twice said as we went into the house, "it's come Friday, come Madame Zora. Mattha's got a kitten."

"Aye, Ah huv that," said Mattha, materialising in his uncanny way from the back passage and putting a match to the fire, for, although August, it was a cold, dank evening. "Ah jist got tae auld Jeanie's in time to stop her gettin' Chairlie Mair tae droon them, or yin o' them onywey. . . . Weel, hud ye a gidd day in Glesca?"

"Very nice, thank you, Mattha. . . . Madame Zora is coming to tea on Friday, by the way. I am just telling you so that you can stay away and not have to see her."

"Whit wey should Ah no' see her?" he asked belligerently. "Ah wis here at Crook-mill afore Lizzie Fintry an' if you think Ah'm gaun tae rin awa' an' hide frae that

123

yin, ye're awa' up the Clyde in a banana-skin, that's whit ye are!"

"Dash it, Mattha! I didn't think you'd want to see her."

"Ah widnae care if Ah niver saw her atween here an' eternity, but ye cannae get a' ye want in this life. Ah'll be here on Friday, till the Lad wins hame, onywey!"

He always referred to Twice as "the Lad" in moments of stress or excitement.

"If ye're haein' a Fintry aboot the place, ye're needin' a man aboot it as weel. They're no' safe. There's no a Fintry born that widnae steal the sugar oot o' yer tea!"

"Mattha, don't talk rubbish! Madame Zora is—"

"Madame Zory ma back—"

"Mattha! You told me yourself that her father was a man of standing and that she was his heiress—is she likely to come here and steal the teaspoons?"

"Heiress ma back—Aw, a' richt!" He turned to Twice. "Ah dinnae mean tae speak vulgar tae the Mistress, Lad, but whiles she's that damt pig-heidit an' aggravatin'!"

Twice grinned at me in a malicious way

124

which made me feel more "pig-heidit an' aggravatin'" than ever.

"I don't see why you make out that Madame Zora's going to steal the teapot," I said.

"Ah niver said she wad steal nae teapot. It's jist that wi' a Fintry ye niver ken whit they'll dae an' Ah'm gaun tae be here tae see that she disnae!"

"Look here," said Twice, "what are you two arguing about? Does it matter if Mattha is here or not?"

"Not a damn," I said.

"Och, the Mistress an' me has mony a bit argy-bargy," said Mattha in a soothing tone. "It disnae mean onything much but it's the only wey Ah can get things like Fintrys through her heid. Ah'll be here on Friday!" he concluded to me in a threatening tone.

"All right!" I snapped. "And see that Dram doesn't kill anything else before then!"

"Ye ken fine that that dug'll no' kill onything unless he's tellt!"

"And who told him to kill Madame Zora's cat then?"

Mattha looked at Twice. Twice turned

125

his back on both of us. "Weemen!" Mattha then said with strong disgust and retired to the kitchen.

"Look here," I said to Twice, "now it seems we've got a kitten. I meant to tell you the other night, but it is sort of embarrassing and then Sir Andrew and Cousin Egbert came in and I didn't get round to it. Madame Zora doesn't want a kitten—she wants ten shillings compensation for the dead cat. She doesn't want a replacement."

"Ten shillings?" Twice asked. "Are you off your chump?"

"You feel it's too much? Twice, I'm awfully sorry. I'm a fool about things like that—I mean, I've never done business over a dead cat before and when she said ten shillings I just sort of said all right but I hadn't any money with me on account of having given my purse to Daze to pay the butcher and forgetting to put it back in my bag and you see when she said ten shillings—"

"Hold on and calm down, for Pete's sake, Flash! It's not a question of it being too much or too little—it's—it's—well, the ten bob is an absurdity. It's simply not relevant, I should have thought. It's too much for the cat it was, qua cat, and too little to compensate for the loss of a valued pet. It's—it's—I can't explain what I mean. It's out of kilter—It's like a piece of broken glass in an oil bath!—How did the ten bob come into the thing at all?"

"I just said, 'My dog killed your cat,' and she said, 'Ten shillings'."

"Just like that?"

"Yes. Just like that."

"Well, I'm damned!"

"Twice, I think she's terribly poor. I think she needed the ten shillings."

"Oh, rubbish, darling! Nobody of her age in this country in these days is in want to that degree! Besides, you said she had a houseful of stuff and furniture is highly saleable. I must say, I'm looking forward to seeing this old dame."

"You'll have every chance," I said, "because there's another thing I've done that I haven't told you yet."

"What now?"

"I said you would drive up to Dunroamin and fetch her."

I always imagine that other people, and especially Twice, will resent the things that

I would resent and, had I been in Twice's position, I would have resented this commandeering of myself and my car to pick up a guest that I did not really want to entertain.

"I wouldn't have said it," I told him, "but she suddenly seemed so pathetic and so old! And I thought of what Monica had said about old people and—oh, drat Monica!"

He grinned at me. "A stranger, hearing you would think I was one of these chaps who get a sadistic kick out of not co-operating with their wives. Of course I'll pick the old girl up. No need to look so apologetic and careworn. . . . Meantime, I'm going to tell Mattha to get rid of that kitten before we are any older. In theory we are trying to get rid of a house, not acquire a cat."

4

AUGUST was now turning into September and Twice and I had been back in Scotland for about four weeks, but I still had a feeling of disorientation, as if I were suspended between two worlds with no secure foothold in either. Thinking of this, I told myself that we had made a mistake in coming for a holiday to this house which, formerly, had been our home—a mistake from my point of view, being the kind of person I am, for I like everything connected with the mechanics of life to be clearly outlined. Crookmill was no longer our home—our real home, as always, was Reachfar and our temporary home, now, was Guinea Corner, St. Jago—and yet Crookmill could not be regarded in the impersonal light of a hotel either. To live in it now gave me a feeling of transitory insecurity which was made no better by the fact that, although we had decided to sell it, we had been too cowardly as yet to take the initial step of telling Loose-

129

an'-Daze of our decision. Daily, my mind became more muddled; daily, the weather became more grey, dreary and depressing and, daily, I became more and more aware of being caught in some uncanny vortex that was developing, some eerie change in the climate of life that was outwith my control.

"Twice," I said, "do you ever get the feeling that something queer is building up round you, only you don't know what it is?"

"I have it right now," he said. "Whatever you are building up with that question is very queer indeed and I don't know what it is. What are you getting at?"

"I don't really know." I looked out at the grey mist of rain that hung like gauze between the windows and the hills. "There's something that has been there since the beginning of this leave, almost, and it's getting more intense all the time."

"What sort of thing?"

"That's what I don't know! It's a lot of things all jumbled together, like Monica having that time-slip in the churchyard at home and Dram and the cat and Loose-an '-Daze saying it was an omen and seeing that picture of Poyntdale Bay at Madame

Zora's—I mean, they're all queer sort of things that you wouldn't expect to happen. Monica's not the sort of person to have time-slips—"

"Agreed. But Dram is the sort of person to kill cats. He's been hell on cats all his life—"

"But Loose-an'-Daze saying it was—"

"Flash, don't be silly! It's exactly the sort of thing they would say, with their horoscope football—"

"That's just the point! They weren't all horoscopish eighteen months ago! I get the feeling that a sort of climate of—of sort of black magic is being built up—"

"Flash, you are being absolutely absurd! You're letting that Highland temperament run away with you! . . . D 'you know what I think is wrong?"

"What?"

"You are disappointed in this leave and you won't admit it and the disappointment is finding this way out. I don't blame you for being disappointed. The weather is hellish and it's been monstrously dull for you here since we came down from Reachfar. I'm disappointed myself. There's a feeling of flatness about it all. The Works here is horrible—a lot of little bureaucrats spitting and snarling behind each other's backs—I'm fed up to the back teeth with it and the sooner we can get away south the better. The truth is, Flash, that you and I have shot our bolt here in Ballydendran and at Crookmill. We've got to face facts. This house was our first home; we were happy here, but we've been away from it for eighteen months and in that time we've seen a lot of new people and found another way of life. But during the eighteen months we've sentimentalised this place. I have, anyway. Out there in St. Jago, I thought of this room either in frost with a big fire or in the summer sun. I never visualised it on a dreary day like this when it's neither cold nor hot, bright nor dark, but just a miserable, airless half-light."

I looked round the room. "I suppose you are right, Twice."

"I think I am. I think we've sentimental-ised it out of a mistaken sort of loyalty, loyalty to a place where we've been happy. But we've got to accept the 'have been'. I think that's what one hates to do. One wants to believe that everything lasts for ever, but it doesn't. One has to move on.

132

And it is time we moved on from here. I've been thinking about all this a lot, Flash, trying to sort it out. I've been pretty miserable off and on since we came back here and I think it's because of this conflict— the sentimentalising loyalty that makes me not want to sell the place against the knowledge, now that I face it, that we've outgrown the place and it's time we sloughed it off. But once you face the truth —and I think this is the truth—and face the fact that loyalty to a few stones and some mortar is just a lot of sloppy auld-lang-syne, you feel much better."

"I suppose you are right. Maybe I feel better, but I am also so depressed I could burst into tears," I said.

Twice smiled at me. "And another thing that's wrong with you is that you are not getting enough action. Once you make up your mind, embark on the selling of the place, get into gear and get the sparks flying, you'll feel like a new woman."

"It's still sad to think of parting with it," I persisted. "I know you are right, Twice, in all you say, but isn't it a little sad that one should grow away from something that once meant so much?"

"It would be sadder if one got stuck and didn't grow at all. That's the worst thing. I think one has to do the growing, even if it hurts a bit here and there. The alternative is to get stuck—accept a myth, like—like the old lady at Achcraggan believing that her grandson is still alive, or grow inwards like this old Madame Zora or get airborne on your horoscope like Loose-an'-Daze. After all, by growing away from Crookmill and putting it behind us, we don't lose what it once meant to us. That is part of us now. I can think of no better words for what I mean than the Army phrase: We've had Crookmill, chum. That's what it is, really. . . . And what I think we should do is do something, right now."

"Such as?"

"Tell Loose-an'-Daze we're selling, give it to the house-agents and be done with it."

"All right, we will, but let's have another cup of tea first, because although you say 'we' in that lordly way, you really mean that I have to tell Loose-an'-Daze. And I have to—you are quite right. It's domestic —although anti-social."

We drank tea in silence for a little while the grey misty rain drifted past the windows, until I said: "I don't think I'm very good at this thing of moving from one sort of country to another, Twice. I was just getting used to all the bright glare and black shadows of St. Jago when we came away and now I'm finding it difficult to get used to this grey light and wreaths of mist again. In spite of all the eerie, jungly feeling of the tropics, Scotland has more real mystery about it. It has a feeling of age and history and an old wily cunning instead of the new, brash, explosive sort of atmosphere you find in St. Jago. I wasn't aware of this age-old mysteriousness when I lived here all the time, but it's come home to me terribly strongly since we came back, as if the rain out there were screening all sorts of secrets and the hills were brooding over masses of hidden knowledge."

"I think you've responded a bit too strongly to your interview with Madame Zora," Twice said. "You spoke of things building up round one. This old woman is building up in my mind in such a way that I don't know that I won't strangle her on Friday."

"None of it is Madame Zora's fault. What happens to one and how one feels is always partly one's own fault," I said, and stood up and tightened the belt of my skirt. "All right. You said do something and I'm going to do it and you're quite right. I feel better already." I looked firmly at Twice. "But you have to write to the house-agents, remember."

"Right," he said. "That's a bargain."

I went out to the kitchen, perched myself on the table, explained to Loose-an'-Daze as lucidly as I could our situation and then told them straightforwardly that Crookmill would have to be sold. Daisy was the first to speak.

"I'm sorry," she said. "No good saying I'm not. I've been happy here. We've all been happy, but I can see that when you're away out there—"

"—it's an expense—"

"—and a worry—"

"—and a nuisance, us being here and not paying anything—"

"—and we've been very lucky to have been here for so long."

I did not know any more which one of them was speaking which words. All I wanted to do was get away from their kindness and courage.

"But we're not in a hurry about it," I said. "We needn't sail until the end of November and I'd like to see you both settled before then. We're going to take our time to find a nice buyer and we want you two to take your time to find something really suitable and a nice place to go."

"Oh, we'll find places—"

"—housekeepers are always wanted—"

"—although it would be nice to be together—"

"—but hardly possible, likely—"

They both looked round the kitchen of which they were so fond and proud and their eyes seemed suddenly to grow very large. I slid from the table, feeling like a monster.

"Anyway," I said, "try not to worry or get in a state about things. It will all work out."

It seemed cold and banal to leave them there with those words but I could think of no more to say to them, so I went back to the living-room and said to Twice: "Well, that's that. It's queer—you get fond of people, you do all you can for them, it all seems happy and right—but the time always comes when you have to hurt them.

At this moment I wish I had never laid eyes on Loose-an'-Daze.''

"I don't think they wish that about you," Twice said. "I think they've been happy here and they'll always appreciate it."

"But to have to end it for them?"

"Tout passe—" he said.

"I suppose so, but I never want to believe it. It makes everything so insignificant. I like to feel that every moment, everything, no matter how small, that one does is building up into something permanent. I don't mind being just a tiny mollusc or whatever you call them if, eventually, I become part of the Great Barrier Reef, but I hate this thing of being like a flake of snow on a river—there for a moment and then nothing at all. That thing of the moment mattering, of it being important or unimportant, is the difference between happiness and unhappiness, I suppose. After lunch in Glasgow the other day—I suppose I was just full of good food and good wine and in pleasant company—I was full of well-being and I suddenly felt in Mr. Fisher's club that thing of How did I get here? And it seemed right and important that I was in that place at that time. But through there just now, it was all disinte-gration—all tout passe, as you said. It's very odd. It's as if the things that one plans are no good, like planning to sell this house, and the things that just come along, like lunch with Cousin Egbert, are the real things of life. Oh, well, there it is. You'd better go and phone those house-agents or write to them or something."

Twice got up. "I will, right away, darling. I now feel that we are heading somewhere."

"As long as we're heading and not just oscillating, or do I mean vacillating?"

"Rusticating. If we don't look out there'll be none of this so-called leave left. We'll go back out there, never having been to a theatre or heard a concert or anything. I wish you'd get on to Monica and find out when she's going to Beechwood and then we can build round that."

"I'll write this evening," I promised.

I had told Mattha that I had asked Madame Zora to tea, but I had not told Loose-an'-Daze and I knew that Mattha would not mention it to them. It was part of my Crookmill policy never to tell Loose-an'-Daze anything until it became essential to tell them, a policy that had been beaten out in blood, sweat and frayed nerves. Different people are irritated by different things. Or perhaps I am an unusually irritable, short-tempered woman. In any event, although I am a great admirer of the house-keeping capabilities of Loose-an'-Daze and can register like a Geiger counter their true and sterling qualities of all kinds, they have more irritating habits woven into their composite personality than any other twenty people I know. Habits that are irritating to me, that is. When they receive a letter they say:

"A letter for me?"

"Yes, it says Mrs. Ramsay so it must be for you," says Loose in an amazed voice, as if Daze had never had a letter in her life before; as if nobody knew, even, that her name was Mrs. Ramsay; as if the house were hotching with Mrs. Ramsays. Daze then takes the letter, turns it over, holds it up to the light and tries to see through it, and then the conversation continues.

"I wonder who it's from?"

"Do you know the handwriting?"

"It might be my cousin Maggie—no, I don't think it's Maggie." She then lays it down on the table, stands back a couple of yards, puts her head on one side and begins to walk sidewise round the table. Then:

"No. I don't know who could be writing to me. What day's this?"

"Monday."

"Then it can't be from anybody at home in the north because they always write on Sundays and it wouldn't get here till tomorrow."

Loose becomes inspired now. "What's the postmark?"

They both fall upon the letter and find, of course, that the postmark is illegible. I do not know how, in the end, they get to the point of opening the letter and discovering the identity of the correspondent because my temper has become so frayed that if I waited until the end of the performance I would crack their heads together.

I never tell them of the arrival of guests, either, until the very last moment because, by the time they have discussed what kind of sandwiches to make; whether they should make a currant tart; which table-cloth they will use; which dress they will wear; what clothes the guest will probably wear; either Just fancy her coming for tea after all these years or Just fancy her coming to tea because her poor pussy got killed—quite romantic you could call it, really—I know that I will be so sick of the sound of the guest that I shall be rude to her when she finally arrives. So, at lunch-time on Friday, I said in my breeziest way: "Oh, Loose-an'-Daze, Madame Zora's coming to tea this afternoon. There's that Dundee cake and could you make some scones and a few sandwiches and put on a good fire?" with which I burst into song and went off and shut myself in my bedroom.

I came out at about twenty-five minutes past four to find the tea-table laid in the living-room in front of a blazing fire, while in the kitchen were the sandwiches, the scones, the cake and some jam tarts all ready to be carried in. This is the reliable, respect-worthy side of Loose-an'-Daze. Also in the kitchen were Loose-an'-Daze themselves, dressed in their prettiest flowered silk dresses and wearing their frilliest "tea aprons" and—

"We're so excited—"

"—Madame Zora—"

"I've always wanted to go to a fortune-teller—"

"—but it's sort of frightening—"

"—if you've never been before—"

"Will she read our cups?"

"What is she like?"

"Or is it palmistry she does?"

This is the other side of Loose-an'-Daze, and Twice and Madame Zora were a quarter of an hour late. Loose-an'-Daze have a lot of irritation value in fifteen minutes and I was just about to crack their heads together when the car came up the road on the other side of the stream.

The visit was, I think, a success. It may have been the down-to-earth attitude and influence of Twice on the short journey between Dunroamin and Crookmill, but Madame Zora, although very eccentric in appearance, being dressed in exactly the clothes I had seen her wear before but with yards of dusty black voile draped over her head and billowing all about her, was in her practical mood. She did not keen or bleat; she ate an enormous tea, for which I was thankful, and then she accepted a cigarette, put it in the long holder which she extracted from a large black cloth pouch which hung over her arm on two black, bangle-like rings and bent her intense glance on Loose-an'-Daze. "A most delicious tea," she said. "I feel sure that you ladies are sympathetic to my gifts."

They giggled a little and smiled but, although they made little rushes of words, they did not make much sense and were clearly overpowered by Madame Zora and her panoply.

"Mrs. Wilton and Mrs. Ramsay wondered if you could foretell the future out of your own—sanctum and without your crystal, Madame Zora," I said.

"The future," she said in her intoning voice, "is visible to those who can see it in all sorts of symbols."

Why does she only intone at me? I wondered, annoyed, until I caught Twice's astonished glance at her and then his look at myself of mute apology for not having believed that Madame Zora did thus intone. She reached forward, picked up Daze's teacup and carefully ran the liquid out of it into the slop-basin. "Place it upside-down," she chanted, "and turn it completely about in a clockwise direction three times, then hand it to me. The Eastern races use grains of sand—"

"My grandmother used barley yaavins," I thought.

"—but all materials are under the influence of the stars which reach them through the medium of our earthly being. Your hand now, that turns that cup, is exerting upon its contents the influence you draw from the stars in their courses, Mrs. Ramsay. What is your birth date?"

"May," Daze breathed. "The twenty-fifth of May."

"Ah, Gemini!" sighed Madame Zora and closed her eyes. "Your cup!" she commanded.

Daze reached across and placed the cup in her hand; Madame Zora continued to sit with her greasy, shadowed eyelids making two black patches in her white face; Twice and I suppressed our desire to giggle and, after a moment, she opened her eyes and looked into the cup.

"If you have not already heard," she said in her intoning voice, "you are about to hear of a great change that is to come in your life." Loose-an'-Daze exchanged a glance that was at first startled and then pleased. "This also involves a very dear friend. This friend will find a similar change—I see great happiness for you both. And I see great good fortune. When you first hear of this change, you will be sad and disappointed, but do not be downcast. Have faith, believe that all things work together for good and your stars will not fail you."

There was a great deal more in this vein, the artificial, high-pitched, whining voice spilling out words without effort, and also without much meaning. Then: "You are also a link in a chain of important events, but you will not be aware of the importance until the chain is complete. But I can advise you—I can advise you! Listen now to what I say. If, within the next three months, a relative or a friend calls upon you for help, go to that person. Go, I say! If you heed not that cry you will be conspiring with the devil!"

On the last phrase she had raised her voice to its full keening note and had thrown her head back so that the sound seemed to travel round the room. Indeed, I think that she was something of a ventriloquist. Loose-an'-Daze were sitting

146

close to one another, coming closer at every vibration of sound, their eyes popping out of their heads, when there came an unearthly howl from the kitchen as Dram joined in the supernatural chorus, and this was immediately followed by the door bursting open, Dram bouncing in and Mattha saying: "Fur the love o' Jimmy Johnson, whit's up wi' yeez? Ye've the pare dug driven haufdementit!"

Twice grabbed Dram who was sniffing in an ugly way round Madame Zora's draperies which, no doubt, to his sensitive nostrils had a savour of his favourite enemy, and I rose and said: "All right, Mattha, we're coming. Madame Zora, do stay with Mrs. Ramsay and Mrs. Wilton and please excuse us for a little."

Twice and I retired with Dram to the drawing-office while Mattha went to continue his suspicious guard-duty outside the living-room door, and after half an hour or so I went back to the living-room and broke up the star-gazing party. Loose-an'-Daze were almost in a state of trance with pleasure and Madame Zora seemed to me to be looking a good deal the better for her outing, so, of course, happy that all had gone well, in I plunged again with both feet.

"I hope you will come again, Madame Zora," I said, and then I felt Twice's eyes upon me. "My husband and I may not be here, but Mrs. Ramsay and Mrs. Wilton will be very pleased to see you."

"Oh, yes!" said Loose.

"Indeed we will!" said Daze.

"It's been lovely!"

"It really has!"

Twice, with his ten-shilling note in his pocket ready to press into the hand of Madame Zora, went across the bridge and got into the car; inexorably I led Madame Zora in the same direction while Loose-an'-Daze chattered behind and Mattha, standing in the doorway, spat on the path and sent after us his most malevolent glance. In the middle of the bridge over the little stream Madame Zora stopped suddenly and, in a dramatic way, raised an arm and pointed a skinny finger at the lowering evening sky.

"I hear the sound of running water!" she keened shrilly, as if a bridge over a mill stream were the last place on earth where one would expect to hear the sound of flowing water. "The waters of time run on as the stars turn in their courses, and drawn by the stars our friends have come home to us across the wide waters—"

I think it was at this point that Twice—accidentally, I hope—leaned on the horn button of the car, causing it to emit a very rude noise, but Madame Zora, looking more like Merlin in an unusually vengeful mood every moment, caused her lean, up-raised finger to tremble dramatically so that all her many veils floated and swirled, and her voice rose in an eerie, eldritch crescendo: "No matter how wide the waters, no matter how we try to escape our fate, we are bound to it by our governing stars, and where they send us we are bound to go! We are but links in a great chain girdled about the universe! Let there be love and friendship among us! Let us work for the eternal goo-ood! For the living and eternal goo-ood!"

On the last note, which went echoing down the valley of the stream, Dram, shut in the drawing-office, raised his voice in a blood-curdling howl; Loose-an'-Daze screamed; Mattha began to jerk in a threatening way down the path and I, almost with physical violence, crowded against Madame Zora and bundled her unceremoniously into the car which Twice caused to shoot away down the rough road.

"Goodnight, dear friends!" the voice floated back to us. "Goo-ood ni-ight!" and the car disappeared round the corner with a long streamer of black voile flying from its side window.

What with the comments of Loose-an'-Daze and Mattha and trying to control Dram who was rushing about in a threatening way suspecting us all of cat-harbouring, I did not realise how long Twice was away until he came back an hour later, but when he came in I looked at the clock and said: "I'm sorry, darling. I should have gone with you. Couldn't you get away?"

"I got away in the end," he said, "and with what I wanted."

"What?"

"Poyntdale Bay. Mattha's bringing it in."

"Twice! How on earth did you manage that?"

"Simplest thing in the world. Since you told me about that ten bob thing, and

150

listening to Mattha carrying on, I've been thinking about that old woman. I'm not as clever about people as you are as a rule, but there's one weakness in them that I can usually pick up—the love of money—coin—nice crisp clean notes. Anyway, I developed an idea and I drew fifty quid from the bank this morning, all in nice clean fivers, just in case. Then I had a go. I offered her twenty, let her see the notes, let her beat me up to twenty-five—Good, Mattha! Stand it on that table against the wall. . . . Well, darling, still like it?"

"Twice, I love it! Thank you very, very much, but you shouldn't have done it. Twenty-five pounds is a lot of money and—"

"Will you be tired of that picture in a year and want to burn it?"

"No! Of course I shan't. Why?"

"We spend that much in a year on newspapers and magazines and burn the lot. I don't know a thing about painting, but if you get a year's pleasure out of it, it's a bargain. . . . Seen that place before, Mattha?"

"Jist haud on a meenute noo, Lad," said Mattha. "The pent's a bit lumpy in places

151

—the fellah maun ha' been workin' wi' a dirty brush."

"Come back here where I'm standing."

Mattha came over to us and looked at the picture again. "God sake!" he said. "That's yon bit watter that's doon ablow Reachfaur wi' the wee kirk on the ither side on the road tae the pub at yon wee place on the hill whaur ye took auld Tam an' me yon nicht! There's the wee kirk there on the shore!"

"That's right, Mattha," I said. "It's Poyntdale Bay."

"An' ye got it frae Lizzie Fintry, Lad?"

"Aye, Mattha."

"Noo, whaur in the name o' auld Nick himsel' did she come by that pictur', think ye? It's ma belief, Mistress, that she stole it, jist like Ah tellt ye!"

"Mattha! She could have bought it anywhere!"

"Bocht it? Awa' an' no' be daft! Nae Fintry iver spent a bawbee they could keep. She niver bocht nae pictur', lassie!"

"Well, wherever she got it I'm glad she got it and I've got it now! Twice, I'm delighted with it!"

"So am I," Twice said. "I don't know

what Cousin Egbert would say about it but it suits me."

"Oh, poop to Cousin Egbert!" I said.

Twice and I spent the rest of the evening looking at the picture and talking about Madame Zora.

"How mad do you think she is, really?" I asked at one point.

"Not mad at all," he said. "I don't think she is mad astrology-wise as the Americans would put it. I think her crystal-gazing stuff is the worst sort of ham act myself, but I think that she is mad in that she is a sort of miser. Did you look at all those cats? They're half-starved and she is half-starved herself. We had to get the kitchen steps to get Poyntdale Bay off the wall and I went through to the back of the house with her. I could swear that no more than a cup of tea has been cooked in that kitchen for the last year. You could see a quarter-inch of dust on the keys of the old gas stove."

"You are sure she is not really in poverty?"

"No, poverty has a different look and a different—smell."

"I could smell nothing at Dunroamin but cat."

"There was a lot of that, all right, but the rest was miserliness, not poverty. I shouldn't be surprised if she's got thousands in the bank myself."

"And we've given her another twenty-five!"

"But we have got Poyntdale Bay!"

"Yes, indeed we have! Twice, I am pleased with it! This is the sort of thing that I was trying to explain about yesterday —how these wonderful moments just come along, not planned at all! Dram killed a cat; I got involved with Madame Zora; you got the idea of buying the picture! And it all adds up to being so happy I could burst!"

"We are all links in a great chain that is girdled about the universe!" Twice intoned. "Listen, let's have one more tot before we go to bed. This leave is getting better as we go along, don't you think?"

I agreed with him. It seemed to me that, now, the leave began to take on the character of a map spread before us, with a road of some three months of time wandering about over the space that was Scotland and England. It was decided between Monica, Twice and myself that we would go down to Beechwood, from which

154

place Twice would be within easy reach of the firm's main factory near Birmingham, for the last week of September and the first week of October and that, after that, we would all three move on to London, where Torquil would join us. Monica would have a spasm of clothes-buying and we would all do a round of restaurants, theatres and concerts. After that, Twice and I would come back to Crookmill which, we hoped, would be sold by then, pack up the things we were shipping, consign them to the shippers and then spend a little time in Edinburgh before going up to Reachfar for what remained of our leave.

The thought of what would happen to Loose-an'-Daze lay like a small black cloud on the far horizon of my mind and when I found myself looking inwards at it I at once lost patience with myself, for there were obviously no black clouds—large or small —in the minds of Loose-an'-Daze. They were muddling along, from day to day, as they had always done, with their minds all woolly-warm and comfortable in their own peculiar golden haze.

"We came to ask—"

"—if you wouldn't mind—"

"—you see, we thought—"

"—we thought we'd like—"

"—we'd like to ask—"

"—MADAME ZORA—" they said in chorus.

"—to come to tea next Thursday!" Loose ended.

"I don't mind," I said.

Actually, I did, for Madame Zora was company too exotic for me to want a great deal of it, but Loose-an'-Daze had a nice kitchen, or they could have tea in the garden if it was fine, and I need not even see their guest.

"But why?" I asked. "I think she's rather a queer old woman."

"Well, we thought—"

"—if we went about it the right way—"

"—we could get her to—well—"

"—well, she might—might give us guidance—"

"—WITH   OUR   FOOTBALL COUPON!"

I could only stare at them. Loose-an'-Daze are utterly exasperating, for half the things they do and think of and generally take up their time with seem to me to be beyond all sense, and yet they have a kindly innocence and an innocent kindliness that force me to keep my exasperation and my sharp tongue under control. To me, their composite personality is an embodiment of frustration.

"I see," I said. "By all means, ask her then. But how will she get here and back again? We can't ask Twice to—"

"Oh, no!"

"We've thought of that—"

"—and Robbie at the garage—"

"—will lend us his car—"

"—and I'll fetch her and take her home again," said Loose.

"Then that's splendid. Go ahead and arrange it all to suit yourselves," I said.

Thereafter, the visits of Madame Zora became a weekly occurrence and in some weeks she came twice to Crookmill and each time she came another two of Loose-an'-Daze's many friends from the Women's Institute or the Church Guild would come too and have their fortunes told, while with each tea-party Mattha became more and more scathing and embittered.

"Ah help ma Jimmy Johnson!" he would say to me, "Ah've niver seen a wumman like you in a' ma born days, Mistress, wi' yer kitchen fu' o' they cacklin' auld bitches tellin' fortunes! Ye wid think ye were nae better nor a ludger in yer ain hoose!"

"Mattha, Loose-an'-Daze can entertain their friends, surely? They provide all the food themselves, and look how they look after everything and how much they do for Twice and me!"

"They get this gidd riff ower their heids, divn't they? But it's no' that—it's them twae that cannae afford it feedin' cream buns tae that cadgin' auld bitch Lizzie Fintry that could buy an' sell them! It fair gies me the scunner, that's whit it diz!"

"Well, Mattha, that's their own business. And anyway, I'm not sure that Madame Zora is as well off as you say."

"Lizzie Fintry has mair money nor ony ither yin body in this toon an' there's a few in this toon that's gey warm folk! . . . Och, weel, it'll no' be fur lang. Whit's them twae ben there gaun tae dae when the hoose gets sellt?"

"I don't know, Mattha. I wish to Heaven I did!"

"Ach, dinnae fash yersel', lassie! There's a special providence fur lookin' efter they kin' o' folk! . . . Here, ye'll be needin' a

158

wheen gidd boxes tae tak' a' that cheeny tae this St. Jago place. Ah ken whaur Ah can lay haun's on the very thing!"

"You do, Mattha?"

"Aye, Ah dae that! Ah'll hae a word wi' the Lad aboot it when he wins hame the nicht. It's Baxter the Unnertakker that hiz them—the boxes, Ah'm meanin'—he gets them wi' the coffin fittin's an' that. Ye aye get a bit gidd widd roon' aboot a funeral business, but Ah suppose they'll sune hae plastic coffins as weel. . . . Weel, Ah maun awa' an' cut a wheen kin'lin' sticks."

Without Mattha, I felt, Crookmill would be a dreary house these days, for I had begun the dismantling of the rooms and the clearing of cupboards and drawers. Twice was out all day, Loose-an'-Daze thought of little but football pools and fortune-telling, and south-west Scotland was recording an all-time high for a cold, wet, miserable summer, which means a very high high indeed. In St. Jago I had been so tired of the eternally blazing sun that I had been wont to close my eyes and visualise the fine grey rain smearing across the green sheep-hill above Crookmill, but I was now closing my eyes and visualising the trunks of the palms barring and criss-crossing the brazen sky of St. Jago.

About the middle of September, Mattha did not appear for the whole of one day. This was unusual, for although he was entirely a volunteer worker, and quite unpaid, Mattha's sense of responsibility always made him tell me that he would not be coming on the next day to carry in the coal and why. When by lunch-time on the second day he had not appeared, I changed into my heavy shoes and found my rain-coat. Twice was in Glasgow that day and Mattha's cottage where his daughter kept house for him was half-a-mile away through the mud and fine, misty rain.

"Mrs. Alexander!" Jessie said to me when I arrived at the door. "I was going to get wee Mary Binnie to run up with a letter to you when the school came out. Come in, you must be soaking!"

Mattha was in his big bed in the little warm room off the kitchen, looking very old, very grey of the skin, and with the malevolent gleam in his rheumy old eyes very dimmed he looked up at me much too sadly.

160

"This is a fine carry-on!" I told him. "What's happened to you, Mattha?"

"Ach, it seems Ah got a richt glisk o' the cauld, lassie." He was very hoarse and wheezy. "It's kind o' got intae ma chist." He began to cough.

"You'll have to be quiet and hold your damned old tongue for a day or two," I told him. "I'll come down to see you again tomorrow."

"Aw richt, lassie."

I shut the door and said to Jessie: "What does the doctor say?"

"It's this 'flu that's going about. What can you expect with the summer we've had? Sit down, Mrs. Alexander—I'm just makin' a cup o' tea. Father's not bad, the doctor says—he's past the worst of it already."

"Your father is a wonderful old man, Jessie."

"It wouldnae be polite to argue," she said cautiously. "He's all right with folk he likes. But he's wonderful in health, right enough. The doctor's real pleased with him —apparently this flu's going real hard with some of the old folk."

When I went down the next day, Mattha

was sitting up in bed; on the following day he was still in bed but quite extraordinarily bad-tempered even for him and accusing Jessie of grudging to him the brandy which I had brought for him and which the doctor said he could have, and the day after that I found him sitting up in his big chair beside the fire. In another few days he arrived at Crookmill, as hale and hearty and unrepentantly malevolent as ever, and had a particularly vicious row with Loose because, in his absence, she had chopped up for kindling wood a plank of pine which he had been saving to repair the tool-shed. He could not have the row with the composite Loose-an'-Daze, because Daze had gone down with the 'flu two days after he himself had and she was slower to recover than he had been, and then, the day she got out of bed for the first time, Loose went down. Then, that same evening that Loose took to bed, Twice came home sneezing, sniffling and wheezing and looking the colour of stale putty, which was the effect of the influenzal grey on his St. Jagoan sun-tan.

By this time, I thought I knew the drill for this disease and ordered Twice to bed at once and called the doctor. The doctor dealt with Loose first and wrote the prescription for the tablets and the mixture in record time, but when he came to examine Twice he became less brisk, frowned and ran the stethoscope over his chest for the second time.

"Ever had a chest illness before?" he asked.

"Pneumonia when I was a kid of six," Twice croaked.

"I see."

He applied the stethoscope again and I felt a horrid chill creep up my back from my waist to the nape of my neck. Then the doctor nodded and smiled at Twice, nodded to me and we came out into the living-room.

I am a coward about illness. I have a loathing for it and for all the paraphernalia of the sick-room, and my instinct is to attack it as if it were the bitterest of enemies, but not to attack it bravely. I want to attack it insidiously, treacherously, creep up behind it in the same way that illness creeps up behind its victim. I stared at the doctor, half-afraid, half-angry.

"Try not to worry, Mrs. Alexander, but

you want to take great care of your husband. There's a lot of bronchial congestion in the chest. He hasn't only got 'flu— he has bronchitis as well. . . . You've just come here from the tropics, haven't you?"

"Yes. At the beginning of August."

"I would say the bronchitis has been developing for some time."

"He's been wheezing and coughing a bit ever since we landed—we thought it was the change in his pipe tobacco."

"He shouldn't smoke at all until he's well over this anyway." He sat down with his prescription pad and began to write. "He's a fairly energetic type, I gather?"

"Very."

"Well, you're going to have the fun of keeping him in bed. He won't feel too bad in a day or two, but he'll have to stay in bed."

"For how long?" I asked.

"Ten days at the very least, maybe more. I'll come in and give you moral support whenever I can." He smiled at me. "I'm a little over-popular at the moment, though. Still, if you are worried in any way, don't hesitate to call me. . . . Can you send somebody for these?"

He handed me the prescriptions.

"Yes," I said, and then: "Doctor, how serious is this? I'd rather know, please."

"Serious enough to need careful nursing. Can you get help? Not professional help— the treatment is mostly rest and warmth. But you can't look after him and the other one and Mrs. Ramsay will have to go slow for a day or two."

"Ah'll tak' they papers an' get doon-bye tae Wilson the Chemist," said Mattha who had appeared in the doorway. "An' we'll get help a' richt, Doctor. Ma Jessie's on the road up the noo an' Ah'll get Mrs. Murchison for the morn."

"Splendid!" the doctor said. "Don't worry, Mrs. Alexander. Just look after him."

He went away, Mattha went with him to be driven down to the chemist's shop, and I stood in the middle of the floor trying to pull myself together.

I suppose that most people in the course of their lives suffer from disease of one kind or another, but I, at the age of forty-one, had never suffered from anything worse than a cold in the head. I had had a serious illness a few years before but that had been the result of an accident, which, to me, is logical, while the insidious attack of the marauding germ of disease is not. If you fall over a bridge down into a rocky stream-bed, as I did, it seems natural that the body should suffer injury and have to be repaired, but why, for no reason, had this thing crept up and attacked Twice? The walls around me gave back no answer and I straightened my back, swallowed a few times and walked purposefully into the bedroom.

"What'd he say?" the voice husked from the bed.

"That you're to lie still, not talk and not smoke."

"I don' wanna smoke!"

"Mattha's gone with the doctor to get the medicines for you and Loose."

"You gotta get help."

"I'm getting it. Mattha's Jessie is on her way. Are you thirsty?"

"Awful."

"I'll get some of the lemon stuff we had for Daze."

At last the house settled for the night, with Loose in the room that she and Daze shared, Mattha in the spare bedroom,

Jessie on the big sofa in the living-room and me in a camp-bed across the bottom of Twice's bed. For hours I listened to the wheezy, laboured breathing; at last I fell asleep; with the dawn I woke and day after day and night after night went past until, on the eighth day, the doctor straightened up, stethoscope in hand, smiled and said: "You're a persistent sort of bloke, Alexander, with this bronchitis, but your wife and I are winning. It's beginning to clear."

Hastily, I left the room. The relief that was born in me took the physical form of an uprush of tears that spurted over my lower eyelids and ran down my cheeks.

"He's better the-day!" said Mattha, who was waiting in the living-room. "He's better, Ah'm tellin' ye!" He was almost shouting his defiance of all sickness.

"Yes, Mattha. The doctor says he's better."

"Sit doon, lassie. Whit you're needin' is a dram o' the Article!"

He took the whisky decanter and a glass from the sideboard.

"Wait till the doctor goes, Mattha."

"The doctor ma backside! Here, haud

that ere Ah get a wee drap watter tae pit in it!"

Between Mattha and myself there was some strange bond. We could look at one another open-eyed, be hypercritical of one another and quarrel in a way that was disgraceful, but, like Twice, Mattha could never irritate me or fray my temper as could Loose-an'-Daze who were basically much kinder-natured and incomparably less malicious. I suppose that Mattha and I saw the same world through similar eyes and liked or disliked the same things that we found in it. At all events, although he was the oldest, most rheumaticky, ill-natured and anti-social of the Crookmill circle, it was Mattha who, for me, at that time, was the bottomless well of strength both physical and spiritual.

5

AT the end of three weeks, Twice was on his feet again although he was still inclined to wheeze if he exerted himself a little, and the doctor contrived to convince him that this was not something he could ignore.

"You're forty-one, you know. You have to accept it and act your age. It comes to all of us in different ways and this is yours. You're quite lucky. You've got neither of the modern forty-year-old man's usual ailments—high blood pressure or duodenal ulcers."

"Dreary sort of cove," Twice said when he had gone. "I wonder how blokes take to being doctors? Last job in the world I'd tackle. . . . Well, here we are with the whole blooming leave schedule knocked to blazes. I'm sorry, darling."

"Don't be a fool!" I said. "Postponing things for a couple of weeks isn't knocking them to blazes. We'll have less time at Beechwood, but maybe that's just as well if any of Monica's brothers or sisters are there. Anyway, the house isn't sold yet."

"It would be if you'd agreed to that last offer!"

"She was a horrible woman. Mattha didn't like her either and Dram growled at her."

"Look, if all the buyers have to be screened through Mattha and Dram— not to mention Loose-an'-Daze—and come out well-beloved, we'll never sell the confounded place!"

"Stop bawling! It's making you wheeze!"

"Wheeze yourself! Go and get us some tea!"

The next day was a Thursday, as I remembered when Loose-an'-Daze came in to use the telephone that they might borrow Robbie's car again.

"All right," I said, "and who else are you having tomorrow?"

"Only Madame Zora—"

"—you see, it's football coupon day—"

"—and we never have other people on Thursdays."

"Oh."

"Does Madame Zora do a line in the coupon herself?" Twice asked.

"No. She says—"

"—she knows that a great fortune won't come to her that way."

"But she thinks it might come to you two?"

"Well, if you have faith—"

"—it's because you feel—"

"—sort of—"

"—that it might."

"I see. Well, don't bother Robbie today. I'm here doing nothing and I'll run one of you up to fetch her tomorrow, but one of you's got to come with me, remember."

"Oh, thank you."

"You'll go, Lucy."

"No, Daisy, you go and I'll get the tea ready."

"No, Lucy. You've hardly been out since you had the 'flu—you go!"

"Oh, no—"

"You'd better both come," Twice said. "Get the tea ready beforehand."

They looked at each other with wild surmise.

"WHAT A GOOD IDEA!" they said in chorus and fluttered out to the kitchen.

171

The next afternoon, Twice drove off with the two of them to Dunroamin, and after being away for an inordinately long time he came back alone.

"What's up?" I asked at the door.

"My God, Flash," he said, and I noticed, of course, that he was wheezing very loudly, "what a mercy we went up there! That old woman's got the 'flu—she's damned ill—and those beastly cats were all locked in with her, half-starving. If we hadn't gone up there I believe they'd have started to eat her!"

"Twice! How horrible! But how did you get in?"

"I broke the scullery window in the end. I could hear the cats howling and snarling inside. Gosh, but it was horrible!"

"Darling, come and sit down. I'll get some tea. . . . Mattha, will you put the kettle on?"

"It's on a'ready. Awa' ye go an' sit doon, the twae o' yeez. Ah tellt ye that auld Lizzie Fintry meant bother."

I shut the door upon him in the direct and impolite way that Mattha and I have with one another and came back to Twice.

172

"And you left Loose-an'-Daze up there?" I asked.

"Yes. And I called at the doctor's on the way back—he was in, mercifully, and went right up."

"You're sure it's 'flu she has—not a stroke or anything?"

"I don't know. I just thought of 'flu. She was grey and wheezing and could hardly talk."

"Where was she?"

"In an awful bedroom full of furniture and cats and stink on the first floor. Lord, but it was terrifying!" He shuddered. "Crumbs, I've never hated anything so much! When I started to go up the stairs, I could have turned tail and run at the drop of a hat. I nearly did—and then a great skinny brute of a cat hissed at me and I thought it was going to spring, and then I thought of it springing on the old dame if she had fallen and was lying helpless somewhere and so I went on up."

"Twice, what a blessing you did! Never mind, Loose-an'-Daze will cope."

"Aye, an' a bonnie stramash it'll be!" Mattha chuckled malevolently over the tea-tray which he set down between us. "God sake, I'd gi'e a bonnie penny tae see them twae reddin' up a' the cats' dirt! Ah'll bet ye they'll no' be sae fond o' their Madame Zory noo that they've seen the inside of her hoose!"

In spite of everything, Twice and I began to laugh, for Mattha was right. I am sure the meticulous house-wives, Loose-an'-Daze, had never in their worst nightmares conceived of any house that could be in the state of filth that prevailed at Dunroamin.

"Go and get yourself a cup, Mattha, and have some tea with us," I said. "Loose-an'-Daze probably won't be back for hours."

In the end, it was Loose alone who came home from a Dunroamin that night, and when Twice, who had gone to fetch her, brought her into the house, she looked very strange to me, standing there alone without the familiar other half that was Daze beside her. And she, too, it seemed, felt disorientated and bereft, for as soon as Twice had put the car away, come in and shut the door, she sank on to the nearest chair and burst into a storm of tears.

"Now, look, Loose," I said, "Twice will get you a glass of sherry and I'm going to make a cup of tea and you will tell us all about it."

"I'll get the tea," Twice said and, after pouring the sherry, he went out to the kitchen.

"Come now, Loose, over to the fire. It must all have been quite dreadful."

Both Loose and Daze had, I think, always been the kind of people who find relief in talking about their experiences, telling of their troubles. This does not apply to all people, but with Loose-an'-Daze it applied to a degree that was extraordinary. It was as if, by the mere act of telling, of getting the thing into the spoken word, they shed it completely, cast it off out of their memories and their experience so that nothing remained.

"It was! It was perfectly dreadful!" Loose sobbed, wiped her eyes, took a sip of her sherry and was off. "When Twice got in through the window at the back and opened the door and let us in, there were all these cats and the smell! The smell was just not feasible and he went in front of us up the stairs, hitting at the cats with an old broom, and we went into the bedroom." She gulped and took another sip from her glass. "And I slipped in a cat mess and fell down and there were cats in the bed and Madame Zora looked as if she was dying. Daisy was simply wonderful, knowing everything to do and everything. I wish I'd been trained as a proper nurse, like Daisy. . . . Anyway, we got two of these big old draught-screens and put them round the bed and then opened the windows, but the sash-cord in one of them was broken and it came down with a bang and all the glass broke."

"Where was Twice by now?"

"Oh, he'd gone for the doctor."

"And what about the cats?"

"They all ran away when they knew the door was open."

"That's a mercy anyway."

"They were starving, you see. Then we tried to clean the bedroom, but it just wasn't possible, so when the doctor came we asked if we could move her to another room the cats hadn't been in and he said we'd just have to because she couldn't stay there and neither could he. So he went away and got the district nurse and we got clean sheets and blankets from the Welfare Emergency store at the Cottage Hospital and we carried her into the clean room. Then the nurse stayed with her and Daisy and I lifted all the rugs in the hall and landing and the stair carpet and we scrubbed down the stairs and then we had to do the kitchen and scullery so that Daisy could get a cup of tea."

"Loose! No wonder you're exhausted! This is absolute nonsense—couldn't they take her to the hospital?"

"She won't go! After the doctor gave her an injection and she had some milk to drink she became quite herself—you'd be surprised—although she's got a high temperature and very breathless—and was quite rude to the doctor and said she had every right to stay in her own house if she wanted to and her friends would look after her. She—"

"But, Loose! That's ridiculous!" I said. "What did you and Daze say?"

"My dear, what could we say? After all, we are very friendly with her and you just can't say you're going to walk away and leave somebody who's sick and—Anyway, Daisy is staying the night and Nurse is going in in the morning and I said I'd go over to let Daisy come home."

"Somebody will have to be found to look after her," Twice said. "That's no place for you and Daze, Loose."

"The doctor wanted to send in one of the Home Help ladies, but she got terribly angry and said she couldn't afford it and there was no need for it anyway."

"Rubbish!" I said. "From all I can hear she's rolling in money!"

"That's what the doctor said and he's going to see the lawyer tomorrow and find out what's to be done, and Daisy and the nurse and I said we'd manage between us till they get it settled."

She poured herself a cup of tea with a shaky hand and then raised her wet eyes to my face. "I'm sorry about this for you, Janet. But one of us will always be here to get the meals and Mattha will see to the fires and—"

"Don't get in a tizzy about us, Loose," I said. "We can manage all right. It's simply that I resent this woman thinking that you and Daze exist just to serve her."

"It isn't really like that, Janet. She's old and a bit queer and think what she must have gone through these last days, all alone there with those awful cats. And you know

178

how a thing can get on your mind sometimes. She is an astrologer, after all, and
she had been trying to bend the influence
of the stars to bring somebody to help her
and when Twice and Daisy and I walked
in—"

"I didn't walk in!" said Twice. "I broke
in and the stars had nothing to do with it.
It was the noise those bloody cats were
making."

"But she believes it was the stars and you
never know, you know, Twice," Loose said
in her gentle but tellingly insistent voice.
"It might have been some influence that
was making the cats howl like that and—"

"The influence of hunger!"

"Well, anyway, Madame Zora told the
doctor we were star-sent and it would be a
break in the chain of influence if she was
to send us away and have a Home Help."

"A Home Help would be a break in the
chain of her purse is what she means," I
said. "Is there anything for Daze to eat over
at that house?"

"There was nothing in the house—
nothing we could find, anyway—except a
little tea, but the doctor took me down to
the town and I got some things and some

shillings for the gas meter and Robbie ran me back with them. That was before we scrubbed the stairs—I'm all in a muddle—you see, it was when we were looking for the soap that we saw there was no food either."

"No wonder you're in a muddle!" I said. "And you'd better get off to bed early and get up there in the morning. Lord, I hope poor Daze will be all right!"

"You know how strong-minded Daisy is—nothing upsets her," said Loose.

The adjective "strong-minded" was about the last that I would have applied either to Daze or Loose, for they seemed to me to spend their lives in a fluttering dither of shall-I?-shan't-I? and if-maybe-perhaps, but under this frothy, sickly-sweet meringue that lay on the surface of their minds there was a thick layer of good sound pudding made of the bread of common-sense saturated with the milk of human kindliness. In the course of the next week, they nursed Madame Zora round the corner, rendered her house sanitary and clean and refused with remarkable firmness to allow any cat that tried to come back to cross its threshold. The cats, which were completely wild, met a variety of fates, but most of them were shot by Sir Andrew's gamekeeper although I suspect that Dram and Mattha accounted for one or two of them that came marauding around old Jeanie's chicken coops.

In the course of the week that Loose-an'-Daze were taking the day and night watches over Madame Zora there was, as in every other week, a Thursday, and when I went into the kitchen to make a cup of tea for myself in the afternoon, I found Mattha seated at the table, his glasses on his nose and, in front of him, a bottle of ink, a sheet of paper gridded with printed squares and a magazine called 'Women's Wisdom' open at the horoscope page. His gnarled old hand awkwardly held a pen and his face wore a tortured frown.

"Hello, Mattha," I said, "you're busy, surely?"

"Ach tae damn wi' it!" he said. "That's me lost ma coont again!"

"Mattha, what are you doing? . . . Oh! Is that a football coupon?"

He looked shame-faced. "It's no mines. An wis tryin' tae dae it fur them twae. Loose is awa' up the toon fur the messages an' yae wey an' anither they jist havnae time tae dae it an' they missed it last week wi' lookin' efter that auld bizzom Fintry an' they miss it, ye ken, an '—weel—Ah jist thocht if Ah wis tae dae it by their hoaryscopes an' sen' it in fur them it wid be a kind o' help tae them, like."

"But do you know their system?" I asked.

"Och, aye! Ye jist tak' the words o' their hoaryscopes an' coont an' put an 'o' in the square that's oppysite tae the nummer ye get, but my e'en is no' as gidd as wis fur coontin' they wee printit letters."

"Let's have a cup of tea and I'll help you!"

"Ye wull?"

"Sure. You tell me what to do, though."

We made the tea and then Mattha instructed me in how to fill in a football coupon in the manner laid down by Loose-an'-Daze.

"Noo," he said in a businesslike way, "yin o' them's Jiminy an' the ither yin's Saggytarryus in their hoaryscopes, but Ah dinnae ken which o' them is the yin or the ither an' it disnae maitter a damn onywey.

182

We'll start wi' the Jiminy yin. Noo, read this."

He put the magazine in front of me and pointed to the word "Gemini" and I read: "May 21–June 20. The daytime shows exasperating tendencies but you hit satisfactory highspots in the evening."

"Yes," I said. "Well?"

"Weel, the first word is 'the', isn't it? Weel, they dinnae use 'the's ' or 'a's '."

"Why not?"

"Hoo the divil dae Ah ken—? Noo, count the number o' letters in the next word."

"Daytime—seven."

"That's richt. Noo, here's the copy coupon. It disnae maitter if ye mak' a mistake on this—we've got anither yin fur sendin' tae the pools. Ye see the seeventh teams here? Weel, pit an 'o' in the wee square in the furst line o' wee squares oppysite they teams. That's richt. Noo, whit's the next word?"

"Shows—five."

"Richt, start in the wee square whaur ye pit the 'o' an' coont doon five an' pit an 'o' in that wee square. That's it. Noo, the next word!"

183

"Exasperating—twelve," I said.

"That's a beezer! Richt, on ye go doon twelve wee squares."

With grim concentration we laboured on.

"How many of these o's do we put in?" I asked.

"Eicht tae a line an' we'll dae twa lines fur Jiminy an' twa fur Saggytarryus."

At last the line of eight o's were neatly in their squares and Mattha said: "Noo, fur the sakunt line, ye start at the end o' the hooryscope an' ye coont up frae the bo'om o' the coupon tae start wi'. Whit's the last word o' it?"

"Evening—seven."

"Richt! Ye're daein' fell! On ye go!"

After what seemed to me a very long time, we had thirty-two circles drawn in thirty-two little squares and we had also forecast by the horoscopes that certain matches would be "away wins" and that certain others would end in other ways. I had made a fair copy of our work and filled in Daze's name in the place provided for it, for, Mattha said, the rules were that you tossed a penny for the name to be used, so he was Loose and I was Daze and I called "Heads!" and heads it was. Then he took a

184

postal order and a stamp from his waistcoat pocket, put the postal order and the fair copy into a printed envelope, went through the motions of spitting into the envelope for luck, sealed it, stamped it and set it proudly against the ink bottle.

"Weel," he said, "mebbe it'll please them tae ken it's been sent in, the pare daft gowks that they are, although, mind ye, ye cannae but say that they're gidd-hertit!"

"They are certainly good-hearted, Mattha."

"Here, whit's tae happen tae that auld Lizzie Fintry?"

"Goodness knows, Mattha. These old people who will live alone are an awful problem. There are a lot of them up round Achcraggan and if it weren't for Monica I hate to think what might happen to some of them."

"Aye, the Lad wis tellin' me that the Wee Yin spends a lot o' time visitin' the auld folk." Mattha's private name for Monica had been "the Wee Yin" for a long time. "My, Ah'm fairly lookin' forrit tae seein' her when she comes doon. The Lad wis tellin' me there's anither troot in the well. When's it due?"

"The baby? About the end of January."

"My, it's fair wunnerful the wey she's settled doon—she made a hell o' a steer in her day, yon yin! . . . Yon man Sir Andra brocht yon nicht wis her kizzin, ye said?"

"Yes. Why?"

"He wis a queerlike auld customer, but Ah widnae care tae try an' cheat him."

"No?"

"Naw. He hud a bit look o' auld Gair, the gran'-faither o' Gair the lawyer in the toon. Auld Gair wis as fly as a bag o' monkeys an' had a memory that wid stretch frae here tae the Broomielaw. . . . Och, weel, Ah maun gae doon an' pit that coupon in the box at the road-end an' it'll get the morn's morn's postmark."

"Do," I said. "I didn't play that game of noughts and crosses for you to miss the post with it."

The nursing of Madame Zora had settled into a routine whereby the district nurse came to Dunroamin for an hour in the morning and one of Loose-an'-Daze's many friends for an hour in the evening, so that for a short spell, twice a day, they saw each other at Crookmill as they changed shifts. Twice fetched and carried them when he could, and when he could not the dependable Robbie did his stint. On this evening, Loose arrived home and Daze, who had slept part of the day and then done the shopping, was ready to go on night duty and a cup of tea was being taken in the kitchen with Mattha, of course, in attendance. Twice and I were having a quiet drink by the fire when Mattha's voice began to rise in fury and then bedlam broke loose in the kitchen.

"Lord, what now?" Twice asked.

"Goodness knows, but I'll soon know too!" I said and wrenched the door open. "Look here, you three! What the dickens is going on?"

In a body they poured into the living-room.

"I only said—"

"I didn't mean—"

"It's not that we're—"

"—ungrateful—"

"Ye are so!" bawled Mattha. "Ye're the ungratefullest, damnedest couple o' weemen Ah bliddy well iver saw an' the Mistress an' me skitterin' aboot the hale damnt day wi' yer bliddy coupon! Whit

187

wey wis Ah tae mind aboot yer flamin' X's an' Z's? Ah've a damnt gidd mind tae—"

"WHAT X's and Z's?" I bellowed, for, years ago, as the soi-disant mistress of Crookmill I learned to be heard at all costs and have stronger lungs than any of them.

Mattha lapsed into a mincing voice that he supposed to be an imitation of the voices of Loose-an'-Daze.

"We don't use the eckses and zeds—they are fraightfully unlucky—"

His own voice asserted itself: "Unlucky ma back—"

"Mattha! . . . Do I gather that we've done the coupon all wrong?"

"No, no—"

"—and it doesn't matter—"

"and it was terribly kind—"

"—to do it at all—"

"—very, very kind—"

"Vairy, vairy kaind!" mimicked Mattha. "But it was vairy, vairy unkaind—tae furget yer bliddy eckses an' zeds!"

"WHAT X's and Z's?" Twice bellowed this time, and his lungs were stronger than mine, bronchitis and all.

"X's an' Z's ma back—"

"Mattha, be quiet!" I shouted.

188

There was a strained silence.

"You see, I don't believe in X's—" said Daze.

"And I don't believe in Z's—" said Loose.

"—and there was an X word in my horoscope—"

"—and a Z one in mine—"

"AND YOU USED THEM," came the chorus.

"I'm sorry," I said.

"No, no, it doesn't matter—"

"—and we didn't mean—"

"—and it's not that we aren't grateful—"

"—and we only just said it—"

"—and Mattha got angry—"

"An' hud Ah no' ivery richt tae get angry at yeez? An help ma Jimmy Johnson, it'll be a gey while afore Ah fill anither coupon fur yeez, ye star-gazin' hoaryscopin' auld—"

"Mattha, get yourself a bottle of beer and come in here out of harm's way," said Twice. "I'm surprised at you—gambling on the football pools at your age. You're letting Loose-an'-Daze corrupt you."

"Ye niver spoke a truer word!" said

189

Mattha and with a malevolent glare at them he fetched a bottle of beer, came into the living-room, and shut the door in their faces.

By the beginning of the following week, Madame Zora had quite recovered from the immediate disease of influenza, but she was extremely weak from years of malnutrition, and her heart, the doctor said, which had probably been weak for some time, was now seriously impaired. The doctor, who had called on his last visit to Twice, was persuaded to stay for a cup of tea now that the epidemic in the town had abated and he was loud in his praise of Loose-an'-Daze.

"They are rather a remarkable pair," I agreed with him, "but Madame Zora can't depend on them for ever, Doctor. When we go overseas again we are selling this place and Loose-an'-Daze won't be staying on in Ballydendran, I'm afraid."

"Loose-an'-Daze?" he questioned and we explained to him about their names being Lucy and Daisy and their having this composite personality.

"Your predecessor, Dr. Sullivan, who was here a lot when my wife was ill a few years ago, used to refer to them as the Crookmill Composite," Twice told him.

"What happens in the case of an old person, living alone, who is unfit like Madame Zora?" he went on to ask. "I mean is there any law you can invoke to get them into a hospital or anything?"

"No, not unless they can be certified non compos mentis."

"Madame Zora isn't all that compos really, is she?" I asked.

The doctor smiled. "In this country in particular, Mrs. Alexander, the individual can exercise a remarkable degree of—er—freedom of thought and eccentricity without coming within the meaning of the term non compos mentis."

"But what do you do with someone like Madame Zora?"

"Exercise a great deal of patience and expend a great deal of peaceful persuasion. We usually lure them into a suitable institution in the end except for the very cussed ones and we find them dead in their houses some day. I have an idea that Madame Zora will be lured peaceably and safely into the Old Ladies' Ward at the Cottage Hospital. Mr. Gair the lawyer, who is an old friend of her family, is seeing her this afternoon. That's why I asked you to send up your— your Crookmill Composite in force to Dunroamin for an hour or two. I've told them to take over the persuasion where Mr. Gair leaves off."

"Gosh, I bet she'll liven up the Old Ladies' Ward!" Twice said. "If she gets in there with her crystal and her chart of the Heavens, you scientific chaps might as well pack up. I shouldn't be surprised if you find rejuvenation setting in and all your old ladies starting to skip like young lambs."

"They're lively enough as it is," the doctor said. "It's the company, you know. It's loneliness that kills a lot of elderly people—they've nobody to sharpen their wits on, their minds get dull and the spirit goes out of them. But down there in that ward they all fight like Kilkenny cats and complain to me about the staff and complain to the staff about me and complain about each other to everybody and they're as lively and happy as sand-boys." He rose. "Well, I have to go. Be careful of chills, Mr. Alexander. This isn't the West Indies, you know—"

Loose-an'-Daze, closely attended by Mattha and Dram, burst into the room.

"Doctor—"

"—we saw your car outside—"

"—so we ran up the road—"

"—because Madame Zora"

"—wants to see you at once—"

"—and she's simply furious—"

"—because she can be in hospital—"

"—without paying anything—"

"—and she says you should have had her taken there—"

"—LONG AGO!"

The doctor sank on to a chair near the door and stared in silent bemusement at them and I, for one, did not blame him.

"You mean," I said, "that she is willing to go to hospital if she can get in free?"

"Yes!"

"You see—"

"—she thought they would make her pay—"

"—because she applied for the Old Age Pension—"

"—and they wouldn't let her have it—"

"—and that's why she wouldn't go to hospital!"

193

"She applied for the Old Age Pension?" Twice repeated.

"Av coorse she did!" said Mattha. "Did ye iver hear o' a Fintry that let free money gae by them?—Here, you Daze, this le"er cam' fur ye wi' the efternune post."

"A letter?" said Loose.

"For me?" said Daze.

"D'ye think Ah cannae read?" said Mattha. "D 'ye think it's fur the dug?" and scornfully he tossed the buff envelope on to the table.

Loose-an'-Daze at once went into their letter-opening routine and began to make a wide, slow circuit of the table, glancing sidewise at the letter the while as if it might suddenly rise up and spit vitriol at them. Fascinated as by the movements of a snake, the eyes of Twice, the doctor, Mattha and Dram followed them and I felt the customary irritation bubble up in me as the whole room seemed to begin to revolve round that buff oblong of paper in the middle of the table. I sprang between Loose and Daze, halting their mesmeric march, picked the thing up and said: "Damn it! it's only a circular or something! Daze, open it at once and stop this non—Hi, it's from those football pool people!"

"What?" said Daze.

"Oh, Daisy!" said Loose.

"It can't be—"

"—this is only Tuesday—"

"—and we've got the coupon for next Saturday—"

"—and the one for the next Saturday doesn't come till next Friday—"

"—so it must be from someone else—"

"It will be one of those things that you hand in and get the soap threepence cheaper—"

"It's from the football people!" I almost shouted. "Open it!"

"So it is!"

"Open it, Daisy!"

"I can't. You open it, Lucy!"

"No, it's yours."

"It's yours as much as mine!"

"Give me that!" said Twice, snatched the envelope and ripped it open, whereupon a brightly printed notice and a cheque fell out on to the table. Dumbstruck, we all stared at it for a moment and then: "Ah help ma Jimmy Johnson!" said Mattha, and Dram, feeling the excitement among us all, began to prance round the table, barking as if he had gone crazy.

Twice picked up the folded cheque and handed it to Daze. "Come on! Have a look and tell us, Daze!"

"I can't! Oh, Lucy!"

Loose shied away from the green slip which slipped from between their shaking hands, whereupon Dram caught it in mid-air, ran to Mattha and laid it at his feet.

"Ye're a richt wyce-like dug," Mattha said, picking up the slip of paper, unfolding it and peering at it. "Fower poun' seeventeen shillin's!" he announced. "There yeez are! An' that'll learn yeez tae be ill-tongued aboot the Mistress an' me pittin' in they eckses an' zeds!"

Horse and foot, Loose-an'-Daze fell upon him, taking automatically to their normal release from tension in a spate of speech.

"We weren't ill-tongued—"

"We only said—"

"After all, we didn't mean—"

The doctor continued to gaze at them in silence until Twice clove a path through them shepherded him out to his car. He then looked from one of us to the other as if he were in the presence of two examples of an anthropological type that was new to medical science.

"Yours must be a very lively way of life," he commented as he started his engine, and before we could reply he had driven away.

The next afternoon, the ever-obliging Robbie and his car were commandeered again and Madame Zora, accompanied by her ladies-in-waiting, Loose-an'-Daze, was driven to the Cottage Hospital and installed in the Old Ladies' Ward. Singing about the house, while I packed china into one of the boxes that Mattha had acquired, while Mattha and Dram waited with the hammer at the ready to nail the lid down, I could think of no happier solution to the Madame Zora problem.

"Gosh, Mattha," I said, "it's wonderful to think that that old woman is where she will be properly looked after."

"It's a damnt scan'al!" said Mattha. "An' she should be bliddy well ashamed o' hersel', but there niver was a Fintry born that had ony sense o' shame."

"Och, now, Mattha—"

"Dinnae you Och-Mattha me! When Sir Andra an' a' them—aye an' a' the rest o' us forbye—gi'ed money tae mak' the auld hospital intae a place fur the auld folk o' the toon when the new hospital got pit up, we didnae mean it fur the likes o' Lizzie Fintry! An' by the Auld Hairy, if the day iver comes when she's takin' up a bed in there that some pare auld workin' body o' a wumman is needin', the Toon Cooncil will hear whit Ah think o' them!"

"Mattha, you can't be certain that Madame Zora has any money!"

"Whit wey can Ah no' be certain? Whit dae ye need tae mak' ye certain o' onything? Are ye needin' it tae come up roon' yer lugs an' droon ye? Lizzie Fintry is the last o' a bad lot. Her faither wis yin o' three brithers an' they a' made money, but her faither wis the only yin o' the three that wisnae ower mean tae mairry a wife. But the wife, pare sowl, dee'd when Lizzie wis born an' nae damnt wunner! When the auld Fintrys dee'd, Lizzie got the lot. Auld Chairlie, that wis her uncle, left her fower hooses up the Back Loan an' Jockie Jamieson the retired sergeant pit in an offer o' fower thoosan' five hunner fur yin o' them, but that butcher frae Glesca offered five thoosan' an' Jockie didnae get it. Ah'm tellin' ye, Lizzie

Fintry has mair money than maist o' Bally-dendran!"

"Well that means that she must be a miser," I said. "I didn't think there were misers nowadays. I thought they were out-of-date like organ-grinders and old maids and things."

"The things that folk can be niver gets oot-o'-date. There's aye been misers an' there'll aye be misers in spite o' a' yer new-fanglit ideas aboot social service an' prolet-ariats. Aye, an' there'll aye be auld maids as weel an' Lizzie Fintry's yin o' them. Whit'll happen tae a' that money when she dees, think ye? For she cannae tak' it whaur she's gaun—there's nae pockets in shroods. Will it be the Government that'll get it?"

"The Government will take a good whack of it," I said. "She's probably made a will leaving it to the Cat and Dog Home."

"Cats an' dugs! Lizzie Fintry widnae gi her money tae a cat or a dug!"

"But she loved cats. That's the sort of thing these wealthy old women always do."

"Loved cats ma back—Weel, onywey, Lizzie Fintry niver gied a damn fur nae cat!"

199

"Then why was her house infested with them?"

"Because there wis a cat there when the hoose wis left tae her! It belanged tae auld Maggie Sangster that kept hoose tae her faither, an' when Maggie dee'd the cat jist stopped there an' then it had kitlins an' they had kitlins till the place wis fair infestit wi' them as ye said."

"But, Mattha, if Madame Zora didn't like them she'd have given them away or had them destroyed or something—"

"Nae Fintry iver destroyed onything an' they were a' ower mean tae gie ye a fricht in the dark, much less a kitlin!"

His old eyes suddenly took on a rapier-sharp gleam as he looked at me and said: "Noo, listen, Ah niver speired at ye afore aboot this because it's nane o' ma business, but hoo much did that auld bizzom chairge ye fur that cat she said Dram an' me killt?"

"Charge me?" I said quickly. "What do you mean, Mattha?"

"Ye're as quick as a knife an' as fly's a monkey but Ah'm an auld man an' Ah've kent a lot o' Fintrys an' whit's bred in the bane comes oot in the flesh. It's aye been the fashion o' the Fintrys tae sen' fur the polis but be ready tae settle fur a conseeder-ation. Conseederation ma back— Weel, ma faither conseederationed them an' auld Fintry rued it till the day he dee'd. Ye neednae tell me! Ye gied her something fur that damnt cat an' efter me gettin' a kitlin bespoken an' a'. It's a bliddy shame, that's whit it is!"

"Mattha, if I gave Madame Zora any-thing it was because I thought she needed it. I honestly think you are wrong when you say she has a lot of money—that's just Ballydendran gossip. She's been living at starvation level."

"An'm no' sayin' she wisnae. But you hark at me, lassie. When ye've lived as lang as Ah huv, ye'll ken that there's naething queerer nor folk an' Lizzie Fintry is yin o' the extry queer yins. As folk gets aulder, there's aye yin thing in them that gets the uppermost o' them. Wi' me, noo, Jessie says it's ma ill-naitur an' that ere Ah'm ninety there'll be naething o' me but a bundle o' bad temper. Weel, that's as may be, although, mark ye, Ah widnae be sae ill-naitured if folk wisnae sich bliddy fools a' the time. But wi' Lizzie Fintry there's jist the yin thing that maitters an' that's money. She'd stairve fur it an' she'd sell her sowl fur it if she hud yin tae sell. She his nae feelin' fur onybody or ony thing except money!"

"Well, maybe you're right, Mattha," I said, for I was tired of the subject and it seemed to me that there was little future danger of Madame Zora recurring in our lives now and I wanted to forget the whole episode, especially since Mattha had made me feel a fool for being robbed of ten shillings by a near confidence trick.

However, I do not forget things easily, especially contacts with people, and, after Mattha had left me and as I went about the dull jobs of packing china and listing furniture, I would find myself, quite often, thinking and wondering about Madame Zora. I tried to imagine her as a young woman and wondered how she had taken to her queer "profession", what had inspired her to take up that particular form of charlatanism. She had always, obviously, been an ugly or, at best, a very plain woman, and probably she had been activated by a need to mingle with her kind in some intimacy, and the receiving of secrets in her "sanctum" had been a means of achieving the intimacy, as well as a certain amount of money for a minimum of effort. It had been interesting to observe the spell that she had cast over Loose-an'-Daze, and those two were in no sense freaks, but examples of very typical women of their age and class. And, as I had said to Twice, I could imagine worried wives and mothers and anxious lovers in time of war or some personal crisis deriving comfort from her spurious outpourings. Of what did the comfort consist? Sympathy? No—Madame Zora gave out no feeling of sympathy. The more I thought about it, the more convinced I became that the comfort was derived from the faith of Madame Zora's clients. All she did was to provide a symbol to which they could attach that faith, on which they could concentrate it so that, as it were, it became harnessed instead of wasting its energy wandering down the winds of the world. Harnessed like this the faith generated comfort and security in the mind as the harnessed waters of a river can generate electric power.

In the case of Loose-an'-Daze, I knew that they had been hoping in their vague way to win enough money on their football coupons to buy Crookmill from Twice and me, but ever since the first day when Madame Zora had told Daze from her teacup that she could see "great good fortune" ahead for her, that vague hope had crystallised into a definite faith. Looking back at it, that first day of fortune-telling had been a very neat piece of work on Madame Zora's part, I thought. She had obviously grasped right away the "composite" personality of Loose-an'-Daze in their close friendship and had included both in the coming good fortune. She had made the stock fortune-teller's remark about the "great change" to come in their lives, a forecast, I thought, which cannot be wrong, for life is one long process of change and death is the greatest change of all. And then there was her "if a friend should call upon you for help", which was a brilliant touch. Loose-an'-Daze, at sight, would strike any average person as two leading members of the world's corps of helpers of friends who were liable to be called upon for help at any moment, but as they interpreted Madame Zora's words, they were a forecast of her own illness and her own call upon them for help.

But the important thing was that Madame Zora had engendered in Loose-an'-Daze this faith that their heart's desire would be theirs and this nagged badly at my mind. The disillusionment that must come would be hard for them. Faith should never lead to failure, I felt—faith should always triumph. Or were there different qualities of faith? Was faith induced by a fortune-teller less powerful and of poorer quality than the religious faith that was reputed to move mountains? How were the poor human mind and soul, when moved to faith, to choose the symbol that moved them? The faith was born; there it was and the manner of its birth should not condition its power for moving mountains. The fact that Loose-an'-Daze could be moved to faith by Madame Zora while I could not be did not strike me as being to my credit. Rather the reverse. It seemed to me that to generate faith so easily must make life very comfortable for Loose-an'-Daze. It must make life almost a paradise, indeed. A fool's paradise? What did it matter? To the fools, if fools they were, it was still a paradise and more comfortable than the wilderness in which the doubter wanders. One would rather have the truth among the hard rocks of the wilderness? But what is truth? The thing in which you believe with all your heart and mind and soul is truth—the thing, indeed, in which you have absolute faith. And so it all came back to faith and I thought again of all the different kinds of faith and degrees of faith and, inevitably, I went back in memory to the church at home, when I was a child, and our tall, impressive, black-bearded minister, the Reverend Roderick Mackenzie, was in the pulpit, his strong hands clasped upon the big Bible while he leaned forward and spoke the words: "Have faith in God. I say unto you, what things soever ye desire, when ye pray, believe that ye receive them, and ye shall have them." Faith, I decided, was faith, however it was awakened or induced—it was not conditioned by the instrument of its awakening, whether that instrument were Madame Zora or the Reverend Roderick Mackenzie. Its power was conditioned by the mind and soul in which it was born—the purer their fire, the greater its power.

And Loose-an'-Daze, I thought, were unlikely to win their fortune on the football gamble, for the desire to possess Crookmill was not, I felt, a very pure fire to light a mind and soul—or two minds and two souls. It would be much more likely, I thought, if my interpretation of faith and its power were accurate, that old Granny Gilmour's Guido would come back from the dead, for Granny Gilmour had a faith that was born out of a pure and selfless love, not an imitation of faith spawned out of tea-leaves by the cunning words of Madame Zora. Unless the reward was in ratio to the selflessness of the faith? Crookmill might be the reward for the impurer faith of Loose-an'-Daze while Guido, alive, might be the reward for the faith of Granny Gilmour. I wished with all my heart that I could believe that the rewards came into it and, deep in my mind like a far echo, I heard again the Highland voice of the Reverend Roderick: "How is it that ye have no faith?"

I was rudely shaken back to the present by Loose-an'-Daze returning from the hospital. Expecting, as I always do, the reactions of other people to be similar to my own, I thought they would return from the installation of Madame Zora in the Old

Ladies' Ward full of satisfaction at this eminently suitable conclusion, and I was therefore much taken aback when they came into the house, looked at Mattha and me for a moment, and then dissolved quietly into tears.

"Mattha," I said automatically, "would you go and put the kettle on for some tea?"

Mattha went out and I looked at them, standing side by side, their pretty, silly faces under their pretty, silly summer hats drooping as the pretty, silly tears trickled down over the plump cheeks.

"What's wrong?" I asked. "Was the journey too much for the old lady? Is she worse?"

"Oh, no—"

"—she's splendid—"

"Then what has upset you both?"

"It was just so sad—"

"—leaving her there—"

"—with nothing—"

"—just a bed and a cupboard—"

"—it must be dreadful—"

"—to have nobody of your own—"

"—and be taken there by strangers—"

"—and left among strangers!"

With the last words, they were completely overcome, turned to one another and fell weeping upon their composite bosoms. I felt the familiar exasperation with them rising in me and I was also haunted by the fear that Mattha would come in with the tea and give tongue with his views of "Lizzie Fintry" and her fate, so I said sharply: "Now look here, you two, pull yourselves together! Madame Zora chose to go to the hospital rather than have someone from the Home Help."

"She can't afford a Home Help person—"

"—she has nothing except that awful house—"

"—with all that dirty old rubbish in it—"

"—that her father left her—"

"—and it's so awful to be helpless—"

"—and poor—"

"—and all alone!"

They clung to one another again and wept a little more.

"But she's not quite alone," I said. "She's got you and you must go to see her all the time. Why, you'll have to go tomorrow—it's football coupon day!"

Loose-an'-Daze had the charming as well

as the exasperating qualities of their child-like nature. They looked at one another, thinking of football coupons, and blinked. The tears ceased to flow. They began to smile.

"Oh, yes, the coupon—"

"—we were talking about it last night and we're not going to do it by our horoscopes any more."

"You're not? Have you found a new system?"

"Oh, yes! We're going to do it—"

"—by Mattha!"

I am quite sure that there comes a moment in the lives of the cleverest generals—like Napoleon—or the most guileful statesmen—like Machiavelli—when they feel that they are beaten, and this was my moment. I went to the far end of the room and sat down, leaving them to it.

"Mattha, we were wondering—"

"—we mean, it's only a suggestion—"

"—but if you would we would split with you—"

"—just like this time, and it's not difficult—"

"—and it doesn't take long and we'd do the writing part—"

"Whit in the name o' the Auld Hairy are yeez ravin' aboot noo?" Mattha said. "No' a meenute back yeez wis greetin' like a couple o' weans an' Ah thocht auld Lizzie Fintry wis deid an' noo ye're bletherin' a' through-ither aboot writin'! Whit the hell is it yeez is wantin'?"

Eventually they made him understand that they felt that the spirit of their luck was housed in him, and after all shouting at one another while they drank their cup of tea, he said: "A' richt, but if Ah'm tae help yeez wi' yer coupon, we'll hae tae dae it the nicht. Ah'm gaun tae be sortin' boxes fur the Mistress the morn an' Ah'm no' gaun tae be fashed wi' yer bliddy fitba'." This led to another prolonged argument, for hitherto Thursday had been coupon day and it might break the luck to do it on a Wednesday, but at long last they retired in a body to the kitchen and, fascinated, I followed them.

Daze handed Mattha a large darning needle and that day's issue of the 'Glasgow Herald'. "Think of a number!" she said in a voice very like Madame Zora's fortune-telling one.

"Seeventy-seeven!" said Mattha.

"That won't do—"

"It has to be a number of a page in the paper."

"Hoo mony pages are in the damnt thing the-day then?"

"Daisy," said Loose, "a number has been named—" and she too was using a fortune-telling voice, I noticed. "Don't you think the luck—?"

"Better say page seven," Daze agreed in a hasty whisper, presumably that the luck would not hear this piece of near-chiselling.

They found the seventh page and spread it in front of Mattha.

"Now, shut your eyes—"

"—and stab with the needle."

"Hoo kin Ah see tae stab them bliddy wee words wi' ma e'en shut?"

"Just go ping!"

"On the paper—anywhere!"

Mattha closed his eyes and began to rotate his needle in the air while he recited the following incantation:

"Eenty-teenty ma black hen,

She lays eggs for gentlemen,
Sometimes nine and sometimes ten,
Eenty-teenty ma black hen!"

On the final word "hen" he went "ping!" with the needle, then opened his eyes and said: "Ah help ma Jimmy Johnson, whit a bliddy cairry-on!"

"Zoological!" said Loose-an'-Daze with one voice.

"Gracious! And a zed in it and everything!" and they began avidly to count the letters in the word. I left them to it and went back to the sanity of the living-room.

When Twice came home from the Works, I told him of the events of the day and ended: "It's high time we were back in St. Jago. If I'm here much longer with this lot I'll be going in for fortune-telling myself."

"Oh, well, we'll be at Beechwood by the end of the week, I hope," Twice said. "I must say I'm a little nervous of the whole visit. I've never entered a stately home as a guest before, although as an apprentice I achieved a very seedy inside knowledge of the central heating and electric light arrangements of quite a few Scottish castles. . . . What's Beechwood like really?"

"It'll probably be quite a dull visit and I wouldn't waste our leave time on it if it wasn't that Monica wants us so much to go there with her. The house is interesting though. The first thing that hit me was its sheer size," I told him. "Monica will tell you it's small in comparison with some and it's not terribly old, but bits of it are—it's the fourth house on the site. A persistent sort of family, the Loames. Anyway, the present Beechwood—it's really Beechwood Court—is seventeenth-century and when you cross the bridge over the river in the park and it comes into sight you would think it was growing right out of the ground. The walls just rise out of the grass and there are no trees or shrubs or flowers or anything cluttering it up."

"But I thought you said Lady Beechwood was a keen gardener?"

"She is, but that's a walled garden about a mile and a half away over a hill and she goes to it in her Land-Rover."

"Crumbs, I had thought of an elegant old lady in big gloves pottering about in a rose-bed by the front door."

"There are no roses round the door at Beechwood. Maybe there were once, but Capability Brown probably cleaned all that up when he landscaped the place."

"Who built the house if Brown did the grounds?"

"I don't know. I don't think it was one of the famous architects, but it's very beautiful all the same in spite of its grandiose scale—grandiose to me, that is. There's a room they call the Saloon that goes up through two floors and covers about half an acre. Oh, there's no point in trying to describe Beechwood—wait until you see it."

"I shall probably get lost in it and be found a hundred years hence walled up in a linen cupboard."

"Everybody gets lost in it except the Loames, but there are telephones here and there that ring in a pantry when you pick them up."

"But is there anybody in the pantry? I didn't think pantries existed nowadays, much less pantries with people in them."

"There are always people round Beechwood even in these days. I suppose Loose

215

will end up back there and I suppose Daze will go too. I think that's what's at the back of their minds. Lady Beechwood won't want them but they won't take any notice of that. And Beechwood's big enough for her never to have to see them and they'll be quite useful. It's in a little place like this that they're such a menace. Anyway, they are not worried one damn about their future—they give far more thought to Madame Zora. Gosh, but I'm glad that old woman is safely inside the Old Ladies' Ward. What with fortune-telling and one thing and another, they had me starting to feel that my grandmother had been a witch after all and that I was turning into one too."

"Are you sure you're not?" Twice asked.

"What in the world do you mean?"

"It's very odd that the minute you horn in on the football coupon the only money ever won by Loose-an'-Daze gets won."

"Oh, don't be silly!" I said. "But Twice, I'll tell you something I sort of thought about while I was packing up the china. Don't laugh at this. Maybe it's silly, but don't laugh."

"I won't laugh, chum. Go on."

"I get a feeling sometimes that things go better—things come out right—if one does a thing for a completely unselfish disinterested reason. I mean, that day I went into the kitchen and found Mattha doing the coupon—he wasn't doing it for himself. He was doing it so that Loose-an'-Daze would have the match results to look forward to on Saturday as usual. Then, I started to help him because I thought it was nice of Mattha to be doing it for them. And, well, there you are—"

"You won four pounds, seventeen shillings!" Twice ended. "It would be nice if that theory of yours were true."

"I believe it is true in a queer way. But it's very, very seldom that people are entirely disinterested. With Mattha and me, the filling in of the coupon was a little accident. Mattha had an impulse of affection—he is fond of them in spite of everything—and it was a wet day and he couldn't work in the garden and I was a bit bored too and, well, there you are. We did it. But if one little thing had come up that was more important to us ourselves, that coupon would never have gone."

"One would like to believe that lack of self-interest gets rewards, but one has to doubt it."

"I don't doubt it at all," I said. "I think that selfless love and selfless faith and all the selfless things are rewarded—the trouble is that there isn't much selflessness about so there aren't many rewards showing up either."

6

THE next evening, Twice met the Inverness train at Glasgow and brought Monica down to Crookmill and the next morning we were to leave for Beechwood. As soon as she was in the house she was on the telephone to Torquil, and when she put down the receiver she said: "Well, now I can go to Beechwood!"

"I should darn well think so," I said, "after all this planning and postponing and re-planning that's got gone in for! Is something wrong at Poyntdale?"

"No, it's old Granny Gilmour. She slipped on the stairs the day before yesterday and we thought her thigh was broken, but she's been X-rayed and the hospital at Inverness says she is only badly bruised. What a devil of a job we had to get her to go to hospital, too! She didn't want to leave her little house and, of course, the neighbours were no help, saying they would look after her and so on. In the end, Torquil had to do a Sir Turk"—Sir Turk

219

had been Torquil's redoubtable grandfather with whom no-one in the district had
ever dared to argue—"and bully her into
it."

This led us to give Monica a blow-by-
blow account of the Madame Zora affair
which amused her enormously, especially
when we got to the part about Mattha being
so certain she was wealthy but was a miser.

"I'll put my money on Mattha," she said.
"That old character is never wrong about
people. Do he and Loose-an'-Daze quarrel
as much as ever?"

"More than ever," I said, "and no
wonder. They are an unconscionably silly
couple of women."

I then told her about the football coupon
and our win of four pounds seventeen shillings.

"I wish to goodness it had been four
thousand, Monica. Then they'd be off one's
conscience for good. I have an idea they are
airting towards Beechwood. We'd better
warn your mother."

"Mama will be furious," Monica said.
"Of course, they can always do with people
at Beechwood, but Loose on her own was
such a menace because she would be coy

with Papa and he just can't take it. Maybe now that she's got Daze they could have a room well out of the way and keep each other amused—they could be useful. Anyway, don't have them on your conscience, Jan. . . . I say, where'd you get that picture of Poyntdale Bay?"

She rose and moved to look at the picture from a different angle and we told her how Twice had acquired it from Madame Zora. Monica frowned at the picture, went close up to it and peered into it, came back to the middle of the floor and said: "You know, that's not bad. It's not bad at all. Twice, what did you pay the old dame for it, if you don't mind my asking?"

"Twenty-five quid. Think it's worth it?"

"It could hardly be worth less, could it?" She frowned again, her long eyes slanting at the picture on the wall. "It seems to me you've got a bargain."

"Do you think it's by somebody important?" I asked. "It's not signed or anything—there's just a sort of squiggle in the bottom left-hand corner."

"I haven't a clue who it's by, but it's by somebody who can paint. . . . Hi, Cousin Egbert was here! Didn't he notice it?"

"We didn't have it then."

"Oh. Well, I'm no expert, but I've an idea I've seen something else—" She narrowed her eyes momentarily, searching her memory. "In a gallery—yes, it was in a gallery, with a lot of other pictures—yes, I've seen something else by the same hand."

"It's completely modern surely?" Twice asked.

"Yes—that's what's so odd. I haven't been to an exhibition for years. Darn it, I wish I could remember!"

"Oh, well," I said, "it's not a lost Gainsborough or a wandered Cézanne or anything. We'll ask Cousin Egbert's opinion about it sometime instead of hiding it from him as we thought of doing."

"We'll put it in the car when we go south and let Cousin Egbert see it right away," Monica said.

"Oh, Monica, we can't go bothering him like that!" I protested.

"Oh, yes, we can!"

"We don't care who it's by," Twice said.

"But I care!" Monica said in a pettish way. "We'll take it with us when we go south." She then seemed to repent her vehemence and went on in a lighter voice: "By the way, how did you get on with old Eg? I think he's a tedious old bore myself. Actually, he has no use for anybody or anything unless they're fixed for posterity in paint on canvas. He walks past Papa in the club and never even recognises him."

"You surprise me," I said. "I got the idea that he was the type that prides himself on never forgetting a face."

"Eg? How on earth did you get that idea about Cousin Egbert?"

I told her of his persistence about our having met before and how, in the end, it was all tied back to the portrait of Mr. Fisher's grandmother.

"There you are!" she said. "It was paint on canvas he was remembering—not a living woman. Dried-up old stick! I don't believe he's ever noticed a woman in his life!"

"Not your type of man, lovey," Twice said.

"Quite definitely not!" Monica agreed brazenly. "A few more Cousin Egberts and the race would die out. I wouldn't bother with him at all but for his collection of pictures. Somebody's got to get them when he shuffles off and it might as well be me as the nation—some of them, anyway. But honestly, the longer I live the more convinced I become that people like Eg don't contribute anything!"

"How do you mean contribute?" Twice asked.

She gave him one of her prolonged, side-long stares. "Have you forgotten your English since you've been away foreign?" she asked. "Contribute means 'give'—give along with other people to some common pool or fund. What I said was that Eg doesn't."

"Doesn't give to what pool or fund?"

"This common pool of muddy water that we call life. He's not interested in artists except for their work and he usually waits till they're dead before he interests himself in that. And he's not really interested in pictures anyway, I often think. He's only interested in playing a sort of international game of chess with them—he looks like a fish and has just about as little humanity."

"The trouble is," I said to Twice, "that Monica just plain doesn't like her Cousin Egbert and never has."

"Of course I don't like him, because he's

a fish in human form. I don't like human fish or fishy humans and Eg is both."

"You mustn't write him off entirely," Twice told her. "Even if he only shifts the odd Picasso from Paris to New York and then from New York to London, that is a contribution."

"To what?"

"I don't know exactly. In the end, though, every human activity seems to lead to something—that's why it's important to try to choose one course as opposed to another."

"Where you've got the wrong pig by the lug, as Martha would say, is when you say human activity. Eg isn't human!"

When Monica makes up her mind about anybody or anything, you might as well try to move the Grampians with a knife and fork as move her and, when you meet her parents, it is at first very difficult to understand how, among their eight or nine children, they could have produced one like Monica. Lady Beechwood is a beautiful, faded, frail-looking lady, which is deceptive, for she is very healthy and has boundless energy. But when she was young she was, I imagine, the English rose type of beauty and at the age of about seventy her petals have lost their colour and have become dimmed and transparent, so that the fine bones show through the pale skin, the intervening flesh having fallen away; the hair has lost its springiness and lifts now in delicate silver wisps to the movement of the air, and the voice has lost resonance but retains its music so that it has the fluting yet vibrant note of an old harpsichord. Her favourite phrase is: "Well, do as you think best, dear", pronounced in a soft, faraway voice as if the harpsichord were being played behind curtains of pink silk, and this adds to the impression of frailty, as if the faded rose were bowing helplessly before the winter blast. In actual fact, it means that Lady Beechwood is about to do everything in her power to make the "dear" do precisely what she, Lady Beechwood, wants, and it is very seldom that she fails.

Lord Beechwood is a tall, thin, gentle old man who always wears a withdrawn look as if he had got into the room by accident, but yet he always gives me the impression that a great deal is going on behind his high, serene forehead, and I think it is true that a great deal does go on there, for people of all kinds are always asking him for his opinion about all sorts of things, from what to do for their dogs' worms to what to do about this situation that seems to be getting out of hand in Kenya or somewhere. He makes me very uncomfortable every time I meet him after an interval of time, by making me feel what a fool I am compared with someone with a real brain, and then, as soon as he begins to talk to me, he makes me feel very comfortable and clever by asking me about one of the few things I know a little about and listening with meticulous attention while I tell him about it.

When we arrived at Beechwood, about four in the afternoon, neither Lord nor Lady Beechwood was at home. This was one of the little things that marked so strongly the difference between the way of life to which Monica had been reared and the way of life that had been mine. At Reachfar, one of my family at the very least had always been in the house at all times, and from the time when I left home at the age of twenty-one every one of my visits home has always been a family occasion and seldom were any of the members missing from the welcoming party at the granary gable. But not so at Beechwood. If Lord Beechwood was not out on local County business, he was in London, Stockholm or Rome on Government business, and if Lady Beechwood was not presiding over a County meeting, she was opening a bazaar or superintending some activity in her garden.

We went in through the big doorway into the enormous hall where Monica said to Twice: "Give that a bang or two," and indicated a gong of about three feet diameter that stood in a recess. Twice did as he was told and a deep, booming note droned up and away, echoing along a dozen passages and galleries, and then an aged manservant appeared from a door on our left.

"Hello, Selby! I brought Mr. and Mrs. Alexander." The old man bowed to us gravely. "Is there anyone to take the stuff in?"

"I shall have it attended to, Lady Monica. I hope I see you well?"

"Very well, thank you, Selby. And you look all right. How is Jackie?"

"Wonderfully well, Lady Monica. You

won't have heard our great news? It only happened yesterday—"

"What's that?"

"The chair from the Green Gallery that her ladyship had Jackie's needlework put on has been accepted for the Royal Exhibition of Needlework!"

"No! Oh, Selby, congratulations! Isn't Jackie thrilled?"

"He doesn't say much, Lady Monica—you know his way, but he's pleased all right. You see, it was chosen without the judges knowing anything."

"That's absolutely wonderful, Selby! Tell Jackie I'll be down to see him tomorrow."

"Thank you. . . . You would like to go up? Her ladyship will be back at five o'clock at the latest. You are in your own room, Lady Monica, and her ladyship thought that Mr. and Mrs. Alexander would be happy in the rooms in the Blue Passage."

"Right. Don't you bother, Selby, about coming up. . . . Where are we having tea these days?"

"We are using the West Parlour this

229

month and the dining-room, of course, and the Outer Library after dinner."

"Fine. We'll go up. When Mama comes, tell her we're here."

Having been to Beechwood before and knowing its effect on people like me and knowing that Twice often reacts as I do, I watched him askance as we climbed the main staircase and set out on the journey that took us in the end to the Blue Passage, which was a wide hallway hung with pictures and floored with deep blue carpet from which a door opened into a suite of bedroom, dressing-room and bathroom.

"This is a favourite room for the late summer and autumn," Monica said, "because of the Beech Walk," and she waved a hand at the avenue of beeches that led straight as an arrow over the green grass, drawing the eyes to a small lake with a miniature temple on its further shore. "Tired, Twice, with all that driving?"

Twice sank down into a deep easy chair beside the window. "Tired, no. Overcome, yes. Monica, I've never seen such a magnificent place!"

"It isn't a Chatsworth," she said, "but it has its points. But, I warn you, show the slightest interest in it and Papa will tramp you round every inch of it—he's a Cook's guide manqué about Beechwood."

"I'd love to go all over it!" I said. "I've never seen a tenth of it, Twice—it was always in the war and there never was time—"

"And most of it was shut up because of the black-out anyway and there was hardly ever anybody here. Like now. I'm glad you got ill, Twice, and we had to postpone things. Beechwood's much nicer when it's not all cluttered up with the family but with only Mama and Papa here."

"Are all the rooms kept open?" Twice asked. "How do they manage?"

"They have this thing of certain rooms in use each month. It works quite well except that the first three days of the month are hell. Mama's spectacles and book get lost and Papa forgets which month it is and can't be found for dinner. But it does work and keeps it feeling lived in. Then they have a constant bit—a study each, up beside their bedrooms on the south front." She frowned. "They feel they have a duty to the house but I often think they'd be far more comfortable in one of the lodges."

"Apart from duty, wouldn't they hate to leave it?"

"They think they wouldn't, but they would. They'd stifle in anything smaller. That's why they've only been up to Poyntdale once. Papa told Steff after he came back that every time he turned round in the Poyntdale drawing-room he fell over something and every time he went outside he fell into the pigsty."

"Monica!" I protested, for, after all, Poyntdale was the "Big House" of my childhood days and its home farm and pigsties were a good mile from its front door.

"I know, but that's what he said and he really believes it. It's what people believe that matters. If they believe it, it's true for them."

When Monica left us and a young man who looked like a gardener had brought our bags up, Twice lapsed into a dreamlike state which held him throughout tea, silent and staring about him, so that I began to feel that Lady Beechwood would think that I had married a half-wit, but when tea was over it was Monica who said: "Twice is unusually silent, Jan, even for him." She turned to her mother. "When Twice goes into the silence like this, Mama, it can mean two things. He is either going to have a shocking fit of temper or he is about to come out with some shattering pronouncement. . . . Which is it, Twice?" He was staring up at a picture on the wall above the fireplace. "Twice! What are you thinking about?"

He jerked round in his chair. "Oh, sorry! . . . If I lived in a place like this, I'd believe in ghosts!" which was, from him, the shattering pronouncement that Monica had foretold.

"You don't believe in them now then?" Lady Beechwood asked.

He blinked and looked at her with concentration. "Well, no. Do you?"

"Oh, yes." The musical voice, might have been remarking on the weather. "I have not the sight for them myself, so I have never seen any, but I have often heard the rustle of Lady Freda's dress and heard her laughing on the east staircase and quite a number of people have seen her."

Twice looked round him in a startled way and then: "Have you seen or heard—Lady Freda, Monica?"

"Not me," said Monica. "I've never seen or heard anything like that."

"I think that is quite easily explained," Lady Beechwood said. "I don't know why we accept the fact that every human mind is individual and different and yet insist on thinking that when we four people look across the room with our four pairs of eyes at that lamp over there, we all see precisely the same thing. Painters down the ages have proved that we don't. It is the function of the painter—and of every kind of artist —to broaden our vision by making us see what he sees, feel what he feels. The eyes of great painters see more—and see it differently—than our eyes do. Why should there not be another sort of eyes that can pick up even a vibration of the air, a presence that is not quite material or only very faintly so?"

"That sounds sort of reasonable—in a way," Twice said hesitantly.

Lady Beechwood smiled at the unwilling concurrence. "I should think that you are like Monica, with all your senses about equally balanced—people like you are unlikely to see or hear ghosts. But where one of the senses dominates the others—as my hearing does—the whole case is altered. And you cannot comprehend the things I may hear, any more than I can comprehend the type of eyesight that can descry Lady Freda in visible form. . . . Janet, you are much more the type to be sensitive to spirits. Have you never experienced anything?"

"Never, Lady Beechwood."

"Janet—" Monica and Twice said together and then Twice said:

"All right, you first, Monica."

"Janet has a good touch of her old witch of a grandmother, Mama," Monica said, "but her thing works in quite a different sort of way, doesn't it, Twice?"

"Oh, rubbish!" I said. "I agree entirely with Lady Beechwood that human spirits may linger on around places after their bodies are dead. I'd like to believe that, because I hate to think that three-score years and ten are all we get of this world. I'd loathe to haunt a place in a vengeful, hating way as some ghosts are supposed to do, but Lady Freda laughing and her dress rustling sounds gay and as if she were enjoying herself—"

"She is—the east staircase is one of the

happiest places in the house," Lady Beechwood put in.

"And I agree that Lady Freda is percep-
tible to some people and audible to you,
Lady Beechwood. I don't question that at
all, but I don't think she would be to me.
I haven't any of these super-sensitive or
extra-sensitory gifts at all."

"No, Janet's is a different sort of thing,
Mama," Monica said. "It's a kind of
instinct for people and events. Twice, you
know what I mean!"

"I know, all right, but I can't find words
for it any more than you can."

"This instinct for people and events
those two say I have," I told Lady Beechwood, "is the most earthy and straight-
forward thing. It is compounded of
commonsense and the Presbyterian religion
that was put into me as a child. I think the
Christian religion is a very sound affair and
the more you examine its tenets and the
more you understand them, the sounder it
becomes. I believe in big, general things
like love and faith and I believe that they
can build up into gigantic forces that literally can move mountains and I believe that
hatred and evil can build up forces too.

236

That's the religious side of what those two call my 'thing'. The commonsense side is that if you look at people closely enough to find out what their dominating force is, such as love or hate or ambition or whatever, you can see the thing building up, gathering power, and you can sometimes forecast what is going to happen. But none of this is on a supernatural plane. . . . Talking of things building up, though," I went on, "it's odd how, sometimes, for no obvious reason, one seems to get into a cycle of something. Ever since Twice and I landed in this country on this leave, there has been a lurking air of the uncanny all around. . . . What I would have called a 'palter-ghost' when I was a child, Monica. . . . An air of magic has been paltering in a ghostly way with this holiday of ours. We are just fresh from the antics of Madame Zora and here we are, talking about ghosts!"

"Who was Madame Zora?" Lady Beechwood enquired, naturally enough.

"Oh, a typical Janet jamboree, Mama! Do keen and intone for Mama a little, Janet!"

"Not on your life! After what she has told me of her hearing!"

But Twice and I told Lady Beechwood the saga of Madame Zora and when we had finished she said: "No wonder that you feel your holiday is being paltered with, dear!"

"I don't really," I said. "I think I've noticed all this so much because out in St. Jago I had built up a picture of home that was more sane and sensible, more matter-of-fact and mundane, than home really is. You see, St. Jago seemed to be full of tropical magic and jungle mystery and general black mischief and one was always conjuring up pictures of the sanity of home to counteract it all."

"I've never been to St. Jago," Lady Beechwood said, "but Papa and I once spent a few weeks in Honduras when Cousin Loveday was there, do you remember, Monica? I think that all that part, from the Gulf of Mexico right down over the Isthmus and the Caribbean on to the coast of Latin America is very uncanny, Janet dear. I always get a queer feeling in those places where so much human blood has been spilled and where there has been such dreadful and prolonged human cruelty."

"Mama is very good about the feel of places," Monica said. "I never feel anything at all."

"Oh, nonsense!" said her mother. "Don't try to appear more turgid than you really are, darling. When we took you to the Priory at ten years old, you nearly screamed the roof down and crouched spitting and snarling in a corner of the hall like one of Janet's old lady's skinny cats. It's simply a ridiculous pose to say that you don't feel anything. I believe quite firmly that human actions do build up over a long period into something almost tangible, something that is communicated and can quite definitely be felt centuries later. How otherwise do you explain all the plague houses there are in England alone?"

"They probably all have some quite logical and natural explanation like our disappearing steeple up there." Monica waved at the window. "And that's only gas from a disused coalmine, combined with the direction of the wind and the slant of the sun at certain times. As Martha would say, all these ghostly things are a lotta hooey!"

"Hi," I said, "you are the one that started this spooking up of my holiday! You are the one who had a time-slip at Achcraggan Church and were so peculiar about old Granny Gilmour and Guido! You can't go ratting like this!"

"Granny Gilmour and Guido are quite a different thing!" Monica said quite snappishly.

"Who are Granny Gilmour and Guido?" Lady Beechwood enquired, and Monica, coming out of her snappishness, told her, ending: "What I say is that it's possible Guido is alive, in spite of what the War Office says. Look at that man that was the husband of that friend of Steffi's that wears the awful hats. You two have been saying that when people are terribly cruel in a place like the Caribbean with the pirates and the slave trade, and the destruction of the native tribes by the Spaniards and things, all that spilled blood leaves an atmosphere behind it—like you said, Mama, human feelings building up into a reality of some kind on a super-normal plane that can be apprehended only

240

occasionally and by certain people who are attuned to it. Well, what I feel is that somebody like Granny Gilmour who loved somebody ˎvery much can possibly transcend the normal plane of logical probabilities and letters from the War Office saying: 'Missing—believed killed' and simply know that somewhere, somehow, Guido is alive. After all, think of Selby's Jackie. If those Frenchmen hadn't seen he was alive and hidden him and looked after him and remembered so exactly what the rest of his tank crew looked like and everything, nobody would have known who he was. A couple of identity discs and a paybook don't last long when a tank blows up, and look at the time it was before Jackie's memory came back! It didn't really come back properly till you brought him back here to Beechwood."

"Is this the Jackie who has done the embroidery?" I asked.

"Yes, dear." It was Lady Beechwood who answered me. "It was my cousin Olivia's idea—she is an exquisite needle-woman—and it has worked out marvellously. Jackie was very badly burned and has a spine injury so that his legs are paralysed, but he does the most beautiful work and is really interested in it. It is quite splendid because we have so much here that needs doing and fortunately we have all the drawings of the third Lady Beechwood's designs and things in the library."

"So I don't think you two can have it both ways," said Monica, with her obstinate, terrier-at-a-rat-hole, undistractable ability to stick to her point. "If the evil that men do lives on after them and creates an atmosphere round places like the Caribbean, I just don't believe that all Granny Gilmour's love and faith go out into the ether and fade away like that gas from the old coal-mine!"

"Just as you say, darling," said Lady Beechwood. "You may be quite right. . . . Shall we all have a glass of sherry or a little whisky or whatever you can find over there, Monica? Papa should soon be back. I suppose Twice found the library all right? Shall we call him for a drink? . . . I may call him Twice, Janet? What a very large, charming Scotsman he is!"

"He'll have found the library all right," I said with conviction, "and let's leave him there. And he's not really so big. He's only about my height, which isn't tall for a Scotsman."

"He gives an impression of size, and really it is the impression that one has that's important."

"That's what I mean about Granny Gilmour and Guido," said Monica. "Granny Gilmour has the impression he's alive—that's what's so important."

"Darling, don't be so belligerent if you can avoid it. It reminds me hideously of Great-aunt Sophia. . . . Have you found the glasses? That's right. And what was this that Janet said about you having a time-slip? Was it very frightening?"

"Not at all, Mama." Monica handed her a glass of sherry. "It was very queer, but quite pleasant. And you can't really call it a time-slip—that means when you have a sensation of having seen a thing in a former life, doesn't it? This was just a sudden feeling of having seen Janet in exactly that spot in Achcraggan Churchyard, from exactly that same viewpoint before, and, you see, I haven't. That day is the first time that Janet and I have been up to the church together."

"But you have been in that place many times, Janet?" Lady Beechwood asked.

"Oh, hundreds of times. Ever since I was four years old."

"There is no telling with these things. . . . There are Twice and Papa—they must have found one another somewhere."

After dinner, during which Lord Beechwood held a detailed enquiry into the processing of sugar from the cane as done in Paradise Factory, St. Jago, we moved to the room called the Outer Library and Lord Beechwood said: "It is one of the awkwardnesses of life that it is nearly over before we have anything like a grip on it."

"How very dreary of you, Papa," Monica said. "And, anyway, what do you mean?"

"We have to choose what we are going to do and what we are going to be when we are far too young to know anything about ourselves. At this stage, I have discovered two things I should like to have done, but it's too late now."

"What are they?" I asked.

"I should have liked to be an engineer —the sort that builds dams, like that remarkable scheme we saw on the films about the Tennessee Valley, my dear. Or I should have liked to be a man who paints the white lines on the roads, with the two little red flags stuck in cans at each end of the part he is working on."

"Papa, you have a submerged power complex!" said Monica. "You want to master something vast, like nature or the road traffic."

"Bless my soul! You may be right. I've always thought the man with the can of white paint must feel very happy and content, painting slowly on while the world flies past, but he is really a very powerful person."

"Twice," Monica said, "if it had been absolutely impossible for you to be an engineer—I know you can't imagine it, but try—what would you have been?"

"I can imagine perfectly well," Twice told her. "If I had been born here at Beech-wood and had seen this room when I was a youngster"—he glanced round at the shelves of leather-bound volumes—"I should almost certainly have turned into a historian. I don't know if I could have been a good one, but that's what I'd have wanted to try. All this—this bound essence of human minds builds up a force of its own and I'm sure that's the influence it would have exerted over me."

"We were talking when you left us after tea about these forces that build up—"

"And Janet building up a force in Achcraggan Churchyard that gave me my time-slip!" said Monica.

"A little brandy, everyone?" Lord Beechwood asked. "As for time-slips, do you remember, my dear, that woman that had hysterics at your garden fête during the war and set all the others off?"

"Oh dear, yes!" Lady Beechwood laughed. "That was the most extraordinary thing. We had this huge fête for the Red Cross—it was in September and the Beech Walk was looking quite lovely—it was one of those lovely Indian Summer days. This woman stood at the end of the Beech Walk and suddenly screeched that she had been here before but she hadn't, and went into the most violent hysterics. Before we got her carried into the house, we had about a dozen screaming women rolling about on the grass."

"Mama! I've never heard about this—"

"Darling, you and Janet were in uniform

with those unfortunate large pockets in the wrong places at the time." Lady Beechwood could never think of Monica's and my Air Force uniforms without bringing up the tunic pockets. "The absurd thing was that Selby's pantry was our first-aid post and the women were carried in there and when the poor creature who had had the time-slip came to her senses, there on the wall, facing her, was the coloured picture of the Beech Walk from an old 'Country Life' calendar. The 'Country Life' and 'Field' people have a lot of photographs of Beechwood and when they use them in the calendars Selby always frames them for his pantry. . . . It was a photograph from about 1930 and the fête was in 1941—or it may have been '42, I don't remember—but the Beech Walk doesn't change much."

"Talking of permanent features that don't change, Mama," Monica said next, "have you ever seen a woman change less in ten years than Janet?"

"Never!" Lady Beechwood agreed.

"Oh, but there are changes," I told them. "I have quite a number of grey hairs and certain colours don't suit me any more.

I used to be able to wear yellow, but not now."

"Janet should wear blue," Lord Beechwood said surprisingly. "Like that dress she had last time she was here."

"Papa! When we came out of the Air Force, Janet and I swore a solemn oath never to wear blue again!"

"I don't mean uniform blue. I meant that dark blue dress like the carpet in the Blue Passage."

"You have never seen Janet in a blue dress or anything other than uniform until today, Papa!"

"No? Then I must be thinking of someone else—a girl very like Janet, with dark hair and grey eyes. That dark blue suited her."

Lady Beechwood put her head on one side, looking at me. "You may be right, dear. That deep blue can be very trying, but I believe it might suit Janet."

"We'll find out when we get to London," said Monica. "Twice, your pocket-book is scheduled for a severe slap."

"I've been expecting that."

"As a matter of fact," I said, "I'm not going to buy many clothes. One wears nothing but shorts and shirts all day in St. Jago and a cotton dress or two and I can get those on the island. All I need is a couple of evening dresses and a couple of short sort of cocktail things."

"And shoes!" said Twice. "There's a shoe factory in St. Jago and it's a protected industry, so there's a heavy duty on imported shoes. You ought to see Janet try on an island-made shoe! Both her feet go into one of them with a goodish bit left over. They are made to fit the native feet which are as near to being square as makes no difference."

"Feet are a perfect pest," Lady Beechwood said, "or, at least, getting things to fit them is."

"I am very interested in feet—" Monica began.

"I know you are," I said and turned to the others: "In the Air Force once, she got in tow with a Flight Lieutenant with the biggest feet I've ever seen and his brain was about pin size!"

"What about that Army man of yours that was put into Intelligence because of his bunions?" Monica countered. "He had bunions on his brain as well, come to that."

"I'll tell you who had awful bunions," Twice said. "Madame Zora!"

"How d'you know," I asked, "with those long robes she wears?"

"Saw them when she was getting into the car."

"I've heard it said," Lord Beechwood put in, "that the more relaxed and comfortable people are together, the more sinister the things they find to talk about. I am inclined to believe it must be true. How did we arrive at bunions?"

"Where we go from bunions is what interests me," said Monica.

"I know exactly where I want to go." Lord Beechwood turned to Twice. "Who was this lady with the exotic name and the bunions? I think I heard her mentioned earlier this evening."

And so, back we came to the story of Madame Zora and Loose-an'-Daze and their football coupons filled in according to their horoscopes.

"Really, poor Lucy sounds sillier than ever," Lady Beechwood said, "and isn't it extraordinary how she should have found this counterpart, Daze as you call her?"

"That's an example of one of these forces

250

building up that you and Jan are so keen about, Mama. Aunt Kate at Reachfar sent her down to Crookmill that time Janet was ill and she's been there ever since."

"Actually," I said, "in spite of the horoscopes—and they've given those up now anyway—I don't think they are as loose and dazed as they used to be. And they are terribly kind."

"Lucy is a doormat!" said Lord Beechwood. "No, not a doormat—a bath mat. One of those fluffy, woolly ones that tickle you and then get all soggy."

"Well, anyway, Papa, she'll probably land back here at Beechwood and there's no good shying away like that. . . . Mama, if I were you and she asks to come here, I'd tell her to bring Daze with her and take on the two of them. They keep each other amused and talking and you could give them the old housekeeper's rooms and you'd never see them. And they are terribly reliable and capable."

"If I were you I'd have them at Poyntdale, darling!"

"Mama! Poyntdale's too small!"

"Lucy Wilton was far from reliable on that bicycle she had," Lord Beechwood said, "wobbling about and falling into ditches and having to be fetched."

"She doesn't cycle any more, Papa."

"I'm certain she still giggles," Lady Beechwood said.

"But if you put them away through there you'll never hear her, Mama."

"Just as you say, dear—but one would know those giggles were in the house."

"At least," Lord Beechwood said, "their friend Madame Zora is safely disposed of? There is no danger of her coming too?"

"It might have been quite nice, Papa, to have had a family astrologer. After all, think of old Piers!"

"Who was Piers?" Twice asked.

"An ancestor who is reputed to have been caught up in the search for the elixir of life. He was by way of being quite a scientist," Lord Beechwood told us, "and something of an artist—a very much less gifted Leonardo, if you like. He gathered the most extraordinary collection of charlatans and hangers-on here and they dabbled about with astrology and chemistry and ended up by burning the house down. Fortunately, his wife had got tired of his experiments by then and had taken the children and gone home to her people in Wales. Otherwise the family tree would look different."

"Did Piers die in the fire then?"

"No, he survived and went back into business in the stables, having rescued all his papers and books and charts and things, but a lot of his hangers-on and servants and a lot of the furniture and pictures were burned. He lived to be a very old man quite comfortably in the stables. Never attempted to rebuild the place. I suppose he had a touch of genius, really—he had the single-mindedness of genius anyhow. He poisoned himself in the end, drinking one of his own mixtures which he believed would rejuvenate him. Remind me to-morrow and I'll show you his sketch plan for a submarine—it might have been drawn about 1939."

"A submarine?"

"Yes. It was for deep-sea exploration, not warfare, of course. When I say he was single-minded, that's not quite true. He was single-minded in too broad a sense— he had the ability to be constructive about too many different things. The true genius, the one who makes the real mark, is the one whose mind and powers are canalised to one end, don't you think? Old Piers was single-minded about his experiments to the degree of neglecting his wife, children, estate and everything, but he did not follow any one experiment through to its conclusion."

"I'm extremely glad you didn't take after Piers, Edward," Lady Beechwood said. "Genius, if that is what he had, must be very trying to live with—like Gauguin and people."

"Single-minded people are always a bore whether they have genius or not," Monica said. "Look at Cousin Egbert! Nobody could call him a genius but he is single-minded and what a bore!"

"Egbert has a secondary sort of genius when you think of it," her father said. "He can't create great things but he can identify a great picture, which is more than many of us can do. And it was born in him and how there is no telling, for a less gifted man than my old Uncle Egbert it would be difficult to find."

"And Aunt Taddy with her passion for knitting all those egg-cosies and things all shaped like birds!" Lady Beechwood added. "But when you are in London, darling, you must take Janet and Twice to see Cousin Egbert. He rang me up about it specially."

"Eg wants to see us?" Monica almost screeched. "What's come over him, Mama?"

"He seems to be quite fascinated by Janet," Lady Beechwood said. "If one didn't know Egbert so well one would have thought it quite odd."

Monica stared at me. "Well, your potential is even greater and more fantastic than I thought, Jan!"

I felt myself becoming very self-conscious and awkward. "We won't have all that much time in London," I said.

"Egbert was unusually vehement about it on the telephone, but of course it is just as you please, darlings. You must please yourselves."

7

LADY BEECHWOOD'S gentle "just as you please, darlings" constituted what Monica called the "silken blackmail" with which she had always controlled her large, clever, highly-individual family, and all the way to London I felt this blackmail working on myself. I did not want to visit Cousin Egbert, but I did not want to run counter to any wish of Lady Beechwood's either. On our first evening at our hotel, Monica said: "The way to set about this spree is to make all the engagements we have to make first and then we are free to make the ones we want to make. Well, there's this thing of Cousin Eg. We can ring him tonight and get that fixed right away."

"Monica," I said, "do we have to do that? I'm sort of shy of authorities like Cousin Egbert and the thought of showing him that picture of Poyntdale Bay gives me the willies, and besides it's terribly embarrassing to know that he really has only pushed the boat out about me because of the shape of my skull or something."

"If you've got the willies about that picture, you're a bigger fool even than I thought," she said. "And all that apart, I've got to keep on the right side of Eg or he'll leave that Degas he's got to the National Gallery or something. Oh, Jan, do indulge him with an evening of your skull, just to please me!"

"This is absolute blackmail, Monica, and drat you!" I told her. "But all right. Ring him up."

The four of us were in Monica's and Torquil's bedroom. She picked up the telephone by the bed and after some jerky crackling of Cousin Egbert's voice over the line, she said: "All right. Wait a minute," and she covered the mouthpiece with her hand. "There's a private view of an exhibition of modern paintings coming along at his gallery," she told us, "and he wants us to attend it in the afternoon and then come to the dinner he's giving in the evening. It sounds like quite a party."

"Oh, Monica," I said doubtfully.

"Flash and I will be pretty good fish out

of water at a do like that, Monica," Twice said.

"Oh, let's go," Torquil said. "Eg is less trying among a big bunch of his own kind and Monica will be in her element and she's been out of her element for a longish time!"

"Oh, Jan—and Twice—do!" Monica coaxed.

Twice and I looked at one another and then I said: "Oh, all right. We are being bludgeoned into this, remember, and if we put all our feet in things, don't blame us! I feel that my skull is being led to the slaughter and drat you, but there it is!"

Monica returned to the telephone and made the arrangement and put down the receiver with a "That's that!"

Then she came to me, bent over me and kissed me lightly on the forehead. "Bless you," she said. "Bless you twice over— once for being willing to give Eg an evening of your skull and once for postponing this trip so that we are in London for his exhibition. I haven't been to a decent exhibition since 1946."

"It's Twice you have to bless for the postponement," I said grumpily. "Twice and his 'flu."

"My dear, it's a pleasure," she said, falling upon Twice and embracing him with fervour. "There! Now, from here on, this trip is going to be all holiday. We are not doing one more thing any of us doesn't want to. . . . Twice, we want to go to the ballet—I don't care if you have to buy the theatre, get us tickets. And we want to see the play at the Irving and we want to see the Shakespeare—"

"And I want to hear that quartette—"

"All right. Theatre and concert bookings are up to you. Torquil will attend to transport and meals and Jan and I will dress up and do you credit. . . . Oh, Gerald and Steff are in town but we can see them any time."

"And Twice and I are going to the Motor Show!" said Torquil.

"Oh, my feet!" I said. "Not me."

"Oh—in the mediaeval sense—my belly!" said Monica. "Not me. Just tell us which day and we'll have our hair and faces done."

Not for twenty years, not since I first visited London with an admirer who is now my friend Freddy, have I had such fun as we had during that time. As Twice had said, the leave got better as it went along but it hit its climax in London. During the daytime, Monica and I went about our shopping and such affairs while Twice and Torquil pursued their own strange ends such as the Motor Show, exhibitions of machine tools and visits to Torquil's gunsmith, and then all four of us would meet in the evening, change, dine and go to a theatre, a concert or a dance club. Every day, I rose with a sense of exhilaration to the feeling that this day, again, was going to be another climax. "Monica," I said, during our sherry before lunch one day, "this is being the most wonderful time here in London and it's mostly you!"

"For me it's being wonderful too and it's mostly you! Do you know, I've never stayed in a London hotel before in my life? If you and Twice weren't here, Torquil and I would have had to go to Steff or Philip or Gerald—but we made you the excuse for a hotel and it's such fun. I say, let's have another sherry!"

"Should you?" I asked.

"Listen, the younger these children learn, the better. . . . And then we'll have lunch and go to Paul Caraday's."

"I'll love to go," I said, "if Paul Caraday won't mind my not buying anything. Caraday clothes are not in keeping with the wife of an engineer."

"If I see something that will suit you, I am going to give you a present."

"No, Monica. You mustn't."

"I must! And I shouldn't be crossed in my impulses these days. . . . I want to give you an evening dress anyway and a Caraday will stun St. Jago better than any other. . . . And I'm going to get him to make me an expanding dinner dress—wait till you see his face! I'm sure he believes one finds them in the bulrushes."

Giggling, we ate an enormous lunch before taking a taxi to Paul Caraday's salon that was all a lush hush of pale grey, silver and little touches of old rose.

Sitting on a small grey sofa, I felt subdued. Shaking hands with Paul Caraday, I felt very large, solid and over-muscular. Looking at the models who slunk past, their eyelids heavy and their spines languid, I felt aggressively healthy and that probably some of the Reachfar heather was sprouting out of my ears. And when Monica said: "Go in there, Janet, and take your suit off," and a slinky woman led me away into a fitting-room, I felt that the entire situation had passed away beyond my control and that they might dye my hair blonde or remove my appendix without my being able to utter one word of protest. However, the woman merely measured various bits of me and went away, leaving me standing in my underwear. I lit a cigarette, sat down on another little sofa and waited. I finished the cigarette, put it out and waited. When I was halfway through a second cigarette, I decided that Monica had started to have a miscarriage and that they had rushed off to hospital with her and had forgotten me, so I threw on my blouse, coat and skirt and rushed out and along the hall into the salon. Monica, as large as life and not even looking pregnant, was walking round a tall model who was wearing a brilliant scarlet dress made of folds and folds of chiffon, but which was mostly ankle-length skirt, the top part consisting of only a minimum in the front.

"All right," Monica said, "take it and put it on her."

"On me?" I said. "Not on your life!"

I saw Paul Caraday give a pained shudder

while the heavily made-up eyelids of the model gave a twitch and the willowy vendeuse looked round the room as if a tiger had got in.

Monica rose to her feet. "Now, Janet, I didn't bring you here to be awkward. There's no point in standing there like a mule. All we're asking you to do is try this dress on!"

"Why? What for? Are you demented? I've got grey hairs! I'm forty-one and I wouldn't have worn that colour when I was seventeen!"

"The colour has nothing to do with it! But this dress will fit you and Paul just wants to see you in something!"

"Oh."

"Now, go on!"

"All right."

A minute or two later, feeling a fool, I walked out of the fitting-room in the scarlet dress, with nothing under it except my shoes.

"I feel like the woman in 'Gone With the Wind'," I said, "only I feel really gone with it."

Paul Caraday looked at me quite without comprehension and there was a sickly silence until I realised that all breaths were bated, waiting for the words of the oracle.

"No, no, NO, No!" he screeched suddenly and the vendeuse seized me by the shoulder and ran me in a cloud of scarlet chiffon along the hall and into the fitting-room, but when she let go of me and I came to myself, I strode back into the salon with the coat of my suit round my shoulders.

"I told you this wouldn't do," I said, determined to have no more nonsense with Paul Caraday or anybody else, but he had disappeared. "Well, what now?" I said to Monica.

She lit a cigarette and handed one to me. "Sit down," she said. "Now we'll get something." She glanced at me attired in the tweed coat and the red chiffon. "Lord, you do look a sight!" she said and giggled.

"That's right," I told her. "Have a nice laugh. Look here, Monica, this is terribly generous of you and I appreciate it, but I'm not a woman of fashion. I'm the inexpensive gowns department, tall stock-size, off the peg, and a well-tailored tweed suit for everyday wear. . . . Where's the maestro

264

gone to? No matter what he puts me into, I'll still look like Janet Alexander."

"Yes, but Janet Alexander looking her best," said Monica inexorably. I looked round at the lush room, at the velvet draperies and the crystal chandeliers, at the long gilt mirrors.

"All this makes me feel like a fallen woman," I went on, "and this dress business is all very well, but when it goes to this stage it's a ridiculous fetish. It's a waste of time, someone like me sitting here like this while that little man goes into a trance over how to wrap my body up. With you, it's different—you're beautiful. But for me to be in a place like this—I feel as silly and out-of-context as if I had gone to Madame Zora to have my fortune told!"

"Oh, stop belly-aching!"

"I'm not belly-aching! But it's only to please you I'm doing this. I wouldn't put myself in this situation for anybody else on earth and that's the plain truth. . . . How long will he be? Oughtn't I to go and put my clothes on?"

"Oh, shut up!" said Monica. "All right, you're doing this to please me, which is very nice and kind and unselfish of you and

I'm sure nothing but good can come of it. Tell that to your John Knox of a conscience that grudges you a decent dress for once, but do shut up!"

I lapsed into silence.

"And try not to frighten Paul when he comes back again."

"I won't say a darned word."

"Thank Heaven for that," she said.

I sat smoking and brooding darkly, feeling that I was growing more and more uncompromisingly my plain self with every moment until I felt like an awkwardly-shaped lump of Reachfar rock that had somehow been introduced into this rarefied atmosphere and was making rude rustic dents in the carpet and the velvet sofas.

"By golly," I muttered, "this dress had better be a band-stopper when I wear it."

"Shut up."

"If it doesn't make a peer of the realm fall for me in the worst way—"

"Here's Paul! . . . The victim's getting restive," she told him, "so let's get on."

Some curtains that seemed to come from nowhere closed round the part of the open salon where we sat and the model who had originally worn the red chiffon which now adorned me slipped out of a peignoir and stood in a silk slip. Paul Caraday threw the end of a length of some dull, deep blue silk over her shoulder.

"Oh, Paul," Monica said. "Blue? Mrs. Alexander and I have a bit of a ban on blue."

He struck an attitude and looked down at her with arrogant indignation. "This, black or white," he said, "is all. Preferably this."

"Oh, come now, Paul! I wanted something gay!"

"For her? No, no, NO NO!"

"And not that heavy silk! It's for the tropics!"

"The silk is cooler to wear than that!" He made a disparaging gesture at my red chiffon.

Monica turned to me. "What d'you think, Janet? Black or white?"

"The blue!" said the little man on an eldritch note. "Blew-ew-ew!" he keened.

"Not white," I said.

"And definitely not black," said Monica.

"The blew-ew-ew!" he keened again, reminding me of Madame Zora.

"Darn it," I said, "your father said blue,

Monica, and Madame Zora said it meant happiness. These are two fine mad reasons and this is all madness anyway. I haven't worn that colour since I was in my twenties, Mr. Caraday, and if I look like a gaunt ghost in it I'll come back to haunt you!"

"It will look beautiful on you," he said with conviction and, pleased at getting his own way, he brandished an enormous pair of scissors and sliced into the beautiful silk at the model's shoulder as if it had been cheap butter muslin.

It was all of fascinating interest. From feeling embarrassed and disgruntled, I passed to admiration and then genuine wonder at the skill of the little man as he built the dress, piece by piece, on to the living model who stood there like a beautiful, bored statue while he jumped about her, placing folds of silk here and folds there with uncanny precision, muttering instructions the while to a hard-faced, middle-aged seamstress who stood beside him. At last, the model stood clothed in a full-length robe of shining blue that lay close to her body in front and flowed away in a long sweep from her waist outwards to the floor behind.

"Stand, please," Paul Caraday said to me. "Hold open the coat. Yes. Thank you."

He spoke to the seamstress who went away and came back with a roll of stiff blue taffeta in the same deep blue. From this he fashioned a swag that fell low over the skirt at the front and tied in a great bow at the back, and then he draped a length over the head of the model and conjured up a small cape with a wide hood that framed her face so that she reminded me of the pictures of beautiful peasant girls in old fairy-tale books. He then removed it from the model, turned to me and said: "Please." I stood up and he put the cape on my shoulders and drew the hood up over my hair.

"Janet! That blue is perfect!" Monica said. "Look at yourself!"

I looked in the glass and almost jumped with fright and then I began to laugh.

"What's so funny?"

I pointed to the glass. "That's my grandmother on a wet day with her shawl over her head!" I said.

"Shawl! You are the absolute bottom! And shawl or not, it's the most becoming thing I have ever seen. . . . All right, Paul.

I think it's going to be splendid. How many fittings?"

He shrugged his shoulders. "A final one only." He indicated the model. "Mrs. Alexander is almost exactly Geraldine in figure."

"Am I as tall as you are?" I asked the model, surprised. She smiled and waved a hand at the long mirror and I saw that I was slightly taller, if anything, but that did not mean that I had any of her languid elegance. It is surprising how different two people of the same basic shape can look.

I now got back into my blouse, coat and skirt and spent another interested two hours watching Monica choose clothes for herself while Paul Caraday kept saying: "But that is for later—when you come back —afterwards," and obviously disapproved of one of his most elegant clients voluntarily sacrificing her elegance in order to produce a baby.

When we returned to the hotel and Twice and I were changing for the evening, I could not stop talking about my afternoon and, no matter what my subject may be, Twice is always a very patient and even interested audience to my enthusiasms.

"I could have run a mile at first," I told him, "the whole thing seemed so affected and silly and trashy and vain in the worst possible way—all these people involved in doing nothing but make clothes and being so intense and earnest about it—but I suppose people like Paul Caraday have genius of a sort. There I was, he didn't know me from Adam, and his eye went right through me to the bones and he made me a dress that brings out exactly what I am—a Highland crofter woman, apron, shawl and all!"

"You should tell him that when you go back," Twice said. "I'm sure he'd be delighted to know that his creation resembles your grandmother's working garb of fifty years ago."

"But, Twice, it was odd, wasn't it? It was very startling, that first look in the glass with the hood thing on my head. I really thought for a split second that it was Herself, as Tom would put it, come back to scold me for wasting my time in that temple of vanity!"

Twice smiled. "Herself, as Tom calls her, put into you a lot of things that prejudice you against people like this Caraday.

We all admire elegance in car body design, for instance, or in domestic architecture or table-ware. All these crafts can be raised to border on the arts and we all accept that and admire the master craftsmen who make the things. Why should we feel differently about clothes—especially women's clothes? Somebody like Caraday who has filtered to the top in his own line has a claim to the respect we would give to any other master of a craft. It's only Herself in you that makes you want to deride him because of your guilt-complex about vanity. What colour is this confection?"

"Dark blue—it probably marks the start of the blue period of Janet Alexander."

"So you and Monica broke the ban on blue?"

"Paul Caraday made us break it."

Twice looked at me over the tie he was tying. "I think I ought to meet Paul Caraday. So should Torquil. He's the first bloke I've ever heard of that has dragooned the combination of you and Monica into anything. If he hasn't got genius, he's got something very close to it. When do we see this blue creation?"

"It's to be ready for the night of Cousin

Egbert's party. So is Monica's going to be. Hers is a pale green chiffon—she'll look like a nereid in it. . . . How was the Motor Show?"

"Some very interesting new stuff but too many people. Torquil and I will go back later on when it's a bit quieter."

"Did you see anybody we know?"

"Lord, yes! We were hardly inside the place when we ran into that bloke Ferguson from Happy Vale."

"Happy Vale, St. Jago?"

"That very one. The world is a small place, isn't it? Then I met Taffy Davis—haven't seen him since a drunken party in the club in Quetta in 1943. And I met that bloke that runs that restaurant in Edinburgh where old Alex always goes and, of course, Torquil met dozens he knew, including one old cove that Torquil says is a pillar of the law in Edinburgh. He had a blonde that was very unlike a pillar hanging on his arm."

"He was probably buying her a gold-plated Rolls," I said. "Where did you have lunch?"

"We came up to Torquil's club and went back to the show in the afternoon. Lunch was interesting but a bit over my head. It seems that Torquil's been wanting to have Monica's portrait painted for some time and he'd arranged for Cousin Egbert to bring these two artists—the ones he's having the exhibition of—to lunch. One of them's a Frenchman and one's an Italian and neither of them has more than a word or two of English. With what I don't know about painting, French and Italian, I said to Torquil that I'd better lunch back here—"

"Torquil would be in no better case."

"That's what he pointed out. But anyway, it was all right, because these two characters have a sort of courier-secretary with them who seems to speak everything."

"And what are they like?"

"I wouldn't know," Twice said. "I mean, you can't make up your mind very easily about people who are talking in a language you don't understand about some-thing you know nothing about. They looked like quite ordinary blokes, fond of their food and wine and not boheem-looking in any way. Clean-shaven, dark suits and so on."

"I wish I weren't so nervous of this party of Cousin Egbert's—I've always been scared of important people, especially artistically important ones. They make me feel so uneducated. . . . What are their names?"

"The artists? The Italian one's called Serafini, I think, and the French one's Saint-something—I didn't catch it. But the courier bloke is Marandola. I'm sure of that because it was the name of the ice-cream man who used to come round our way when I was a kid. I suppose he's Italian by birth —the courier, I mean—and not out of the Tower of Babel, although that's what he sounds like."

"How frightening! . . . Did he have one of those lovely little carts with a canopy and all cream and blue and red and gold paint?"

"Who? Oh, the ice-cream man! Yes, and a white pony with a red band on his bridle."

"The one that came to the Highland Games at Inverness had a piebald pony and his name was Fedorio and all the children used to sing:

'Ice cream, penny a clart,
Newly out of Fedorio's cart!'

275

when he appeared on the Games field. . . . Which one is going to paint Monica? The French one or the Italian?"

"The Italian. The Frenchman does landscapes, I gathered."

"Not that it'll matter. Monica would be able to talk to either of them even if they were German and Spanish—she's pretty well multi-lingual. When's the portrait to be done?"

"It depends on Monica a bit. Some time after this exhibition's over and probably up at Poyntdale. These two blokes seem to be on a bit of a spree. They said they'd like to see Scotland and quite took to the idea when Torquil suggested that they should all three come up to the north and Serafini should paint Monica in his spare time, as it were."

"I hope he gets started on it before we go back. I've never seen a real artist at work. Twice, this whole leave is being fun. I'm having the most wonderful time and I ought to place it on record. I placed it on record all right when things seemed to be going wrong at Ballydendran at the beginning."

"I'm having a grand time too, but not at

all what I visualised having," Twice said. "I imagined you and me staying at Reachfar and Ballydendran most of the time and coming down south for a week in Birmingham and a week or so in London. Instead of that, we had Beechwood and this and Madame Zora and—"

"Bronchitis," I said.

"Oh, forget that! That was only a dullish link in the chain and it has worked out quite well—we are seeing more of Torquil."

"We are all links in a chain—links in a chain!" I intoned like Madame Zora.

"Don't do that!"

"This leave is still banshee-haunted when I think of it. I wish you had heard Caraday today, saying: 'The blew-ew-ew! The blew-ew-ew!'"

"Stop it, Flash! The people next door will call the riot squad! If he made a noise like that, no wonder you and Monica broke the ban and gave way to him."

The next forenoon, when Monica and I were having a cup of coffee in the restaurant of one of the big stores, she said: "You were in terrific form last night. I didn't know you got caught up in these bubbles of gaiety any more. What set you off?" I felt shame-faced, remembering my high spirits of the evening before.

"I don't know. And I'm getting a bit old for it, but all of a sudden everything seemed absolutely perfect—being here with you and Torquil and Twice and thinking about the Caraday dress and—oh, I don't know —everything just suddenly seem to boil up. Torquil probably thought I was tight."

"He did, until I told him that when in the mood you could get like that on Air Force cocoa."

"Last night, it was more than Air Force cocoa. It was mostly that Caraday dress. You see, when you've just had ordinary clothes before, Monica, there's something very heady about having a dress specially created for you. And then in my case there are all the inhibitions about vanity—what you call my John Knox conscience. I suddenly discovered last night that it isn't wrong and immoral to have someone make one a dress that really suits one, especially when the someone—Paul Caraday—likes to make the dress. Anyway, the whole point I'm making is that the Caraday dress is the highpoint symbol of my holiday and thank you for giving it to me."

Monica smiled at me, the intimate smile that was rare with her and very beautiful. "I'm glad, Jan. But—well, it's been fun while it lasted, but it's nearly over. Torquil and I will have to get back to Beechwood and then the north almost right after Eg's party. Are you and Twice staying on?"

"Lord, no. That would be anticlimax. No. And, anyway, we have to get back to Crookmill—the agents have a good offer for it and I think it's sold at last."

"In a way, I hate to see it go, but there is no point in your hanging on to it. And don't worry about Loose-an'-Daze. Beechwood is yawning for them. It will take at least the catering and the linen off Mama completely, to have them there. When are you coming back to Reachfar?"

"As soon as Crookmill is settled and we'll stay there almost until we sail."

"Good. . . . Jan, you will talk to the Women's Institute for me?"

"Oh, lord, yes. I suppose so."

"And visit one or two of my old people again?"

"Yes, I'll do that too." I grinned at her.

"You haven't half dragooned me around this leave, but I forgive you. . . . Have you heard any more about how old Granny Gilmour is?"

"Torquil rang up Alasdair the Doctor yesterday. She is doing very well, walking about and everything. . . . That old lady is going to keep going until Guido comes back, you know."

"Monica, I find all this a bit frightening. Where can it end? The probability is that Guido will never come back—I think you lose sight of that sometimes."

"When Granny Gilmour accepts that, she'll die. And I don't want her to die, so I try not to accept the probability either, in spite of all old Kersey at the War Office told me the other day. And it is true that improbable things happen—things that are all against the betting book—and hoping hard that they will happen must be better than just accepting that they won't. The more I see of my old people, the more sure I become that the acceptance that life has no more to offer is the point where they turn towards death. Old Adam Patience the fisherman told me categorically that he was going to live to be a hundred. Alasdair said it was terribly unlikely and hardly even possible—Adam lived to be a hundred plus ten days. Old Miss Graham, I'm quite sure, hung on for nothing but to quarrel with old Sandy Farquharson next door, but the day Sandy died, the fun went out of life and she began looking the other way. And the commonest thing of all are the ones who live in and by their young people—the old Mathiesons watching for the post from Canada, reading the letters aloud to their neighbours and to me when I call. . . . And, by the way, this is Mother Monica's Helpful Hints Column; don't you miss out on your letters to your father and Tom and George. They're not getting any younger and they do a lot of living at second-hand in Twice and you. I don't mean to be impertinent, Jan—"

"You're not being impertinent, chum. But don't worry about the letters from St. Jago—writing them helps to keep me sane, and I've been writing home every week for so long that it's second nature."

"And I will say they're about the best letters I've ever read."

"I say, would it help if I wrote occasionally to Granny Gilmour?"

"Jan! Would you? That would be a splendid thing. . . . It won't alter her thing about Guido, though—at least I don't think so. That faith of hers is the most unshakeable thing—if it isn't rewarded, it ought to be!"

So great was her intensity of feeling that, for a second, the fine sharp bones seemed to be about to break through the pale, delicate skin of her face and her long eyes gleamed with a brilliant light.

"I think her faith will be rewarded in some way, Monica," I said, "because it has to be. If it isn't, the whole concept of human love and devotion falls to bits. The thing is, though, that the only just reward that limited minds like yours and mine can see is that Guido should come back alive. I don't think that that is going to happen. Not now. It's too long. But there may be some compensatory reward that will come to her—it may be there already in her happiness of mind in her faith—a reward that you and I can't see or estimate or appreciate."

"Maybe. . . . Janet, you knew him as a child—"

"Oh, Monica!" I said protestingly, for I

was a little afraid of this intensity of hers about Guido. "How well can a child of ten or so as I was be said to know a child of five as he was? And look at the water under the bridges since then. Anyway, why were you asking?"

"Partly to try to visualise him as Granny Gilmour sees him and partly so that I can talk to her about him. Can you remember any little incidents? Anything she might not know?"

"Monica, it's all so long ago! He came to Achcraggan School just the term before I left. There were extra children coming into the school that Christmas—the 1914–18 war bulge, as they would call it nowadays —and Alasdair and I were commandeered, aged ten, by the way, as part-time teachers for the new ones."

"Alasdair the Doctor? Heavens! What a teacher he'd have made!"

"Alasdair at ten was the whackingest intellectual snob bar none. No. I take that back. I was just about as bad myself. Alasdair taught the little boys and I had the little girls. Yes, it comes back as one talks about it. Guido was a very clever little boy —Alasdair used to boast like anything about him, from the out-landishness of his name to his quickness at lessons. But what I minded most was Guido's prettiness, for all my little girls were terribly plain and one of them was a slobbering idiot—really and truly an idiot, you know, and malformed and everything. She was one of the Smith family—the Bedamneds, you know—and simply frightening and awful and Alasdair was awful about her. And then he would boast about Guido's cleverness and I would think of Guido's prettiness— he had those great liquid Italian eyes and dark curls and pink cheeks, looking like a little brunette angel and here was I with this dreadful Georgie Smith—her name was Georgina. Little Guido caused some hideous fights between Alasdair and myself —we were a horrible pair of children. But there isn't much I can tell you, Monica. After Mother died and I went down to Cairnton, I lost touch with all the people of my own age in Achcraggan. I don't remember seeing Guido again until that absurd time I told you about. There must be masses of people who can tell you far more than I can."

"That's the odd thing—there aren't,"

Monica said. "It isn't that I haven't asked. I think that's part of the reason why I have this queer feeling about him—he lends himself to the strange, the unusual, the improbable. When I ask the people at home about you when you were a child, I get: Janet Reachfar? A proper little limmer— her and Alasdair the Doctor was as thick as thieves as little ones—aye, and later on too. We aye thought that something would come of it, but no—she married this man from the south!"

I smiled at the perfect mimicry of one of our village gossips.

"But when I ask about Guido, it's different. Their eyes take on a faraway look and: Oh, aye, Bella Gilmour's laddie? . . . That's why I thought he was illegitimate. . . . A wee foreign-looking craitur. I mind on him but I never mind on seeing him much with the other laddies. I think he went off south when he left the Academy. . . . And then, Granny Gilmour always says that Guido kept himself to himself, except for his friend Bertie from Edinburgh. Oh, that would be your Valentino, of course! . . . In a queer way, it builds itself up to mystery. He has a different feel about him from all the rest of you around Achcraggan."

"Monica," I said, trying to be rational, "that feel is superimposed on him by the native attitude, that's all. He was a foreigner. In spite of being Bella's child, there wasn't a single Highland feature about him. He'd gone entirely to his father and in that tight community it gave him an outlandish air."

"But they're not unfriendly people, really, Janet! And it's not in an unfriendly way that they talk about him. It's more— more almost regretful as if, somehow, he had eluded them. I can't describe the feeling I get about him, but sometimes when I'm chasing this chimera that is Guido I feel like Jay-ell must feel when she lies in her cot and tries to catch the sunlight that comes through between the bars in her hands. Then she opens her fists and looks astonished because the light is still there and she hasn't trapped it."

"Monica, don't let this thing become obsessive—"

"Oh, I'm not! I don't go round raving Guido at everybody—don't imagine that. Oh, this is just the old thing you and I have

286

always done—me talking to you to try to explain something to me! Look here, if we're going to buy shoes, we'd better get buying."

I am fond enough of Monica to try to help her in any way she may want to be helped and, at odd moments in my bath and while putting on my stockings, I dredged about in my memory for further facts about Guido that I could communicate to her, but I did not find anything until, during the forenoon of the big day of the private view and Cousin Egbert's dinner party, Monica and I were sitting side by side under driers at the hairdressers'. Opposite me, also under a drier, was an elderly woman who resembled my Aunt Kate, and the thoughts of Kate and Guido mingled in my mind and a vague, blurred picture formed.

"Monica," I said in the taxi on the way to lunch, "have you ever spoken to Kate about Guido?"

"Heavens, yes. Often."

"Did she ever speak of what happened at the time of my grandparents' funeral?"

"No. What was that?"

"I don't know," I said, "but something

happened and Granny Gilmour came up to Reachfar to apologise. The whole thing is a blur in my mind. I was working in Kent with old Mr. Carter at the time, and Granny and Granda died within the same twenty-four hours and there was this huge double funeral. I think I was at home for only three days or so and my memory of it is about nil. It was summer—I remember the sun and wind rippling on the grass in the churchyard and I remember—I think it must have been the next day—coming downstairs and Kate was seeing Granny Gilmour off from the door of the house—"

The taxi stopped at the door of the restaurant and I moved to get out.

"Go on. Granny Gilmour was leaving the house—"

"I went into the kitchen—there were cups on the table—she and Kate had had tea—Kate came in and said: 'Poor ould craitur, walking all the way up here for that! As if it made any difference where the laddies were or whether they stopped their ploy or not!'—I don't remember any more." I shook my head. "No. That's all. But ask Kate when you get home."

We got out of the taxi, met Torquil and

Twice, had lunch and set off for Cousin Egbert's gallery, taking with us the picture of Poyntdale Bay which Monica had insisted on picking up at the hotel.

"I'm not in favour of this," Twice said sulkily, jerking his elbow at the canvas in its light crate which stood against the door of the taxi that was taking us up Bond Street. "Let's dump it back at the hotel before we go to the gallery."

"We'll do damn all of the sort!" said Monica. "I didn't bring that picture all the way from Scotland to lug it home again without Eg seeing it."

"Then why the blazes did you two women not get him round to the hotel to look at it before now? You've frittered away all these weeks—"

"And how many weeks have you and Torquil frittered away? Or is your time-scale different from ours?"

"Getting Cousin Egbert's opinion wasn't our bloody idea. And it isn't my idea right now. Of all times, you two would pick a day when a man has a big affair on like this exhibition to walk in asking for an opinion on one of Madame Zora's ornaments."

"Twice is quite right, Monica," I said.

"Let's drop it back at the hotel. After all, Twice and I don't care if it's a picture postcard."

"It isn't a picture postcard!" said Monica with her chin sticking out. "And if you don't care, I do and—"

"Now, Monica," Torquil said, "we don't want to embarrass Janet and Twice—"

"Them? You can't embarrass them!"

"Oh, can't you?" said Twice. "Well, I'm not lugging that thing into this place—"

The taxi stopped. A commissionaire opened the door.

"Good afternoon," said Monica with her most winning smile. "Will you have this canvas taken up to Mr. Fitzhugh's office, please?"

"Certainly, Lady Monica."

While Torquil paid the taximan, Twice and I stared at one another on the pavement while Monica, in high dudgeon, stamped on spike heels up the steps, her mink cape swashbuckling defiantly above her slim hips.

But once in the gallery where the exhibition pictures were hung, Torquil, Twice and I were too busy feeling like fish out of water to remember anything about

Poyntdale Bay. The gallery was crowded with people and more were arriving moment by moment, coming through the doorway and loudly hailing their friends. The thing that struck me most forcibly was that everybody seemed to be doing almost anything other than look at the pictures with which the walls were hung. A tall old lady, wearing a tweed cape that reached to her ankles and a coy little hat with an eye-veil, was telling the young man who was with her that she did not approve at all of this job that Bobbie had taken. She seemed to have come to the exhibition expressly to meet this young man and tell him how strongly she disapproved of Bobbie's job and to convey her disappointment to Bobbie through this young man, and I thought it would have been simpler if she had just given Bobbie a ring on the tele-phone and told him direct. Of course, I have a very simple sort of mind. Then there was a fattish, middle-aged man who stood in a corner facing the wall, writing things very short-sightedly in a little black book with a little gold pencil. Then there was a large young woman in a tweed suit, heavy shoes and with cropped hair who strode up

291

and down from one end of the room to the other, staring straight in front of her, cleaving a way through the crowd, as if she always took her exercise in this place at this time every day and resented us all coming and getting in her way.

I saw very little of the pictures on the walls and I find it difficult to believe that any of the other people saw much of them either, but after an hour or so a door at the end of the gallery opened, exposing a buffet that could supply either tea or cocktails. Monica appeared out of the crowd and said to Torquil, Twice and me: "Us for Eg's office. This way."

We followed her along a passage into a large room where there was another buffet with Cousin Egbert's secretary in charge of it, but the room was otherwise empty.

"Hello, Miss Fawley," Monica said, depositing her mink on a filing cabinet from whence it was lovingly removed by Miss Fawley and put in a cupboard, "you've got a success on your hands. Gluckstein says Serafini is the biggest thing since Modigliani. It's like a zoo outside. May we have tea in here?"

"Of course, Lady Monica."

Miss Fawley began to pour tea and, gratefully, I sank into a chair.

"These are nice," Monica said, indicating some paintings of flowers that stood in a row along the top of the file cabinets. Miss Fawley glanced at them. "Aren't they? They're the work of an ex-serviceman down in Sussex. He learned to paint as part of his occupational therapy. He was a bomber pilot shot down over Heligoland in 1944 and very badly burned. Mr. Fitzhugh takes a great interest in that hospital at Branksmere—they have quite an art centre. A lot of their work passes through here. Wonderful, isn't it?"

"Very wonderful indeed." Monica rose and moved about, looking at one of the paintings. "I like that one of the peonies—that fleshy, blowsy look. You see what I mean, Torquil? . . . What's the price like?"

"It's sold, I'm afraid," Miss Fawley said. "They all are. They are only here for Signor Serafini to see. Signor Serafini is a war casualty himself, you know, and Mr. Fitzhugh hopes to get him down to Branksmere to visit the men."

"Oh, I see. . . . Signor Serafini looks all right to me. What happened to him?"

293

"He's lost his memory. He can't remember anything before the time he woke up in some hospital or another. Queer, isn't it? It gives me the creeps to think about it. It seems that he started painting in hospital, just like these men at Branksmere. Oh, here they come."

Cousin Egbert and the two artists now came into the room and Miss Fawley busied herself with her tea trolley, and Monica at once began to talk to the two guests, passing without effort from French to Italian and back again, while Twice, Torquil and I gravitated into a corner talking quietly among ourselves until Signor Marandola the courier came in and Torquil brought him over and introduced him to me. His English was remarkably fluent with only a slight strangeness of idiom and a slight Italian accent which gave to his words a fluidity that was very charming to the ear.

"I envy you your gift of tongues, Signor Marandola," I told him at one point. "Did you travel a lot as a child?"

"No, I think not. I come from a small village near Montepescali in Tuscany. This is the first time I come to England."

294

"And not a very pleasant time of year to visit London. What do you think of it?"

"It is very strange," he said. "Not beautiful, but like a friend so that one does not see it looking ugly. You live in London?"

"No. At the moment our home is in the West Indies, but our family home is in the north of Scotland, on top of a hill beside the sea, not at all like London."

"Like my home at Montepescali—when the air is clear we look westwards over the sea to Elba, where Napoleon was prisoner."

"It must be very beautiful."

"Yes, very beautiful and peaceful. So beautiful and peaceful that Signor Serafini too has now come there to live for some of the time, but he also has a house in Rome."

Across the room, Monica, with her back to us, was deep in conversation in Italian with Signor Serafini and suddenly, out of the fluid incomprehensible stream of her talk, I heard the name "Guido Sidonio" and knew that she was talking to the artist of this near-obsession of hers.

"Miss Fawley told us," I said to Signor Marandola, "that Signor Serafini was a war casualty, that he has never recovered his memory. That must be a very strange thing. One lives so much by memory."

Signor Marandola smiled at me. "It is very strange, but one grows accustomed. I am another like Signor Serafini. He and I met in hospital in Firenze. He studied painting—I studied languages."

I felt that I had made an ugly intrusion on a personal privacy. "I am sorry," I said. "I did not mean to—"

"There is no harm." The man smiled at me again. "Many men suffer from injuries that are more severe. I remember more than Signor Serafini, however. I remember the place where my home is and go back there."

"Monte—Montepescali?"

"Yes. Near Montepescali."

"And you found your home?"

"No. The village is destroyed and my people—I do not remember them."

"Oh—but people recognised you?"

"No. You see, I do not know what I look like before." He smiled at me again, a strange, half-apologetic smile, as if he knew that he was speaking out of some dimension that was utterly foreign to me and was apologising for this inconvenience. "The surgeons give me a new face. The nurses tell me that my name is Marandola and that my mother is a widow named Maria and that my home is in Milan. They give me the address and when I leave the hospital I go there. The address is not any more, not for people to live. At the place is now a large factory which makes parts for motor cars. But I know something. I look at this place and know that it is not here that I lived at the time I remember, when I am a small boy. I know that I come from beside the sea, not from Milan, so I begin to go about Italy, searching for the home I can remember."

"And you found it?"

"Yes, after two years. I worked as a courier—a guide for tourists, you know, and one day I come to Montepescali and know that this is what I remember—the sea and Elba there to the west. I know that it is somewhere here that I remember but I find nobody who knows me or can tell me about my people."

"But surely someone would remember your name?"

He shook his head. "It may be that we left Montepescali long ago, when I was a child. But I am fortunate. Signor Serafini remembers nothing, nothing."

I was so fascinated and so filled with admiration for someone who was living with a deficiency that I could not even imagine, that I could have talked to Signor Marandola all night, but we were separated by Monica saying: "Janet, we'll have to go. . . . We'll meet again at dinner, Signor Marandola."

I could hardly wait to get into the taxi to tell Monica, Twice and Torquil about Signor Marandola, and when I had finished, just as we reached the hotel, Monica said: "There you are! Two of them, Torquil! And another lot down at the place at Branksmere. I'll bet anything old Granny Gilmour is right!"

"Monica," Torquil said wearily, "this thing is a perfect obsession with you and I'm sick of it. The Branksmere cases are crippled men—there's no question of lost memory. And there's no question of lost identity with men like Serafini and Marandola either. They have lost their memories but their identity is quite certain from their service documents. I know our army is reckoned to be pretty inefficient in many ways, but I'm damned sure we were more efficient than Mussolini's lot. We had our men documented too. . . . Get out of this taxi and into the bar for pity's sake and stop going on and on about this boy Guido!"

But as soon as we were inside the bar, Monica said in her persistent way: "Still, it's pretty odd how one keeps running across these cases of lost memory and things. It gives one a feeling—"

"You and your feelings!" said Torquil.

"I must say," Twice said, changing the subject abruptly, "I'm looking forward to seeing you girls in all this Paul Caraday finery."

"If it has arrived," I said.

"Of course it'll have arrived!" Monica said. "Paul's always at the cow's tail as Aunt Kate would say, but he has never actually missed yet."

When we went upstairs, the dress and its little cape were there in a huge cardboard suitcase full of tissue paper, and when I took them out and the blue silk spilled over the bed in a shining pool, Twice said: "Golly, that does look like quelquechose! Hurry up and get dressed. I can't wait!"

I had my bath and by the time Twice

299

came out of the bathroom I was standing in the middle of the floor in the blue gown. He stopped in the doorway and stared.

"What d'you think?" I asked nervously. "It's terribly sort of grand, isn't it?"

"Flash, it's perfect! This Caraday has got genius. It doesn't attempt to trim you up fancy or scale you down pretty or anything —it just brings out the essence of—of— Janet Reachfar."

"Twice! You really think it's all right? Oh, and here's Granny's shawl."

I put the cape on and drew the hood up, so that it stood out stiffly round my head. "Wet day, see?"

"It's good though! Gosh, I wish I could afford to have Caraday dress you all the time."

"Oh, pish and tush!" I said and threw the cape on to the bed. "Imagine me dancing to Big Maxie's saxophone at the Estate Club in St. Jago in this get-up. It was lovely of Monica to give it to me but Heaven knows when I'll wear it again."

"It's worth the money—whatever it was —just for once. . . . Have I a clean pair of black socks?"

"In that left-hand drawer. And Twice,

you don't need that knife with your dinner clothes. Cousin Egbert hasn't got horses that need things taking out of their hooves."

"You never know," said Twice, and put the knife in the pocket of his trousers before beginning to brush his hair with the usual fierce loathing, standing the while in the middle of the floor and reading the evening newspaper that lay on the bed.

"Go to the glass and get that parting straight," I said.

"Och, it'll do."

"It will not! Here am I taking endless trouble to get all dressed up like a dish of fish and you can't part your hair for reading the newspaper."

"Who's going to look at me, anyway?"

"I am for one!"

This before-the-party exchange was a familiar of our lives together, but at last we were ready and we set out in a body for Cousin Egbert's house in a square off Sloane Street.

8

MONICA, Torquil, Twice and I were the first of the guests to arrive, but Mr. Fisher and Mr. Gluckstein from New York were already there, of course, because they were staying with Cousin Egbert. I was so exhilarated in my new dress and at this climax of the London holiday that, during the taxi-ride, I did not notice that Monica was unusually quiet, but, as we waited for Cousin Egbert's door to be opened, she said: "You are in for the surprise of your little life, chum!"

"Monica, what?"

"You wait and see!"

Monica and I were taken by a manservant up the stairs and shown into a small room that was like a bedroom without a bed and, having disposed of her furs and my blue cape, we came down to the drawing-room. I felt that I was on another visit to a picture gallery, for every wall was hung thick with paintings of all kinds, old and modern. Monica waved at them.

"Eg's bank-book!" she said. "Come on!"

Twice and Torquil were already in the room with Cousin Egbert, Mr. Fisher and Mr. Gluckstein, and the five men were standing in a semi-circle with their backs to the fire as Monica and I came in. My eyes were drawn to Twice's face and his eyes were glittering and he had the about-to-burst look that he gets when he is very excited. I stopped in the middle of the floor but Monica went on and joined the ring of men.

"Want to sell a picture?" Cousin Egbert jerked at me.

"What picture?" I asked, looking at Twice.

"Poyntdale Bay," he said.

With the events of the afternoon, I had forgotten all about Poyntdale Bay. "Poyntdale Bay?" I repeated. "Is it—is it good then?"

"We think so," said Mr. Fisher, and I could only stare at the three experts.

"But—" I pulled at myself, trying to be intelligent. "You have identified the artist then?"

"As far as an unknown painter can be identified, yes," one of them said.

The manservant offered me a tray with sherry and I took a glass and sank on to the nearest chair. Cousin Egbert, Mr. Fisher and Mr. Gluckstein all began to talk at once or, at least, they formed among them a continuous patter of explanation in the manner of Loose-an'-Daze. What I gathered was that less than a dozen paintings by this artist were known to exist and that Poyntdale Bay was a discovery and, they thought, a fairly early work among those that were known.

"Don't mistake us," Mr. Fisher said. "It isn't a Van Gogh but it is a very interesting picture. We have no idea who the painter is. It was Fitzhugh here who first noticed his stuff just before the war—he picked up a canvas at some hole-in-the-wall second-hand shop in the Fulham Road. Then, after I saw his, I found another one in the south of France—that was in the summer of 1939."

"Gluckstein here was my partner at that time,"

Cousin Egbert said. "You found the next one, didn't you?"

"Yes, in an antique dealer's shop in Cambridge."

"Anyway, since then they've been a hobby with the three of us," Cousin Egbert went on. "How many you got, Fisher? I've got three. Four, you have, is it? And Gluckstein's got three. Then there's the portrait of a peasant girl that that old madman in Chicago had—"

"That one doesn't count any more," Mr. Gluckstein said. "Old Schaffer's house went on fire," he explained, turning to me, "and half his collection went up in smoke and the Peasant Girl was one of them."

"And now I've got one, have I?" I asked.

In a body they spun round on me. "Yes. Want to sell? Hundred guineas!" said Cousin Egbert.

"Hundred an' ten!"

"Hundred an' twenty!"

I looked at Twice. "Poyntdale Bay is not for sale, gentlemen," I said, and we grinned at one another.

But we told them the story of Madame Zora and how we came to acquire the picture and we also told them that Loose-an'-Daze would undoubtedly be able to obtain entrance to Dunroamin for them if they wanted to search it for more examples of their hobby, and then the other guests began to arrive.

Cousin Egbert, of course, had only one subject of conversation, which was Poyntdale Bay, and I should have been embarrassed had it not been that all the guests seemed to find the story of our acquiring it as fascinating and exciting as he did. He had taken down one of his own pictures, had hung Poyntdale Bay in its place, and the guests as they came in joined the semi-circle that was formed about it. The French artist, himself a painter of landscapes, took great interest in it and discussed it at great length and in great technicality with Cousin Egbert to his enormous gratification, but it seemed to me that everyone was tiring of the subject and of Cousin Egbert's enthusiasm. He, however, was determined to continue his joy-ride on his pet hobby and, with the second glass of sherry, he said: "Come up to my study and see the other Smiths!" and, more or less dragooning the main body of his guests, he led them out of the room and up the stairs.

"Old bore!" said Monica. "Sit down, Jan. We'll see them later if you want to, but not now. I want my dinner."

"Hungry, ducks?" Twice asked. "You have to eat for two, you know!"

"Ow, Mr. Alexander, you are a one! And me in me best and most concealing garment!"

"I wish you two would remember that you are in cultured company tonight," I said.

"Yes, indeed," Torquil agreed.

"And indeed, indeed," said Monica, looking at me with her head on one side. "I must say that your first sortie into the picture-buying racket has been a mad success. Not everybody makes hundreds per cent of potential profit on their first gamble."

"It wasn't a gamble," I told her. "It wasn't even picture-buying. What I liked and what Twice bought was Poyntdale Bay. If the painting had been of Beachy Head, we wouldn't have it, so just you get your feet on the ground and face facts, my girl."

"Anyway, Jan, don't part with it to Eg or Fisher or Gluckstein. If you want to sell, Torquil and I will outbid them."

"But I don't want to sell, my pet. You can see Poyntdale Bay all the time from your drawing-room windows and Smith's version of it is going to St. Jago with Twice and me and that's that."

"So there!" said Twice. "I'm afraid, Monica, that Flash and I don't buy pictures for the right reasons. . . . What about this portrait of you? When's it to be done?"

"Now or practically never," Monica told him. "In a month or two, this baby and I are not going to want to be bothered with having our portrait painted."

"I think Serafini will come north after the exhibition's over," Torquil said.

Cousin Egbert now returned with his rout of guests and we all went in to dinner, I very nervous with an eminent art critic on one side of me and an unidentifiable gentleman on the other who delivered to me a dinner-long monologue on Jane Austen, with special reference to the number of people who wrote books about her.

"They say her art was this and her art was that," he concluded testily, "as if she talked and thought Art with a capital A like themselves. She didn't. She sat down with her pen and said what she had to say and had done with it and that's why she's still readable."

Had I listened in detail to all he had to say, I might now be something of an authority on books about Jane Austen, but Signor Serafini and Signor Marandola were across the table from me, being entertained in their own language by Monica, and most of my mind was concentrated on them or, rather, on wondering what it could be like to be as they were, with a memory that went back only seven years or so, or, as in the case of Marandola, was full of gaps and patches.

Friends like Twice and Monica who know me well have often remarked on the strength and clarity of my memory for details of conversations and incidents that have happened long ago, and even Tom and George, who have never regarded me as being in any way remarkable, have often used my memory to check incidents that took place at any time after I had reached five years of age. Until now, I had never given much consideration to this memory of mine; it was a feature that I accepted just as I accepted the physical feature that my hair was dark instead of fair; it was something that I had always had. Now, though, looking at those two men, I tried to imagine what their situation must be, personalising it to myself. If what had happened to them had happened to me, I would not be able to remember my childhood, my grandparents, my home at Reachfar—I would not have recognised that picture of Poyntdale Bay in Madame Zora's house that day. I think that was the point at which my imagination boggled. I could not, for the life of me, imagine myself being in that cat-ridden room and failing to find relief in recognising the familiar and beloved in that picture.

When dinner was over, Monica led the women to the drawing-room and here the talk was all of the picture of Poyntdale Bay again and the subject was continued for a little after the men joined us, but then the talk moved away into the higher flights of greater pictures and Twice, Torquil and I became silent, although very interested, members of the party.

Too soon, the evening which had taken on a halcyon quality for me began to draw to an end and, as the other guests began to leave, Monica said to me quietly: "We four will stay and have a last drink with the boys and tease them a little more about

Poyntdale Bay. And I take back all the nasty things I've said about Eg's dinners —Serafini and Marandola are fascinating." Her face took on again that sharpened look of intense concentration and she added tensely: "Darn it, Granny Gilmour's Guido will come back! I'm sure of it!"

"Now, Monica—" Torquil began in his big gentle voice.

"There's a chance, isn't there?" she said, swinging round on him so that her pale chiffon swirled round her like water. "Look at Serafini! Can't even remember his own mother. He had to get to know her all over again—and he had identification papers and everything. If he'd been like Jackie Selby with no papers—Gosh, I'm dying to get home to tell all this to Granny Gilmour."

Cousin Egbert, followed by his two friends, came into the room in his brisk, jerky way, rubbing his hands together and very pleased with himself, and I think that Twice and Torquil were as glad to see him as I was, for Monica's intensity on the subject of Guido was unnatural and a little disturbing.

"Well, well," he said, "we'll all have a

311

little brandy and go up to my study, Mrs. Alexander, and see the Smiths. You didn't come up before dinner."

Monica and her relations for persistence, I thought, and aloud I said: "Why Smith, by the way?"

"Commonest name with the initial S of course," he said impatiently, and I resigned myself while we all sat down with our brandy and the talk about the "Smiths" and about painting in general began again, but once more half of my mind was engaged with Serafini and Marandola.

Again, my mind went back to Reachfar and the people there who reared me, and especially did it go back to my grandmother who was a memory so clear and strong that even now, nearly thirty years after her death, I tend to return to that memory of her for guidance in any situation that is unusual or frightening. When she scolded me for doing something that I should not have done, her words were always something like this: "Janet, have you lost your senses? Do you ever mind on your mother doing a thing like that?"

Or: "Janet, use your senses! Do you not

mind on being shown how to fold the table-cloth?"

Or: "Janet, come to your senses and pay attention! If you don't watch what Kate is showing you, how do you expect to mind on it?"

From my very early days, it had been impressed on me to observe, and too, the importance of remembering what I had observed had been laid down as a necessity for the practical living of life from day to day. And so, down the years, I had observed and remembered effortlessly and as a mental habit until, now, it was imposs-ible to imagine the mental void in which these men must live.

"So there's no hope of a sale at all?" Mr. Fisher was saying.

"Jan, wake up!" said Monica.

"Sale? Oh—the Smith? No. I'd like to keep it."

"Has no great intrinsic value, you know," jerked Cousin Egbert. "Only a curio, really. Of no value except to us three in the way of friendly rivalry. . . . Give you a hundred and fifty. My last word."

"Don't sell, Jan!" said Monica. "I'll outbid any of them for it."

"Monica, don't interfere!"

"I'll interfere as much as I like, Eg, my sweet. I'll do all I can to stop you three making a corner in Smiths. Old Schaffer, or whoever he is, in Chicago and I are blood-brothers in this. He wouldn't sell to you either, Eg. Don't you sell, Jan. Twice bought you Poyntdale Bay because you liked it and you hang on to it. A fig for all this stuff about curios and no intrinsic value and friendly rivalry! I haven't ever seen an art dealer who offered a hundred and fifty guineas out of sentimental friendly rivalry and I don't see him among those present here now. Friendly rivalry my you-know-what-Mattha-says!" and Monica laughed into the thin, buttoned-up face of her Cousin Egbert.

"You've made enough trouble today," he told her. "Had no right to take that Head of a Girl off Serafini at the gallery like that."

"Did you want it for the attic landing here, Eg?" she asked him. "Never mind, there are lots more."

"Humph!"

"And I've no doubt he'll do you my portrait at a special price, you old swindler. . . . Do I get a model's fee out of it?"

"You don't," said Torquil. "And you have to entertain Serafini and Marandola at Poyntdale while it is being painted."

"Serafini can come to Poyntdale for as long as he likes. He's really nice and so is Marandola, isn't he, Jan? You seemed to get along very well with him."

"He's a charming man," I said, "quite apart from the fascination that this thing of his lost memory has for me in particular."

Torquil Daviot is a big man with a big but gentle voice and he seldom has a great deal to say and, even when he does speak, he speaks thoughtfully as a rule, as if the words were spoken in soliloquy and not addressed to any particular person or to any company which may be gathered about him.

"I agree with Janet," he said now. "It must be damned queer to be like Serafini or Marandola. I mean, a lot of us spend a lot of time thinking about the here and the hereafter and all that and there are whole religions and philosophies about the after-life and reincarnation and so on, and here are these chaps who absolutely know they were alive for about—what?—thirty-five years before the bit of being alive that they can remember. Queer, that, when you think of it."

"Very queer, Torquil," I said. "In fact, so queer that I just can't imagine it."

There was a short silence while everybody, quite obviously, tried to imagine themselves with their memories curtailed to the short span of the last seven years and after a moment the defeated minds began to take refuge in uneasy speech.

"You'd think with all these drugs they have now—" said Mr. Gluckstein.

"You'd imagine they'd have habits of wealth or poverty that would give some clue—" said Mr. Fisher.

"You'd think if they ever worked at anything they would remember something about it—" said Twice, looking down at his own hands as if it were impossible to forget the things they had built.

"Imagine not knowing where you were born!" said Torquil, speaking for me as well as for himself with the Highland blood-earth tie that was in both of us. "Marandola at least remembers his home village, but Serafini doesn't."

316

"I wonder most about the painting," Monica said. "I mean, before Serafini was injured he might have been a very ordinary youth, working in a shop or in an office or something, and then wham!—this terrible war injury gets him, his whole metabolism is changed and he emerges as an artist. After all, genius—and I think he has a touch of it—is a sort of inexplicable freak —a spark that's struck occasionally out of human clay by a sequence of accidents as far as one can see. This war injury might have struck it out of Serafini." She took thought for a moment. "You know, if I could paint as he can, I don't think I'd mind having forgotten the schoolroom or that ghastly convent in Paris."

"Humph!" said Cousin Egbert, who had been patently bored by the whole discussion. "Let's go upstairs and look at the Smiths."

The study was up one flight of stairs and next door to the little boudoir where Monica and I had left our things, but it took the party of seven of us the best end of an hour to reach it, before Mr. Fisher and Mr. Gluckstein had examined all the pictures on the staircase walls, compared them with other works by the artists, argued about them and told anecdotes about them. In my own homes, at Crookmill and in St. Jago, the conversation always tended to have the hum of turbines and the warm oil smell of running bearings just below the surface, with a permanent threat that they would develop a strength that would overpower every other subject, but in Cousin Egbert's house, with connoisseurs of painting in the ratio of four to the wordless three of Torquil, Twice and myself, the smell of paint and canvas became overwhelming. Also, I was growing very sleepy after my exciting day and by the time we reached the study my mind was a blur of colours, lines, lights and shades and I could not remember in detail any one of the host of pictures I had been shown.

In the study at last, confronted by more rows and rows of pictures, I leaned against the end of a sofa in a state of almost half-trance, very like the state that comes when the thoughts flow into one another and superimpose themselves on one another just before sleep overtakes the brain. The mists that were gathering rapidly round my mind were suddenly dispelled by a shriek from Monica: "Jan! There's my time-slip!"

I jumped awake, my limp spine stiffening. "Huh! What?"

"Wake up, you clot! Look! Achcraggan Churchyard!"

I looked where she pointed and there on the wall was the churchyard at Achcraggan on a summer day, the wind rippling the grass between the graves so that it looked like a sunlit sea. And near the centre of it, on the path by my family's plot, stood a single small black figure. It was all very simple, easy to interpret, with nothing of the obscure depth of some of Cousin Egbert's other pictures, but it shone with the clear, northern summer light of my own countryside.

"A Smith?" I asked.

"Yes—and then these two."

"I like this one," Mr. Fisher said. "It's the best of the lot we've seen so far."

He indicated a peaceful picture, pale with the grey of beech trunks.

"Rubbish!" snapped Cousin Egbert. "Old Schaffer's Peasant Girl was the Smith of the lot!"

"That's what I'd say," Mr. Gluckstein

said, and the endless wrangling broke out between the three of them again.

"It's time we all went to bed," said Monica. "Come, Jan, let's go and get our things." Thankfully, I followed her. "You look asleep standing up," she said. "You feel all right?"

"I feel splendid but terribly sleepy. I think it was meeting Serafini and Marandola—trying to imagine how they must feel, you know."

"You would, of course, have to go having a go at being a person without a memory. No wonder you're tired. You are about the unlikeliest person for it that I know—you've got a memory like one of these awful holograph systems they're developing. I bet you would never have seen that picture through there and then go to Achcraggan and think you'd had a time-slip! Golly, I'm relieved about that, you know. That thing that day gave me the most uncanny feeling. . . . Ready?"

"Yes."

"Let's put your little hood up and give the boys a treat!" She adjusted the wide blue hood over my head. "Janet, it does suit you! Are you happy in it?"

"Monica, I love it. It's the loveliest dress I've ever had."

The men were standing in a group in the hall, Cousin Egbert leaning on a large black umbrella.

"Pouring with rain outside," he said.

Suddenly Mr. Gluckstein stepped forward. "Darn it!" he said. "I must have seen Mrs. Alexander before. It's been bothering me all evening."

"I thought that—" said Mr. Fisher.

"I knew it! And, by Heaven, I've got it!" said Cousin Egbert and threw his umbrella aside. "It's Smith's Peasant Girl!"

He made a jerky run across the hall to the stairs and, like bloodhounds picking up a sudden scent, the other two elderly and rather portly gentlemen shot past us, puffing and blowing, up the stairs and back to the study.

"What do we do now?" Torquil asked mildly. "Our taxi's here."

"Give him something and say it was our mistake," said Monica. "I'm seeing this through to the bitter end."

"Me too!" said Twice and they too went galloping up to the study while Torquil and I wearily brought up the rear.

Inside the room, every flat surface was now being covered with big portfolios which Cousin Egbert was hauling out of large, flat drawers like map-chests that stood round the walls and Mr. Fisher, Mr. Gluckstein and Monica were turning over the heaps of reproductions they contained. At long last, Mr. Fisher came up with a "Here we are!" and stood a cardboard-mounted reproduction of a painting of the head and shoulders of a young woman against the wall. Across a corner of the mount was scrawled in ink: "Happy Christmas! H. G. Schaffer. 1938." The reproduction, mount and all, was about two feet square.

"Quite a Christmas card!" said Torquil.

"Humph!" said Cousin Egbert. "Old fool! Sent all three of us one of these and then let his house go on fire and burn the original!" which made me at once feel akin to Mr. Schaffer and I thought I would have a reproduction made of my Poyntdale Bay and send a similar card to Cousin Egbert, Mr. Fisher and Mr. Gluckstein this Christmas. I felt I fully understood the mood that had made Mr. Schaffer send them his.

"Gosh, it is like Janet, though!" Torquil said.

"It is Janet, I would say," said Twice and turned from the picture to me. "Listen, this Smith must have been around Achcraggan at some time. Wake up, Janet! You must have heard of him! Nobody could have been sitting around up there painting like this without Tom and George coming to hear of it even if you were too dim to notice. Think!"

They all turned away from the picture and I moved in to have a closer look, at the same time sending my mind back, as it were, down the long winding road of my memory. Then I turned round to face them all. I pushed back from my head the blue hood that was so like the blue shawl over the head of the girl in the picture and said: "I suppose it is like me, but it can't be me, and, anyway, that girl could be any one of hundreds of girls in the Highlands of Scotland. My face isn't a distinguished one —it's one of a type. Mr. Fisher, you know that. You spoke of my resemblance to your grandmother. Anyway, I've never met a painter in my life that I know of until tonight and I've certainly never sat for my portrait."

I looked round at them all. They were all looking from me to the picture, with the exception of Twice, who was staring at the picture steadily, his eyes narrowed, his head on one side.

"Honestly," I repeated, "women with faces like mine—broad foreheads, rather wide-set eyes and strong noses—are ten a penny in the Highlands. Monica, Torquil, Twice, you all know that!"

My voice was rising a little. I felt tired and overwrought in an unusual way and everything I said seemed to bounce off a wall of disbelief in their minds.

"This Smith must have been up at Achcraggan once all right," I went on, trying to keep my voice level, "and in the summer—about June, I'd say, because the steading of Seamuir here"—I went to the painting of the churchyard where the slope of Seamuir Farm rose away to the right— "is complete in every detail but the stack-yard is empty—"

"En avant Air Force Photographic Intelligence!" said Monica. "Now just tell us,

Flight-Officer Sandison, from the orientation of the shadows, what o'clock it was, double-summer time, Greenwich, when the painter painted it. . . . Balloons, duckie! If that young woman isn't you, then you've got a double, which I don't believe and I'm sure Twice won't."

Feeling that I wanted to burst into tears, I looked at Twice, and looking back at me he smiled and said: "Oh, I don't know, Monica. As Janet says, she is very typical of her countryside. I never like to shop with her in Inverness—I'm always going up behind the wrong woman and saying: 'Darling, where have you been?'"

The excited tenseness broke down into a spatter of laughter and, with everyone in high good humour, especially Cousin Egbert who had laid the persistent ghost that I had been to him, another taxi was called and we plunged through the rain into it and drove back to our hotel.

When Monica and Torquil had gone away to their own room on the other side of the landing and we were alone in ours, Twice sat down on his bed, looked at me standing in the middle of the floor and said: "The blue period of Janet Alexander forsooth! Come along, my pet, sit down and take your ease and tell me how you came to get your portrait painted."

I took off the blue cape, threw it on my bed and stood looking down at it. Twice stood up and faced me across the bed, frowning a little, his eyes serious now instead of amused.

"Flash," he said, "don't speak a word you don't want to."

I looked up at him. "Twice, I've nothing to tell. You think I am hiding something from you and so does Monica—I could feel it there in Cousin Egbert's study. I never came to get my portrait painted as you put it. That thing may be like me—it is like me, I can see that for myself—but I did not ever sit for it." I sat down on my bed. "Unless I've started to lose my memory like Serafini and Marandola," I added.

"Darling, don't talk rot! You're sure though—"

"Of course I'm sure!" I snapped crossly. "Good Heavens, if anyone had ever asked me to sit and have my ugly mug put on canvas I'd have been so flattered I'd never have forgotten it!" I stood up and began to unpin my hair, pulling the pins out crossly and throwing them at the dressing-table. I suddenly saw my own face in the glass above the blue dress. "I don't like this!" I burst out. "I hate all this—this queerness that's suddenly going on—these men not remembering their lives that did happen and people trying to make me remember things that didn't happen! I hate it, I tell you! I hate it!"

"Flash, sit down and have a cigarette and calm yourself."

"But it's not my portrait, Twice. I didn't sit for it."

"Darling, if you say you didn't sit for it, I believe you. Don't be absurd. Of course you would remember if you had sat for it and of course you would tell me if you had."

"But it's still all very queer, isn't it? Like all these other things. Monica's time-slip and things."

"What other things? Actually, there's only one queer thing and that's this unknown painter, Smith. Monica's time-slip was only her having seen that picture before—"

"Yes, yes, that's right!" I agreed with

relief. "I'm in such a muddle with every-thing. That picture must have been painted in summer, on a day like the day when Monica and I called at the church—on a day when the hay-wind was blowing and rippling the grass. But, still, there's a queer feeling about it all—"

"It's only Smith," Twice repeated. "And, after all, the district at home is a sort of sketcher's and painter's paradise, I should think. There are probably all sorts of daubs of it—it's just that Smith was good enough to attract Cousin Egbert and his chums. I suppose the poor devil was killed in the war."

"He could have been killed at Waterloo, for that matter," I said. "Poyntdale Bay and Achcraggan Churchyard haven't changed much in two or three hundred years."

"But the technique is modern appar-ently and, besides, what about the one of you?"

"It isn't me!" I almost shouted. "I tell you I didn't ever sit for—"

"Darling, I'm sorry. I didn't mean to say that."

"But you don't believe me!"

"I do believe you!" Twice almost shouted back at me and then he sat down beside me on the bed and said: "Look, let's get to bed. Darling, I do honestly believe what you say—that you didn't sit for the portrait, but I honestly think it's a portrait of you all the same."

"But who could have painted it, Twice? I've never known anybody who painted."

"I don't know. I don't suppose we'll ever know. I don't even know how artists work. It might have been someone who saw you and did it from memory."

"Well, whoever he was he had no business!" I protested. "I don't like this, with these men—Cousin Egbert and Mr. Fisher—looking at me as if I were a horse in a sale ring and saying they've met me before and looking as if I were a half-wit when I say they haven't. I don't think people have any right to go painting people—"

Twice began to roar with laughter. "I wish Smith or whoever he was could see you now. Peasant girl, my foot! With all that hair hanging down and that long dress you look like a very angry Highland witch about to jump on your broomstick and put curses on the whole lot of them."

"And that's exactly how I feel," I said. "Unhook me out of this confounded dress and let's go to bed."

9

AT breakfast the next morning I felt, and life looked, much more rational, as people and life tend to do in the morning, but the breakfast table was still dominated by the question of the "Smiths", for painting was Monica's favourite of the arts, and one of her favourite aspects of life, it seemed, was that somebody should be in a position to deny her Cousin Egbert a picture that he coveted.

"He was probably killed in the war," she said of the artist as Twice had said the night before.

"Or at Waterloo or in the Crimea," I said grumpily.

"Don't be stupid, duckie," she said. "These paintings are no more than thirty years old. . . . I suppose you would remember if you'd sat for that portrait?"

"Don't you be stupid! You are the one who has always said that I have a fantastic memory and why should I try to conceal that I sat for it?"

"I'd hate to try to work out how tortuous your reasons could be. Oh, all right. Put that toast-rack down. I believe you. But it's a most entrancing mystery."

"I'm sick of mysteries," I said. "And I'll tell you something else. I'm not built for this sophisticated life of Caraday dresses and the realm of the high arts. I was born among the heather of Reachfar and if you take me too far away from it I stop making any sense at all. I had the high heebie-jeebies before I got into bed last night, what with one thing and another, and it's a good thing this spree is over and I have to get back to earth. . . . Did Twice tell you that Crookmill's practically sold?"

"No! Who to?"

"A couple from Glasgow called Galbraith," Twice said. "They sound like the right sort. He is an engineer with Macdonald, Mullholland and is retiring—"

"Oh, definitely the right sort!" Monica was mischievous. "What a tragedy it would have been if he'd only been a retired doctor! What a snob you are, Twice!"

"And so, on Monday, we're pulling out for Crookmill to pack up," I said.

"But you'll be north again before you sail?" Torquil asked.

"Of course! As soon as we've got Crookmill taken apart and that won't take long."

And so, early on the Monday morning, Twice and I drove out of London on to the north road, and as soon as we reached the open country, the luxurious period in London, with its excursions into the worlds of music, the theatre and painting, began to take on, for me, the character of a dream that I had enjoyed but whose frail fabric was no part of the day-to-day business of living. I did not regret leaving it behind. I had enjoyed its rarefied atmosphere but I found it less effort to breathe the earthy air of my own element.

The dream receded even further into the past on the evening of the next day when we drove in to Crookmill, expecting the entire household to be there to meet us as usual, and found that the reception party consisted of only Mattha and Dram.

"Them twae," he greeted us, "is awa' oot. The doctor sent fur them."

"Loose-an'-Daze? The doctor? What's wrong?"

"Whit d'ye expeck? Auld Lizzie Fintry's run awa' frae the hospi'al again."

We sat in the car and stared at him while Dram galloped round, putting his paws on one open window and then on the other, sticking his head in and licking our faces.

"What do you mean again?" I asked.

"Get down, Dram!" said Twice and swung his door open. "Flash, get into that madhouse over the bridge. It's too cold to sit here and discuss a bunch of crazy women."

In the living-room, where the fire was roaring up the chimney, Mattha had the whisky and water and a bottle of beer for himself already on the sideboard, and when we all had drinks I said: "Now tell us about Madame Zora."

"Madam Zory ma back—Weel, it seems that she up an' ran awa' frae them at the hospi'al again the-day."

"Again? Has she done it before then?"

"Och, aye, twa-three times. Did them twae no' tell ye when ye wis on the phone tae them?"

"No."

"Ah michta kent as much. They're thed amntest coupla blethers on that phone an'

334

they niver mind tae tell ye the richt things an' then they complain that ye only get three meenutes. Ah help ma Jimmy Johnson, in 1939 auld Chamberlain startit a war ower the wireless in less nor three meenutes! An' Ah'll bet ye they niver tellt ye aboot me an' Dram catchin' the fox either?"

"No, they didn't," Twice said. "Where did you get it, Mattha?"

"In auld Sammy Beadle's hen-run ower the hill there. An' jist imagine them twae forgettin' tae tell yeez. Jist you wait ere Ah see them the morn's morn," he said vengefully.

"When did Madame—Lizzie Fintry run away?" I asked.

"What interests me is how she can run!" said Twice.

"Rin? Ah'll warrant ye she can rin! Since she's been in that hospi'al an' gettin' her dinner reg'lar, she's as spry as a bliddy auld kangaroo!"

"But why does she do it?" I asked. "I thought she was delighted to be in hospital and—"

"Ach, so she is, when she's richt in her heid, but aboot three weeks back she startit takin' they daft turns. No' but she wisnae aye gey daft, but it seems she's gettin' fair daunert this last wee while. She tak's a notion that she his tae gang back tae her hoose an' see that folk is no thievin' her stuff an' she locks hersel' in an' when the the nurses go tae get her she shouts: 'Murder! Polis!' oot o' the windae at them."

"But why don't they take the keys of the house away from her?" Twice asked.

"They've din that noo—Gair took them awa' frae her the last time. But when the doctor rung up the-day he said she wis in the shed oot at the back wi' the door barricadit and shoutin' 'Murder! Polis!' harder than iver."

"But what do Loose-an'-Daze do with her?" I asked.

"Och, them twae can work her tae a T. Ah huv tae gie them that. She'll open the door tae them an' then they sit doon an' say they're needin' a cup o' tea an' then they ask her fur the money tae buy some sugar an' then she ups an' says she's gaun back tae the hospi'al fur her tea. An' oot she goes an' intae the doctor's car or the ambylance an' awa' they go wi' her. 'Deed, ye widnae ken whiles whether she's daunert or no'. Maybe this rinnin' awa' is jist badness an' mischievyousness, for she's no' daunert enough tae pairt wi' a ha'penny o' her money, the auld bitch. . . . Weel, Ah'm gaun oot tae bring in they bags afore it gets ony darker. There's a supper a' ready in the oven fur yeez, ye ken, an' Ah'll bring it in when yeez gie me the word."

"We had tea only about an hour ago, Mattha," I told him. "Don't you bother about supper."

Twice went out with him to the car to bring in the luggage and I sat patting Dram's head and wondering if London, Cousin Egbert's party, the exhibition and the Smiths were indeed all a dream, until Mattha came in and set Poyntdale Bay on the table where it had stood before.

"Ah see ye brocht yer pictur' back wi' ye," he said to me.

"Aye, Mattha," Twice said, "and I'll tell you a secret about that picture. A gentleman offered Janet a hundred and fifty pounds for it."

"Ach awa!" He looked from one of us to the other. "A hunner an'—fur auld

Lizzie's pictur'? Is that the God's honest truth, Lad?"

"The God's honest truth, Mattha."

Mattha creaked his old joints down on to a chair, clasped his hands over his stomach and began to laugh with a noise like an ill-fitting wooden spigot turning uneasily in its socket. At last, when he could speak, he looked up at Twice and said: "Ah've aye thocht ye were a smert yin, wi' yer heid screwed on richt, but Ah thocht ye were daft when ye gied Lizzie Fintry twenty-five poun' fur that pictur'. An' then Ah mindit that Ah yince wis daft enough masel' tae gie ten bob fur a pot plant the wife had a notion fur so Ah niver said onything. But Ah help ma Jimmy Johnson, Ah'll tak' ma bunnet aff tae ye noo, fur ye're the only man Ah iver kent that got the best o' a Fintry on a bargain!"

Then Twice said: "Talking of pictures, what do you think of this, Mattha?"

He drew the reproduction of the Peasant Girl from its cardboard folder and handed it to the old man, who moved across the room with it until he stood directly under the light.

"Where did you get that?" I asked.

338

"Borrowed it, to show to Tom and George."

"My," Mattha said, "that's a richt fine photy. Aye, it is so. Ah aye thocht the mistress maun hae been a gey bonnie lassie when she was young!"

He continued to look at the picture for a few seconds and then Twice returned it to its folder. We did not tell him how we had come by it or any of the story connected with it, and he came of his own accord to the conclusion that Monica had had it and that Twice had borrowed it from Beech-wood.

"Is that them twae comin' noo, Dram, think ye?" he said next, as the dog cocked his head, listening, and then we too heard a car drive up the road. "Aye, that'll be the doctor bringin' them back. They maun hae got that auld bizzom back tae the hospi-'al."

And with that Loose-an'-Daze burst into the house and, of course, into speech simultaneously.

"We'd never have gone out—"

"—and we were all ready and expecting you—"

"—and the doctor rang up—"

339

"—and it was Madame Zora again—"

"Ah've tellt them a' that a'ready!" Mattha bellowed. "Whaur wis the auld bitch hidin' this time?"

"In the coal shed—"

"—with the door tied with wire on the inside—"

"—but Mr. Gair is having it nailed up."

"It's Lizzie Fintry they should nail up—no' the coal-shed door. Noo, listen tae me, yous twae—ye're a pair o' damnt auld leears, that's whit yeez are!"

"Mattha!"

"Well!"

"Really, I never—"

"What a thing to say!"

"Reely! What a thing!" mimicked Mattha. "Yeeze swore tae me so yeez did that ye tellt the mistress on the phone aboot Dram an' me catchin' that fox—"

"Owff!" said Dram indignantly, joining forces with Mattha at the sound of his name.

"Stop it, Dram!"

"Dram, be quiet!"

"You let that dug be, the baith o' yeez!"

"Owff-owff!"

"Outside, Dram!" said Twice. "In fact,

340

outside the whole lot of you! Finish it in the kitchen!"

He shooed them through the passage, Dram and all, came back into the room and shut the door.

"Honest to goodness," he said, "there's something wrong with us, Flash. Nobody else's house is like this. Think of Beechwood."

"Yes," I said. "Just think of it. . . . Let's have another drink. This may be a bit of a madhouse but in a way I'm very glad to be back here. Given a little more of Cousin Egbert and his Smiths I'd have been climbing the walls down there in London."

"I see what you mean. To every man his own sort of madness. Oh, well, it was fun while it lasted but it's over. Lots of things are nearly over. I vote we get this place sorted out and packed up as quickly as possible and then take off for Reachfar without a care in the world."

"But it's been a wonderful leave, hasn't it?"

"Wonderful, my pet, even if a little haunted by Smiths and Zoras."

Twice and I first met in an engineering works where he managed the workshops and I managed the office and we are capable of a joint life that moves on two separate planes. In our home and private life we can be dilatory and disorganised beyond words, bringing out in each other, it seems, all the worst in the way of indecision, incoherence and general muddle, but move us on to our other business plane, when decision has been taken and organisation and achievement of material results are required, and even our worst enemies will tell you that we can move from point to point in a combined operation that is almost terrifying in its efficiency.

In the early part of the week following our return from London, we not only got our packing-cases for St. Jago ready for the shippers, but this way and that we sold all the furniture in the house, even the beds we were sleeping in. Mr. and Mrs. Galbraith, the purchasers of the house, agreed to take certain items and of the rest we sold some privately to friends and arranged to send the remainder to the local auction rooms. Then, Loose-an'-Daze and Mattha, in the intervals of packing, shifting furniture, taking down curtains and, of course, visiting Madame Zora at the hospital, had a meeting with the reliable Robbie and invited all four of themselves for a holiday at Reachfar.

"Just for a change before we go to Beech-wood—" said Loose.

"—and to see the folk up there," said Daze, who had never even thought of going to Achcraggan in all the years she had been at Crookmill. "Lucy and I will stay with my cousin, Maggie Gilmour."

"Granny Gilmour?" I said. "She's not fit to have visitors!"

"Oh, we're not visitors—"

"—we'll look after her—"

"—and the house—"

"—and be company for her—"

"—and I've had a letter from her and she's real pleased we're coming!" said Daze conclusively.

"An' Robbie an' me will be fine in yon wee room Ah hud the last time Ah wis at Reachfaur," said Mattha.

"Oh, well, please yourselves," I said. "It's getting late in the year for a Reachfar holiday, but if that's what you want it's all right with me."

Tired as I was of them and their petty quarrelling, I was grateful to them all for taking this business of the sale of Crookmill so well and for putting such a cheerful face on it all, for they had been fond of the place and had served it and Twice and me well during our years there.

"This is Thursday," I said. "Better lay off for a bit and go and do your football coupon. You can't pack up any more anyway or we'll be eating off the floor with our fingers."

"What about filling in a line in the coupon for Janet and me this week, Mattha?" Twice said, driving the last nail into a packing-case. "Just for luck?"

"Aye, if ye like," Mattha agreed. "Ah've been spen'in' a tanner on it masel' the last week or twae. It'll cost yeez a tanner apiece."

"And the winner splits five ways," I said.

"Och, aye. If Ah get fifty thoosan' the rest o' yeez is welcome tae forty o' them," he said and, having collected a shilling from Twice, he creaked off to the kitchen, the coupon and the darning needle.

The mystic silence which emanated from the kitchen was still reigning over the house about an hour later when the telephone rang angrily from its new place on the floor, the table on which it used to stand having been sold to a neighbour.

"Hi, Jan!" said the voice.

"Monica! Where are you?"

"At the Shepherd's Crook Hotel. We'd have gone to Uncle Andy but he's away. You all packed up?"

"Pretty well," I said, and to Twice, "It's Monica. They're over at the Shepherd's Crook," and into the telephone again: "Are you spending the night there?"

"Yes. I'm bringing Torquil and Serafini and Marandola over to you for a drink."

"Monica, you can't do that! The house is all packed up—"

"I bet the bottle isn't packed up—it never is with you two! Well, we'll be right over—"

"Monica, listen to me! This is absolute nonsense. It's a terrible night, this place is ghastly and Twice and I are coming up to the hotel for dinner anyway—"

"I want Torquil to see Crookmill—he's never seen it."

I almost began to gibber with impatience. "Monica, don't be idiotic! This place isn't Crookmill as it was—it's just—"

"I don't care. See you in ten minutes or so."

There was a sharp click as she put down the receiver. I sank into one of the easy chairs with its label tied to its leg.

"Monica really is the end these days, Twice. She's so unreasonable." I looked round the room. "What a place to entertain people, and just listen to that wind! Why does she have to leave the hotel to bring these men to this dump on a night like this? I honestly could brain her!"

"Oh, what does it matter? She is pretty unreasonable, but I suppose that's the way her condition takes her. We'll just explain that we're birds of passage."

"Even at that, it's a pretty untidy transit twig," I said, and looked round at the packing-cases, the rolls of carpet, the labels hanging from drawer-handles and lamps. On the bare mantel, Smith's Poyntdale Bay and Peasant Girl stood side by side, leaning against the wall. The only personal things in the dismantled room, they exaggerated in it, with their air of imminent departure, the abandoned look, as if the spirit of the dwelling had already taken its leave while the November wind whistled round the chimneys and hurled the rain in gusts against the black glass of the curtainless windows. Dram raised his head and gave a short, gruff bark.

"Here they are," Twice said, and went to open the door. As soon as he did so, smoke poured down the chimney and billowed in a choking cloud across the room.

"Are you setting it on fire?" Monica's voice enquired brightly from beyond the cloud. "I thought you were selling it."

"Shut up, you, and come in and shut that confounded door!" I choked back at her.

The door closed, the cloud subsided and I saw Torquil, Serafini and Marandola in the little passage that led from door to room.

"I'm sorry," I said. "Good evening. Do come in," and I gave Monica a glare charged with all the venom I felt towards her for bringing strangers to my house at such a time. The glare had no effect whatsoever.

"You've been busy, I see," she said in a bright, encouraging way. "That's good. And we came to take you both out to dinner at the Shepherd's Crook, just for a treat. Torquil, have you got that bottle of sherry? Have you any glasses, Jan? Or are they all packed?"

"I'll get some," I said, and opened the door to the kitchen passage, with which there was another cloud of smoke and everybody began to cough.

"Oh, dammit!" I said. "Oh, drat you, Monica!" and banged the door shut again.

"It's this southwest wind that's the trouble," Twice said, "and all the curtains being down."

The front door at Crookmill opened directly into the living-room from the end of a small hallway and normally we had a heavy curtain across the end of this in winter, but, of course, it had now been packed up like most other things so that the door was exposed at the end of its little recess.

"I tell you what," Twice said, "I'll bring in that old screen—it'll deflect the draught a bit anyway."

He went to the kitchen to get the screen, there was another cloud of smoke, but with the screen in place and all the doors at last closed, we were able to sit peacefully around the fire, drinking sherry and talking, while the wind howled outside and the rain lashed ever more frequently against the window-panes.

"So this is Crookmill," Torquil said. "I've heard a lot about this place and I'm glad to see it at last."

He seemed obliquely to be begging me to be indulgent towards Monica and I responded with: "This was Crookmill, Torquil. Twice and Monica and I had a lot of fun here one way and another."

"Depending, of course, on what you call fun," Monica said, and with a smile at Torquil she turned to Signor Serafini and broke into his own language.

"But you are not selling the pictures?" Signor Marandola said to me, glancing upwards at the two Smiths on the mantel.

"Oh, no! The Peasant Girl is going back to Mr. Fitzhugh in London and we are taking the other one abroad with us."

"I like that landscape," he volunteered, indicating Poyntdale Bay. "It is a good painting, I think. It is a strange thing that a painting that is good seems to become very quickly familiar and yet to have in it something that is new and exciting. I do not explain well what I mean. But I have seen that a good painting never seems strange or—or foreign. I do not explain well—"

"I know exactly what you mean," Twice said. "It is like a great invention, like the wheel—so obvious that you say to yourself: 'But this thing is so simple, so obvious—it could not be invented—it must always have existed!'"

"Yes—yes—"

"Mr. Marandola is thinking of staying over here for a bit," Torquil said. "That's why he's come north with us."

"Oh?" I looked at Signor Marandola.

"Yes. For two years now I am a travel courier, but I think that I would like to be a schoolmaster, to teach—the languages, you know. And I have heard that many teachers are required here in England—or here, now, I should say Scotland."

"Are you still on the County Education Committee?" I asked Torquil.

"Yes." Torquil grinned at me. "We'd thought of that one already, but we've got to wait to see what Signor Marandola thinks of our wild countryside first."

"Well, he'll see it for the first time at its

wild worst," Twice said, as another angry bluster from the south-west shook the windows in their frames and swept, howling, round the chimney-pots. He refilled all our glasses and went on: "Drink up, everybody, and let's go over to the Shepherd's Crook and civilisation. This place is like a scene from 'Wuthering Heights' tonight—"

There was a sudden frightful crash, the sherry that Twice was pouring slopped over my wrist, and Dram, who had been lying at my feet, sprang up and rushed towards the door, barking furiously, and no wonder. The front door was open, the rain blowing in sheets into the hallway round the gaunt, black-robed figure of Madame Zora, who stood beyond the old draught-screen which the sudden gale had blown inwards on to the floor. The effect was theatrical, but shockingly so, inducing silence even in the bounding dog, a silence through which the wind shrieked and howled. Then the room seemed to me to turn into an outpost of hell. The draught was causing smoke to pour back down the chimney and swirl in choking eddies round the room; Loose-an'-Daze and Mattha, startled by the crash of the screen, ran in from the kitchen to stare at the apparition but causing another cross-draught and more smoke; Dram began now to bay in startled protest and the rain blew in sheets down the wind-tunnel of the small hallway round the gaunt figure of the witch-like woman in the long wet black robes. It seemed to me a long time before Twice sprang past her and banged the door shut; then I sprang at Dram and dragged him by the collar back to Mattha. The smoke began to go up the chimney again and Loose-an'-Daze began to give tongue.

"It's Madame Zora—"

"She's got out again—"

"—and what a night—"

"And she's soaking—"

Twice hauled the flattened draught-screen out of the way, whereupon, with all the aplomb in the world, Madame Zora sailed forward, her long black dripping-wet garments trailing about her, extended her skinny white claw of a hand to me and said: "How very kind of you to invite me to tea, Mrs. Alexander!"

The hand was as cold as ice and the black veil-like scarf was plastered to the wet black hair. Over her shoulder, I looked at Twice who stood behind her still clutching the screen, and he pointed to the telephone on the floor near the fire and then to the door to the bedroom.

"Loose-an'-Daze," I said in my most housewifely voice, "now that Madame Zora has arrived, we'll have tea in about ten minutes. . . . Come, Madame Zora, and take your things off. What a wet evening!"

I took her into the bedroom. Lying in a heap on a chair were a number of old sweaters belonging to Twice which were to be given to Mattha for disposal and from the heap I picked up a long heavy one of thick navy-blue wool.

"Please take your wet coat off and wear this, Madame Zora," I said.

"Thank you! Thank you!" she said, snatching the sweater as if I were offering her cloth of gold. She took her cape-like coat off, pulled the sweater on and then replaced the wet coat on top of it.

"And now," she said, re-arranging the wet veil over her hair, "the others will be waiting for us."

Weakly, I led her back to the living-room and Twice at once came forward to greet her, which indicated to me that he had telephoned the hospital and had also contrived to give the others some inkling of the situation, for when I said: "Madame Zora, may I present Signor Serafini and Signor Marandola?" they came forward and bowed very formally over the white claw of a hand and generally behaved as if gaunt, mad women blowing in on storm winds were an everyday feature of their lives in Italy. What the poor men were thinking of me, Twice, Crookmill and Scottish hospitality in general I could not imagine. At Monica I did not dare to look in case I might break into speech.

Madame Zora, however, was in her most practical and gracious mood and behaved with such ease and aplomb of a near-royal quality that I began to wonder if she were perfectly sane after all and whether I myself had had some lapse and had indeed invited her to tea at nearly eight o'clock on a cold, wet November evening. Eating an enormous amount of sandwiches and cake, she chatted amicably with everybody, asked Twice and myself how we had enjoyed our trip to London, remarked that we were all ready to move out, that she knew the house had been sold, and told us that, now she was living at the hospital, she was thinking of selling Dunroamin. Then, having finished her tea, she rose and said: "And now, if you will excuse us for a little while, Lucy, Daisy and I will go and have a little chat," and with Marandola holding the door open for her, she swept through to the kitchen.

"Signor Serafini, Signor Marandola," I said when she had gone, "I can never apologise enough for this carry-on in this madhouse tonight!"

They both smiled when Monica had conveyed to Serafini something of what I had said and Marandola looked across at the screen which was now restored to position and said: "It was a moment of great drama!"

With that, he, Serafini, Torquil and Monica began to laugh and Twice and I, with gratitude, joined them and we all laughed together until Mattha came in, looked at us sternly and said:

"Ah help ma Jimmy Johnson! It's high bliddy time this hoose wis sellt! The things that happens in it is no' tae be lippened tae! That auld Lizzie Fintry is nae mair daft nor Ah am! She's ben there tellin' fortunes like a band playin'. A' she wis needin' wis a damnt gidd tea an' when she kent ye were back she cam' fur it. An' noo she's got that weskit o' the Lad's as weel—Ah wantit that weskit fur masel'." He glared at me. "God kens whit yer veesitors thinks o' the place!" he added spitefully.

"Have a drop of the Article, Mattha," Twice said.

"And come and tell me you are glad to see me," said Monica.

The doctor and the district nurse now arrived, shaking the rain from their clothes as they stood in the little hallway while the latest cloud of smoke eddied round the room.

"This is just about it," the doctor said. "I'll have to get that old woman into the general hospital. I'm very sorry, Mrs. Alexander."

"That's all right, Doctor. She's in the kitchen telling fortunes and probably having another tea. Come to the fire for a moment."

We told him of Madame Zora's dramatic arrival and he said: "The Old People's Home isn't equipped for this sort of thing.

356

They haven't the staff. She got away when the staff supper was on and only a junior in the ward. It's very difficult, the whole business. She is as sane as you or me, really, most of the time. So sane, in fact, that I suspect this nonsense of being deliberate, just to liven things up, you know, but it can't go on. . . . Nurse, we'd better go through and get her."

But Madame Zora did not have to be fetched. She swept back into the living-room with Loose-an'-Daze in attendance, saw the doctor and said: "Oh, Doctor, how fortunate! You will be kind enough to drop me back to the hospital? Such a wet evening, but I did want to see Mrs. Alexander again before she leaves."

She then made me a pretty speech of thanks for my invitation to tea, bade Twice a languishing farewell, ignored Mattha in a pointed way and turned to Loose-an'-Daze.

"Now remember, girls, great good fortune is on its way—you are coming close to your heart's desire. Come and visit me after your holiday and bring my sweets as usual." She then turned to Monica, Torquil, Serafini and Marandola and, in a grand-duchess way, arranged the shabby veil over her hair and held out her hand to each in turn, bidding them all a gracious farewell, until she came to Signor Marandola.

"So nice to see you again after all these years," she said. "So nice! Goodbye, Mr. Sidonio."

Without waiting for anyone, but like a grand lady taking rightful precedence, she went away round the screen, Mattha rushed to open the door for her, and she swept out followed by the doctor, the nurse, Loose-an'-Daze and Mattha, who slammed the door shut behind him, causing the smoke to eddy and swirl about the room once again.

As the smoke cleared away, we all stood there as if glued to the floor. I think that my own main feeling was one of fear, fear of moving, fear of speaking, fear of looking at any of the others, but after what seemed to be a long time I had the courage to look at Twice. He, in turn, was looking at Marandola, and Marandola was looking down at his own right hand which he still held in front of him, as it had been relinquished by Madame Zora. Then I saw that Monica, Torquil and Signor Serafini were also looking at Marandola and at that out-held hand. Then, suddenly, as if he too were stricken with this fear to move, he began to speak in a quiet, tentative voice, still standing rigidly where the old woman had left him.

"Sidonio—that is my name. Guido Sidonio, care of Miss Fintry, one hundred and eight Carnarvon Road, Fulham." He raised his eyes from his hand and glanced about the room. "Bertie? Bertie? The 'Rawalpindi' was sunk. Bertie was drowned. Bertie was lost—"

The wind howled round the box of silence that was the house while the dark eyes looked searchingly into the corners of the room.

"Guido," Monica said very gently, "who was Bertie?"

"Bertie?" A fleeting smile crossed his face. "Bertie?" He looked bemused for a second. "He had no money for his rent. Bertie never had any money. Bertie—" He swung round suddenly to the fireplace and pointed to Poyntdale Bay. "He gave her that!"

"What? Gave it to whom?" Monica whispered.

"Miss Fintry." He pointed to the door.

"The old grey woman that nobody loves, Bertie called her."

"Guido, who was Bertie?" Monica persisted in the same gentle voice.

"Bertie Stubb!" I said, and my voice sounded harsh in my own ears, as it spoke the harsh, ugly name.

"Yes! Bertie Stubb!" the man said eagerly. "My friend Bertie! You knew him?" he asked me with wonder.

I was afraid to speak but Monica had more courage.

"Janet knew him at Achcraggan, Guido," she said.

"Achcraggan? Achcraggan! Granny! I remember—"

He swayed a little, looking down at his hand, turning it palm upward, then palm downward, then palm upward again.

"Here, sit down, man!" Torquil said.

They put him into a chair and Twice and Torquil listened to his jerky little nuggets of speech, mined out of the dark recesses of his returning memory, while Monica, in a torrent of Italian, explained to the astonished Serafini what was happening. I was too much out of my element and too much frightened by it all to be of any service and

360

could think of nothing to do but be of use in my own mundane way. I went out to the kitchen where Loose-an'-Daze and Mattha were sitting round the big hot stove.

"Loose-an'-Daze," I said, "we'd intended to go to the Shepherd's Crook for dinner but it's such an awful night—"

"Uh, you're not going out—"

"—and us with all this macaroni cooked—"

"—we thought it was the best thing—"

"—when we heard Monica talking foreign like that—"

"—and there's plenty of soup—"

"—and an apple pudding with the last of the puree—"

"—an' if yeez gae oot yer fit-length this nicht yeez are even dafter than Ah thocht yeez wur!" Mattha ended.

"Well, that's splendid," I said and sat down weakly on a chair beside them. "Have we enough spoons and things?"

"Och, aye. Ah drew the nails o' that crate ower there an' got the canteen oot. Hey, yoos twae, whaur'd ye pit they nails?"

"Up there on that shelf!"

"They were on Madame Zora's chair!"

"Madam Zory ma back—Ah help ma

Jimmy Johnson! Can ye imagine that daft auld bizzom breakin' oot again on a nicht like this?"

"On a night like this," I said, as the wind made a new onslaught on the chimneys, "I can imagine anything," and began to tell them about what was happening in the next room.

"So Monica was right after all?" Daze said at last.

"Jist imagine! She wis tellin' me afore yeez went doon tae London aboot hoo she wis gaun tae the War Office again tae see aboot the laddie," Mattha said.

"But it wasn't the War Office that found him!" said Loose and then she and Daze came in in chorus: "No! IT WAS MADAME ZORA!"

"Madam Zory ma—An' whae brocht Madam Zory, as ye ca' her, here? Eh? It wis the dug an' me, that's whae it wis!"

"Look here," I said, "never mind that now. My head's in a big enough muddle already without you three starting another argument. If you'd just look after the supper and see it doesn't spoil—it may be some time before we feel like eating."

"Just let us know when you're ready—"

"—and there's plenty of time."

"An' Ah'll bring ben a wheen mair sticks fur that fire in a wee while," said Mattha. "By the Auld Hairy, Ah aye suspeckit that auld bizzom wis nae mair aff her heid than Ah am masel'!"

10

EARLY the next morning, Monica, Torquil, Signor Serafini and Guido Sidonio left for Achcraggan, seen off from the hotel by Twice and myself.

"Well," Twice said, as the car disappeared down the driveway into the sweeping rain, "there goes as big a car-load of happiness as will ever hit Achcraggan. God bless old Monica!"

We got into our own car to go back to Crookmill and I said: "God bless Monica, all right. It's a queer thing, Twice, but it almost seems as if she brought this about by a sheer determined, unshakeable desire to prove that old Granny Gilmour was right. For these months since we came home, she seems to have thought of little else but Guido and goodness knows how much mental force she had put into it before that. . . . She said a queer thing this morning too."

"What?"

"She said she felt a queer compulsion to

do certain things, like the day she insisted on taking Poyntdale Bay into the gallery when we all wanted to take it back to the hotel. She said she felt she was acting stupidly but just had to go on doing it. And last night, it seems, she and Torquil had quite a row because she insisted on coming to Crookmill and bringing them all with her. She said she knew she was being unreasonable, dragging them all out to a packed-up house on such a night but she still insisted on doing it. . . . Oh, I don't know. I suppose she was just full of contrary tantrums because she's pregnant, but it's all very queer all the same. I wonder how it feels to be Guido Sidonio this morning?"

"Don't!" said Twice, stopping the car at the end of the Crookmill bridge. "It feels queer enough to be Twice Alexander this morning without wondering about anybody else." He leaned across me and opened the car door. "Get out and run for it and don't fall. Lord, what weather! I'll be glad to take ship for St. Jago!"

"It'll be better than this at Reachfar," I promised. "Our weather may be severe sometimes, but it's never as damned dreary as this," and I sprang out and ran over the bridge into the house.

The next morning and still in driving rain, Twice, Dram and I pulled out of Crookmill for the last time and set off on the journey from Ballydendran to Reachfar, which is a diagonal drawn across Scotland from south-west to north-east, leaving Loose-an'-Daze and Mattha to get the crates away to the shippers, the odds and ends of furniture to the auction rooms, clean and close the house and follow us north when they were ready.

"I'm glad it was raining when we left Crookmill," I said, "and everything looking its very worst. And I'm glad we're headed for Reachfar. I wouldn't have liked to leave it for the last time for anywhere except Reachfar."

"And I think Reachfar is going to welcome us properly," Twice said. "What'll you bet it's not clear weather and sunshine on the other side of the Grampians?"

I did not bet against the clear weather and just as well, for when we passed through Inverness it was pitch dark, but it was the hard, clear dark of frost that would be brilliant under a white moon later in the night. In another hour, we were at Reachfar where, despite the sharp cold, the welcoming committee of my father, my aunt, George and Tom were at the granary gable in the circle of light shed by the old stable lantern which my father was holding. The lantern light died away in the glare of the headlights of the car as we stopped and the uproar of Dram's salvo of greeting to his friends the collies began.

"All right," Twice said, opening the back door of the car. "Out and see them!"

Dram sprang out and all four dogs disappeared round the corner of the steading in a commotion of barks and waving tails.

"Well, you made good time on the road," my father said.

"We was thinking you wouldn't be for an hour or two yet," said Tom.

"Or that you wouldna know the road to Reachfar with being down in London an' a-all," said George.

"And have you heard about Monica finding Guido for Granny Gilmour?" asked my aunt.

"Mercy me, Kate! Let them get into the house out of the cold first!" my father said.

Twice had opened the boot of the car and everybody dived into it, dragging out what came to his hands.

"Leave that heavy suitcase to me, Tom," Twice said. "You take this picture and carry it canny. . . . Flash, leave me that rug to put over the radiator."

"Tom an' me has a puckle bags all ready here in the shed, lad," George said. "It looks like being frost before morning."

"Aye"—Tom sniffed the air—"I wouldna be surprised if a few o' the lazy ones wasna catched with their tatties the year. . . . Is this a-all the baggage, then?"

"Yes. Off you go inside. I'll just run the car in."

Over supper and round the fire afterwards, when the four dogs had settled down into a furry heap under the table, the enduring topic was the return of Guido.

"It must have been a fearful shock to old Granny Gilmour," I said.

"No, no shock!" said my aunt. "Monica and Sir Torquil went and got Alasdair the Doctor to go along with them to the house, but she recognised Guido at the door and never blinked an eye."

"Recognised him?"

"Surely! Why not? Ten years or so is not so long for a grown man to make much change. It's funny you didn't know him yourself!"

"So you haven't seen him? Well, wait till you do! You won't know him either—the plastic surgeons have given him a new face. I don't know what his granny recognised, but it wasn't his face."

"But then," Tom said, frowning, trying to understand, "his granny's known him from a bairn. She would know him different like from the rest of us."

"Yes, Tom," Twice said, "she might know him in a way that we can't understand."

"There's a thing I've never understood right although I've been among sheep all my life," George said. "Sheep is awful stupid sort o' brutes in a lot of ways an' chust terrible for being awful much like one another, but an old yow will pick her own lamb out of any hundred you like to put in front of her. It's a very queer thing, that."

"Yes, George, man, it is that," Tom agreed. "But what I canna come at is Guido wakening up in the hospital and them telling him he was this Eyetalian and him believing them."

"But do you not see, Tom, that he didn't know who he was?" Kate asked. "He might have been anybody!"

"It's like the time the old laird went up the glen in his motor car for the first time," said George, "and old Rory Ruach's wife shut the door in his face and then looked out through the window and said: 'Oh, it's yourself that's in it, Sir Torquil! And it's myself that shut the door on you, for I said to myself nobody can come up the glen on wheels without horses so I thought you was nobody and so I shut the door.'"

"Och, be quiet with your clowning, George!" said my aunt.

"Guido must be a brave fellow," my father said next. "Alasdair was up the-day and was telling us about him being dropped behind the lines in Italy, dressed in an Italian uniform."

"So that's what he was?" Twice asked.

"Of course!" I said, remembering. "Guido was a teacher—modern languages, it was."

"Well, let's all drink his health," Twice said. "Flash, where did you put my case?"

"I left it in the passage."

Twice found the case and extracted from it a bottle of whisky and then opened the folder which contained the reproduction of the Peasant Girl.

"Man, Tom," George said, "that's a grand wee baggie that Twice has."

"Aye, man," Tom replied. "They will be telling me that that kind o' baggies is for to be carrying important papers in and Twice a-always has important things in it, although not a-always papers."

"I have an important paper this time too although it's too big to go into the bag," Twice said, pouring whisky from his bottle into a row of glasses on the dresser. "I'll show you in a minute." When he had given everybody a drink, he took out the picture and propped it against the old clock on the mantel. "Who d'you think that is?" he asked.

The four faces in the semi-circle round the fire looked up and Kate was the first to speak.

"That's Janet!"

"Aye, surely!" said my father.

"Aye—and in her early twenties!" said Tom.

There was a little pause. "Aye?" said George on a questioning note. "And a good likeness. Where did you get it, lad?"

Twice then fetched Poyntdale Bay which he had left in a corner and we told them how we had come by the two pictures and also that one existed of Achcraggan Churchyard.

"Kate," I said then, "do you remember a friend of Guido's called Bertie Stubb? He used to come up here in the holidays when Guido was at the university in Edinburgh."

"Surely I mind on him," Kate said. "A big, tall, foreign-looking fellow that looked more Italian than Guido himself even. A good-for-nothing big rascal he was! That's the one that went off without paying old Miss Tulloch for all the tobacco he had—"

"—and poor old Granny Gilmour had to foot the bill!" my father ended accusingly.

"Well, he might have been careless about money," Twice said, "but if he hadn't paid for his digs in London with this picture" —he set Poyntdale Bay on the dresser—"I don't think Monica would have found his friend Guido and have brought him home to Granny Gilmour."

All eyes now turned to the painting and

Twice and I told the family about Madame Zora and the whole story of the "Smiths".

"And this cousin of Monica's has the one of the churchyard downbye at Achcraggan?" Tom asked. "And is it as bonnie as that one o' the Bay?"

"Just as bonnie, Tom," I told him. "And you can see the Seamuir steading away up behind on the hill and everything. It must have been painted in the summer because—"

"I'll tell you when it was painted," said Kate suddenly. "It was painted the day of the Old People's funeral. Poor old Granny Gilmour was in a terrible state about it—she came up here the next day to apologise about the laddies being up on top o' the church porch while the funeral was going on. I never minded a word about that until this minute. I never noticed them up there during the funeral and I don't think anybody else did, but old Granny Gilmour was black, burning ashamed about it. She went a fearful length about Bertie Stubb that day and how he had no respect for anything and how worried she was about him and Guido always being together."

"Well"—George knocked his pipe out

against the side of the fire—"it looks as if she wasted her worrying. It seems to me that Bertie Stubb was the best friend Guido and Granny Gilmour ever had an' well worth the little she paid for his teebacca, the poor fellow."

"And he made a right fine chob of pentin' Poyntdale Bay, forbye," Tom added.

My aunt rose to put some more wood on the fire and as she went to the big box under the little table in the corner, she said: "Oh, Twice, here's this wire of yours that came this afternoon! You haven't opened it! I told you about it, didn't I?"

"Lord, I forgot!" Twice opened the envelope, glanced at the message and then stared wide-eyed at me.

"What's up?"

"Crookmill's fallen through," he said and handed me the slip.

"Cancellation of Crookmill sale requested on sudden death Galbraith," the message said. "Writing, Crawford."

"Oh, poor Mrs. Galbraith!" I said. "Oh, confound Crookmill! Oh, well, there it is, Twice, and the hell with it!"

"Janet!" said my aunt.

374

"Sorry. But anyway, there's nothing we can do tonight and there's no point in worrying. It'll all straighten out in the wash."

"But you've sold everything," my aunt protested.

"Och, well," said George, "that's a-all a little less they have aboot them to bother them."

My father laughed and rose. "I must be getting down the hill to the cottage. . . . Janet has more of George in her than she has of me, Twice, lad. You're the one who'll have to do the worrying, for God knows she won't."

"Maybe that's why people still recognise her in that picture painted about twenty years ago," Twice said.

"It is myself that would not be surprised," said Tom. "Worrying aboot things is very, very bad for people and I have never seen much sense in it myself."

"All the two of you have got to worry about in the way of houses or money," said my aunt, raking Tom and George with her wicked dark glance, "is neither here nor there. You've aye been a pair of happy-go-lucky tramps and it's not better you'll be getting now."

My father laughed, took up his hat and stick and set off for his cottage in Achcraggan where he lived with my stepmother, and when Gcorge and Tom had seen him off they came back to the fire.

"Man, Tom," said George, "that's not bad, that whisky that Twice has in that bottle."

"George," said Tom solemnly, "there is no bad whisky, but some iss a little better than others."

This was a routine which meant that they could do with another drink and Twice, without comment, refilled all our glasses and we prepared to talk the fire out.

The following morning, at breakfast, my aunt said in an-over-carefully over-casual voice: "I was wondering if you would run me down to Achcraggan today, Twice?"

"Of course, Kate. What time?"

"What for?" I asked, just for the fun of it.

"Well, I have a bittie butter and a few eggs I'd like to take down to Granny Gilmour."

"It would be a terrible peety, Tom,

man," said George, "if a-all but Kate had had a look at Guido."

"Indeed and that is chust what I was thinking myself, forbye, George," Tom agreed solemnly.

"Oh, be quiet, you two!" said my aunt, and to me: "And don't you sit there showing your teeth like Jock Skinner's old horse. Pour out some more tea!"

But when midday dinner was over she accepted with alacrity Tom's and George's offer to wash up the dishes, and she, Twice and I set off for Achcraggan.

It was a brilliantly clear, frosty day and as we went down the hill through Poyntdale to the County Road the Firth lay before us like a sheet of cold, polished silver, while away to the west Ben Wyvis lay huddled down for the winter under a first blanket of snow.

"It's a day very like the day of the Armistice in 1918," I told Twice as we passed the Plough Inn with the pier jutting out into the water on the opposite side of the road. "The world's all bright and beautiful!"

At Granny Gilmour's little house the geraniums were still in position on the window-sills, but without flowers now and all cut back for the winter, and I could feel myself trembling with excitement as we rattled the brass knocker on the front door. It was Murdo Dickson of the Achcraggan firm of "Dickson, Ironmonger and Seed Merchant" who opened the door and, behind him, we heard the voice of Granny Gilmour: "That'll be some more of them coming to see Guido, but chust you tell them he's out for a walk, Murdo, and I'm busy."

"It's the Reachfar people that's in it!" Murdo called back to her when he saw us, and her voice came again.

"So it's yourselves! Come in then. Come right ben to the kitchen, for as sure as I'm here it's myself that won't leave this contraption here on its lone."

We went in through the passage, through the living-room and into the kitchen at the back where Granny Gilmour was sitting at the table cleaning the brass candlesticks from the mantel and various other odds and ends of polished metal while, along with little Minnie Davidson who had just left school, she kept an alert and wary eye on the new electric washing-machine which was churning away in a corner beside the sink.

"You're very busy this morning, Granny," Kate said to her.

"It's with Guido being home. It makes a fine steer about the house. Murdo is chust learning Minnie and me how to work this contraption and if it can do all it says in the bookie that's with it we'll be doing the washing for the whole of Achcraggan. Sit down, now, the three of you, and get a fly cup. Minnie and me was chust going to make it. Put the Tricity kettle on, Minnie —it's fine and quick."

"My, but this is a splendid thing that's happened, Granny," Kate said.

"Aye, it is that," said Granny contentedly, putting her head on one side to examine the brass teapot-stand she was polishing. "But I aye knew her young leddy-ship would get Guido back sooner or later—it was chust a question of time. . . . That pottie's too wee for six, Minnie, lassie. Go ben to the room press and you'll see a big brown one with blue floweries on it. . . . They was all telling me that if the War Office people said that Guido had been killed there was nothing anybody could do about it, but I chust somehow was a-always of the belief that her young leddyship knew like me that Guido was still alive and that she never took much heed of that War Office, for as her and me said to one another often: How could they be knowing for sure with a-all the hundreds of men that was in that terrible war?"

"I'm sorry we've missed Guido," my aunt said. "Is he looking well?"

"Och, yes. Chust the same as ever. And he's minding on things something wonderful." She looked at me. "He came back from his walk this morning fair excited and laughing something terrible and he told me he had minded on the time you and Alasdair the Doctor found the old dead rotten hare on the moor and warmed it at the Smiddy fire and sold it to that poor silly Mrs. Cruikshanks from Edinburgh that was here for her holidays and got sixpence for it."

"Janet!" said my aunt. "Is this true?"

"Och, be quiet, Kate!" said Granny Gilmour. "The whole of Achcraggan has been laughing about that hare for this thirty years, if not more."

Calm, cheerful, a pink-faced, serene

380

little monument to faith vindicated, Granny Gilmour chatted on over her cup of tea. She did not try to imagine or understand Guido's state of mind; she did not question the justice or injustice of what had happened to him; she did not bewail the long years of loneliness while she had missed him; she accepted everything and forgot all the heartaches in her happy gratitude that he had come back.

"He is having a grand time to himself chust walking about the place," she said. "Isn't it a blessing it is such grand, bright weather for him?"

Twice and I, after we had had our cup of tea, left my aunt with Granny Gilmour, Minnie, Murdo and the washing-machine which had now turned itself off and was absorbing the interest of all three of the ladies, who were challenging Murdo, its sponsor, to prove to them that it had made the clothes as clean as "it said in its bookie".

"Well, I don't know," Twice said when we were in the car, "Mattha once told me that the older you are the harder it is to be surprised at anything, but I'd have thought a return from the dead would have raised a little excitement even in Granny Gilmour."

"You forget one thing," I told him. "For her, it isn't a return from the dead. She always knew he'd come back. . . . I say, let's go up to the Cobbler. We'll be able to see for miles today. It'll be something to take back to St. Jago and I haven't been up there for years."

"I've never been at all. How do we go?"

"Right through the Fisher Town and out the road at the east end."

"Right."

With the whitewashed houses of the Fisher Town behind us, Twice set the car at the steep road made during the 1914–1918 war and renovated during the 1939–1945 war, that led to the now abandoned heavy-gun sites on the South Cobbler, which, with its northern counterpart, guarded the narrow entrance to the Firth. I think these black cliffs had a mystic quality for the fisher people, for they would seldom refer to them by name, but always by some oblique description, such as "where the guns were in the war" or "away up the top there". These cliffs, to the returning fishing boats, had meant safety, security from the wild seas beyond, and it was as if the fisher folk felt that to call these guardians of their homes by their geographical names was a blasphemy against the sea gods.

The road wound round and round the hill and eventually ended on the summit in a circle of chipped concrete from which narrower tracks led out to the emplacements where the guns had been. There were a few tumble-down huts, a lot of coils of rusty barbed wire, a few derelict concrete water-tanks, a heap of tin cans and bottles and an air-raid shelter covered with rotting sandbags which were rapidly being overgrown by the strong brown heather. On a few bricks at the end of the shelter Guido was sitting, an outlandish figure in his light-coloured, foreign-looking overcoat and dark blue suit. He rose as we left the car on the concrete circle and walked over to him through the withered heather.

"You've had quite a walk, Guido!" I greeted him.

"Yes," he said, smiling.

"It's a long way to the top here."

"Yes, a long way."

"But you can see a lot of Scotland from here."

"Yes, a lot of Scotland." He looked smilingly from one of us to the other. "Mrs.— Janet," he said, "do you remember that first day we met at the gallery? You told me about the place where you were born and you said that the country round it was a part of you."

He moved his arm in a wide sweep, a gesture that embraced the Moray coast to the south, round Ben Wyvis and the more distant mountains of Ross to the west and on to the hills of Sutherland to the north. On the east of us lay the open North Sea.

"Yes," I said. "It was when you were telling me about Montepescali."

"It was not Montepescali I remembered," he said. "It was this. See, here we stand on the hill west of Montepescali and down there, you see, is the village and the sea." He pointed to Achcraggan and the waters of the Firth. "And then you look west, across the sea, and the sun is setting behind the island of Elba." And he pointed westwards up the Firth to where the sun was going down behind Ben Wyvis. He then dropped his arm, turned and looked away east, out over the grey of the North Sea to the far horizon. "At Montepescali," he said after a moment, "out there was land and villages and the town. I was always dissatisfied with that. I did not remember it so, but I would not—would not listen to the dissatisfaction. You see, when you have not very much of anything—even memory —you cannot afford to be dissatisfied with what you have. I was glad to have Montepescali, the sea and Elba."

I heard Twice swallow convulsively and I myself felt the tears gather in my eyes as Guido said happily: "But this is what I remembered. There is no dissatisfaction now."

"I'm terribly glad you're home, Guido," was all I could say and then: "Gosh, this wind is cold!" I blew my nose. "Let's go down. Coming, Guido?"

"Yes, thank you. Granny will be scolding me again when I get home."

11

WHEN we arrived back at Reachfar, my father, Tom and George met us at the granary gable and as soon as the car stopped my father said: "Isabel Mackinlay was up with this telegram about half an hour ago," and handed the orange envelope to Twice. My family, the men especially, do not like telegrams, and although Twice gets them frequently at Reachfar, they have never grown used to them nor have they ever learned not to distrust them. "You should have opened the darned thing," Twice said, ripping the envelope. "It can't be anything much. . . . It's from Mattha. They won't be here till Monday. Old Madame Zora's dead, Flash—pneumonia."

"That's the old cat leddy?" Tom asked.
"Yes."

"Och, poor ould craitur!" said George.

"It would be that night she came to Crookmill that she got it," I said. "She was chilled to the bone but she wouldn't take

386

off that ghastly old wet cape coat thing. Poor old Madame Zora."

"It's maybe for the best that she's away," my father said, "with her mind going wrong and everything."

"She seemed to have more mind than some I could mention," said my aunt. "She recognised Guido."

"Are you trying to imply that you'd have recognised Guido if you had met him in London as Signor Marandola?" I asked her.

"Of course I would! D'you think I'm daft?"

"No, but I think you're a self-suggesting liar! It was easy for you, when he came into Granny's today with Twice and me. He couldn't have been anybody else!"

"He isn't anybody else!" she argued.

"Ach, be quiet, the two of you, and come into the house," my father said. "There's some letters in there too. Rory the Post must have turned up by the Smiddy before you got to the road-end on your way down."

"It's just as well Loose-an'-Daze are not coming until Monday," my aunt said when we were in the kitchen. "Granny Gilmour doesn't want them, so I've said they can stop here, though Heaven knows I don't want them either."

"But Daze said Granny had written saying she'd be glad to have them!" I said.

"That was before Guido came home and you can't blame the ould craitur. Their tongues would never lie until they had her and Guido driven half-demented."

"Indeed and your own tongue hasn't been idle about Guido," said George, "and you've little room to speak about poor Loose-an'-Daze. They're a fine, cheery pair, that's what they are."

"Aye, they are that!" Tom supported him.

Nevertheless, I noticed that when, on the evening of Monday, Robbie's car with the Crookmill contingent drove up to Reachfar and Loose-an'-Daze debouched into the house on a flood of words in their usual way, George and Tom were the first to retreat to the furthest corner.

"We're sorry all the plans got upset—"

"—and the house not sold or anything—"

"—so we brought the keys up with us—"

388

"—and poor Madame Zora—"

"—she got a chill that night and just got worse—"

"—and then it was pneumonia—"

"—and not a soul at the funeral except—"

"—the doctor and Mattha and Mr. Gair and us—"

"—and wasn't it nice of Mattha to get dressed and come?"

"Ach, haud yer tongues fur the love o' giddness! Ah niver heard sich a coupla weemen tae blether. . . . Aye, Tam, hoo ur ye livin'? Man, George, Ah'm rale pleased tae see ye again."

My family at Reachfar, like most families, is a microcosm of humanity in general and, after a few more questions about Madame Zora had been asked and answered, we turned away from thoughts of the dead to thoughts of the living or, rather, thoughts of the man who had virtually returned from the dead. Everybody held forth at one time with questions and answers and comments about Guido and Granny Gilmour until the rafters rang and, of course, Loose-an'-Daze, with their remarkable speech endurance, were still in full cry when all the rest of our voices had died away and they came in on a final note of loyal tribute to their dead friend.

"And just to think if it hadn't been for Madame Zora—"

"—we'd never have known—"

"—it just shows that she wasn't mad at all—"

"—remembering his name like that and knowing him after all these years!"

"The doctor said," I interrupted them in a loud voice, "that she probably didn't recognise Guido at all. She simply came out with what was probably the only Italian name she'd ever known by pure accident, because she couldn't remember Marandola."

"I don't believe that!" said Loose.

"And I don't either!" said Daze.

"Madame Zora was not one bit queer in her mind really—"

"—and able to tell fortunes right to the end—"

"—and Mrs. Gilmour has her to thank—"

"—for Guido coming back—"

"—for if it hadn't been for MADAME ZORA—" their voices began to rise in

390

chorus when Mattha broke in: "Madam Zory ma back—If it hadnae been fur me an' the dug killin' that damnt cat—"

"So you and Dram did kill that cat?" I asked.

Mattha closed his eyes in a pained, dramatic manner and said in a feeble voice: "Robbie, Ah'm gey tired wi' a' that traivellin' the-day. Whaur did ye pit that bo'le o' the Article we got frae the Royal yestreen?"

Loose-an'-Daze were quite happy to settle at Reachfar instead of going to Granny Gilmour's; content to share a small attic bedroom and to accept the fact that Granny Gilmour would not want them now that Guido had come home. After supper, they forced my aunt and me to sit down by the fire while they cleared the table and washed the dishes, and then they chattered to one another contentedly in the scullery while they boiled kettles to fill all the hot-water bottles for all the beds. When Twice and I went up to bed and I unwrapped my nightdress which had been wound round my bottle, the plight of Loose-an'-Daze came over me in a cloud of pathos.

"It's a damned shame!" I exploded.

391

"And I can't bear it! Mr. Galbraith going dying like that just proves it. We've got to send Loose-an'-Daze back to Crookmill."

"You know what I've been thinking?" Twice asked.

"What?"

"They've got a little capital and so has Mattha. Mattha's going to miss Crookmill as much as they are. They could furnish it and go in for old-lady paying guests—old ladies with a little money who need a little looking after and people to be kind to them, you know. Mattha's Jessie would keep them right on the accounting side of it."

"Twice! What a splendid idea!"

"Later on, when they have started to make a go of it, they could pay us a little rent. They could buy it eventually, maybe."

"I believe they will make a go of it!" I said. "It's just their sort of thing—people to fuss over. Anyway, one can't just cast them off. Oh, I know there's Beechwood, but they know that Lady Beechwood doesn't really want them. They know, deep down, that nobody wants them and they go washing all the dishes and filling all the hot-water bottles just to get staying and it's simply awful. And they are so afraid of having to be separated—of Loose having to go to some of the Loames and Daze having to go to one of her sons—and of being old and of nobody really wanting them. That's why they were so kind to Madame Zora. It wasn't just the fortune-telling and all that nonsense. What they did for her was a sort of—a sort of prayer, a sort of casting of their bread on the waters in the hope that, later on, they wouldn't be old and alone and unwanted as she was. Twice, it's all so terribly pathetic!"

"It isn't any more, darling, if we let them do the Old Ladies' Home thing. Look, get into bed. You'll freeze."

I got into bed, but I could not rid my mind of the pathos that hung about Loose-an'-Daze and interrupted Twice's bedtime reading with: "And the women are worse than the men, somehow, when they get old. They are so much more irritating than men. Look at Mattha—he's not nearly so kindly and not even so much use as Loose-an'-Daze, but he's not irritating." Twice made a sort of non-committal noise. "What is it that makes the women so irritating?"

Twice raised himself on his elbow and

stared at me sternly. "It's what you're doing now that makes them so bloody irritating—going on and on and on after everybody else thinks that everything is settled. Now, shut up and read your book!"

The next morning Reachfar had an air of being en fête. My father came up from Achcraggan as usual, but he, George and Tom no longer took the farming of Reachfar very seriously. Most of the arable land as well as the moor was let as pasture to the farmer of Dinchory on our west march, but, out of habit more than anything else, Reachfar still kept a cow or two, a horse and a sheep or two and my aunt still had a few hens, ducks and turkeys clucking, quacking and peeow-owing about the yard. It did not take a great deal, however, to make Tom and George come downstairs in the morning in their highly-polished, second-best boots with the declared intention of "having a holiday to themselves" and this was their mood today.

"It iss very cold and greeshach outside whateffer," Tom said, "and not fit for working, but later on, come eleven o'clock, maybe Robbie will be driving us over to the white house on the hill and I will be standing my hand to you a-all."

"That'll be jist the very dab," Mattha agreed. "When Ah saw that pictur' that the Lad bocht frae auld Lizzie Fintry, the first thing An kent in it wis that wee pub ower on the hill there."

"That was the eye of the spirit that was seeing, Mattha," Twice said.

But my aunt put her foot down and said that nobody was to leave Reachfar until after the midday meal, for she said firmly, with her eye on George, "When some men I know get a holiday feeling, there's no knowing when they may come back. There's a man not far from here who went to Inverness to the circus once and kind of accidentally joined the Seaforths and didn't come back for seven years."

"Ach, that was a long time ago, Kate," said George, who had been guilty of this slight lapse in the days of his youth.

"You are no older now than you were then," she informed him firmly. "Move your big feet till I get at the oven." She put her pie in, shut the oven door and straightened her back. "But poor Guido's seven years have left a mark on him though."

"Guido's time was a little different from mine, Kate," George said quietly.

"Did ye like bein' a sodger, George?" Mattha enquired.

"Och, aye, I had a grand time, Mattha."

"Mattha," Twice said, "George always has a grand time."

"I sometimes think he hasn't the brains to have anything else," my aunt said, and at that moment there came a ripple of concerted laughter from Loose-an'-Daze in the scullery. Mattha glanced malignantly at the closed door.

"There's nae doot," he said bitterly, "that the lack o' brains is a big help in gettin' through life withoot fashin' yersel'."

After the midday meal Robbie, with all the men except Twice in his car, set off for the little hotel over on the hill; Loose-an'-Daze set about clearing the table and announced their intention of spending the afternoon baking and my aunt lit the parlour fire and retired through there with Twice and myself, where we told her of our plan for turning Crookmill into a guest-house for old ladies.

"You know," she said, "I believe it might work."

"So do I, Kate," I said. "I think their attitude will be quite different from what it was with the tenants. They were simply awful with them, but I think that was a mixed-up sort of loyalty to Twice and me, really."

"Mixed-up is the operative thing," Twice said. "They'll never be other than mixed-up in some way, but feeding people and looking after them and—ay, Kate, I'm not taking Janet back to St. Jago to worry and grizzle over them. Loose-an'-Daze are hopelessly on her conscience and Janet with a conscience is not fit to live with."

"I can't help them being on my conscience," I protested. "They were wonderful to me all that long time when I was ill and I just can't throw them on the street and go away. Besides, there's a foreboding sort of feeling about Mr. Galbraith dying like that and the sale of the house being cancelled."

"Oh, you and your forebodings and your feelings!" my aunt said impatiently. "You're as bad as the Ould Leddy!"

"You can say what you like," I argued, "but forebodings and things are not all that laughable. Look at Monica and Guido! Monica worked up forebodings from ever since I saw her when I first came home on this leave."

"Nonsense! Monica is not the foreboding sort."

"What Janet means, Kate, is that Monica gave Janet the forebodings."

"Oh, Janet'd get the forebodings if the wind blew the wrong way," my aunt said scornfully.

"I would not! And stop saying forebodings like that as if it was measles."

"You turn your forebodings on to this guest-house for old ladies," she advised me. "You two have enough to do with your income without keeping those two women. Tell them at the end of their first six months that they are to start paying you a good rent for the place and if not you'll have to sell it. They're very lucky to get it rent free to start with."

The three of us were still sitting round the parlour fire when, towards four o'clock, we heard Robbie's car come into the yard. Twice cocked his head.

"There are two cars there," he said.

"Two?" My aunt sprang up. "It's about

tea-time. I hope those two have got the scones baked."

"Don't worry, Kate," I said. "Just count your guests and tell them tea for twenty—they'll manage it."

"What it is to have service in the house!"

The second car contained Monica, Torquil, Guido and Signor Serafini, and Loose-an'-Daze, in their element at having extra mouths to feed, shooed everybody into the parlour.

"Just sit down—"

"—tea is just ready—"

"—we won't be a moment—"

"—and then we'll call you through!"

Very shortly, before Tom and George had finished remarking that they would have known Guido anywhere and that my memory must be failing, Loose-an'-Daze announced that all was ready and we all trooped through to the kitchen to find a table laid in such a way and in such profusion that even my pernickety, Reachfar-trained, Reachfar-hospitable aunt could make no quibble.

It was a happy tea party. Guido was not in the least reserved or shy about answering questions about the recovery of his memory, which was just as well, for Tom and George were so fascinated with the subject that they could not leave it alone.

"And to think," said Tom, "on you taking that island where Napoleon was to be Ben Weevas!"

"And thinking the Mediterranean Sea was the Firth here," George added.

"I don't think, now, that I really did," Guido told them. "But I wouldn't allow myself to believe that Montepescali was not my real home. It was better than nothing, you see."

"Aye. I can see that," my father said.

"When you became conscious in hospital," Twice asked, "did you begin to speak Italian?"

"Yes. Everybody else was speaking Italian, you see."

"Then you started learning English?"

"Not really. I discovered quite soon that I could read English and French and I knew I must have learned them before. I discovered in the same way, later on, that I could drive a car. I discovered that I could do all sorts of things. All that was lost was my memory for events and people and places. My identity papers said I was

Antonio Marandola so, of course, I believed that."

"It is a-all very queer and not canny at a-all," said Tom, "but it is ourselves that is glad to see you back, Guido."

"Aren't we just?" said Monica. "I'm so proud I could burst after all these sensible people like my brother Gerald and Alasdair the Doctor telling me that Guido would never come back. Sense my foot! Things don't go by sense!"

"That's what I've always maintained," I said.

"You've no need to worry," my aunt said. "It won't be the amount of sense you've got that will put things wrong for you. Sometimes I think you've got no sense at all."

"Oh, poop to you and your sense!" I told her. "Who did you see at the pub, George?"

"Old Jock the Roadman was in yonder as full as an egg," my father said, "and— oh, mercy! We met Rory the Post on the hill. Here's the letters. Just one for Lucy and two for Daisy."

He put the letters on the table between them and with one accord they rose to their feet, drew back from the table and stared wide-eyed at the envelopes as if they were poisonous reptiles.

"Two for me—?" said Daze.

"—and one for me?" said Loose.

They fell in, one behind the other, as if by some pre-arranged routine and began to walk round the table and us all, still staring fixedly at the letters, and all except Twice, Mattha and I looked at them with fascinated amazement.

"That looks like a bill—"

"—but we paid every single thing—"

"—even that pint of milk we didn't get—"

"—before we left—"

Against my own will, my own eyes had begun to follow their slow march round the table and all the other people in the room were now as if mesmerised, their heads moving from side to side like a slow-motion film of the spectators at the centre court at Wimbledon.

"Mine are written with a typewriter—" said Daze.

"—so is mine," said Loose.

"Who can they be from?"

"I don't know."

They made another silent circuit of the table.

"They've been forwarded on from Bally-dendran."

"So they have."

"I suppose the post office people did it."

"I suppose so."

Once more they encircled the table in silence.

"Ah help ma Jimmy Johnson!" Mattha shouted suddenly, and it was as if someone had profanely interrupted some solemn ritual so startled were we all. "Ah'll bet ye that yin in the yallah invylope is frae the fitba' folk!" and with remarkable agility he reached jerkily across the table and snatched one of the letters addressed to Daze.

"Give me that!" she said.

"You leave that letter alone, Mattha!" said Loose.

"If it's fitba' it's as much mines as yoos twaes!"

"It's addressed to me!"

"It's addressed to Daisy!"

"Well, open the confounded thing!" I shouted.

Mattha handed the envelope to Daze, but

her fingers did not grip it and it fell to the floor, to lie between the two women, who stood looking down at it.

"Oh, Lucy!"

"Oh, Daisy!"

"You open it!"

"I can't! You do it!"

"I wonder if?"

"Oh, Daisy, it might be!"

"We did the wishing—"

"—and Madame Zora said—"

"Oh, POOR MADAME ZORA!" they ended in chorus and burst into floods of tears.

My aunt, at the end of her never-very-long tether after one day of Loose-an'-Daze and in spite of their kindness and efficiency, rose from the table and made a savage attack on the fire with the poker and Monica said: "This is more than I can stand!" whereupon Twice picked up the envelope from the floor and with a "Darn it, I have a tanner in this too!" he ripped it open. He unfolded the blue slip. "Well, we're in the money," he said. "Fifteen bob. Three bob each!"

With tears trickling down their pretty, silly faces, Loose-an'-Daze sank down on to their two chairs, facing one another, and began to dry their eyes.

"Oh, well—"

"—it was too much to expect."

"It was just the way things happened—"

"—with poor Mr. Galbraith dying—"

"—it was just as if it was meant—"

"But it was too much to expect—"

"Yes. Oh, well—"

They took out their handkerchiefs, dried their eyes a little more, blew their noses delicately and with one accord turned to look at the other two letters.

"Mine's got the Ballydendran postmark—"

"So has mine, as clear as anything—"

"There's a little round badge thing on the back—"

"—with a name in it—"

"I haven't got my glasses."

"Mine are upstairs."

"It's that raised-up printing—"

"—very hard to read—"

Monica picked up a jammy tea-knife and for a moment I thought she was about to make a murderous attack on the two of them, but instead and with incredible speed, she seized each letter in turn and slit the flaps.

"Now," she said in a threatening voice, "will you read them or shall I?"

After looking up at her in a cowed way, they picked up the folded sheets gingerly with their finger-tips and spread them before them on the table. We were all heaving sighs of relief, and Twice had actually begun to talk to Guido again, when the two voices rose in chorus:

"Oh dear!"

"Oh goodness!"

"Oh, Lucy!"

"Oh, Daisy!"

"OH, POOR MADAME ZORA!"

—and Loose-an'-Daze burst into another storm of tears.

In the end, it was I who read the letters from Mr. Gair of Ballydendran that informed them that they had inherited five thousand pounds each from my friend Madame Zora.

GUIDE
TO THE COLOUR CODING
OF
ULVERSCROFT BOOKS

Many of our readers have written to us expressing their appreciation for the way in which our colour coding has assisted them in selecting the Ulverscroft books of their choice. To remind everyone of our colour coding—this is as follows:

BLACK COVERS
Mysteries

★

BLUE COVERS
Romances

★

RED COVERS
Adventure Suspense and General Fiction

★

ORANGE COVERS
Westerns

★

GREEN COVERS
Non-Fiction